the
catastrophist

also by ronan bennett

THE SECOND PRISON

OVERTHROWN BY STRANGERS

ronan bennett

the
catastrophist

review

First published in 1998
by REVIEW

An imprint of Headline Book Publishing

10 9 8 7 6 5 4 3 2 1

British Library Cataloguing in Publication Data

Bennett, Ronan
      The Catastrophist
      I.Title
      823.9'14[F]

ISBN 0 7472 2210 X (hardback)
ISBN 0 7472 7310 3 (softback)

Typeset by
Letterpart Ltd, Reigate, Surrey

Printed and bound in Great Britain by
Clays Ltd, St Ives plc.

Headline Book Publishing
A division of Hodder Headline PLC
338 Euston Road
London NW1 3BH

For Georgina

W HAT SHOULD I be looking at now? The Sankuru is not as wide as the Congo, not at this point at least where the *barque* crosses, but it has the same dull mud colour, the same tinge of rust after rainfall, and there are the floating tangles of water-hyacinth I know from Léopoldville. I have seen them here before, I have seen them in Stanley Pool and at the cataracts below the capital, I have seen them at Matadi where they debouch to the sea. The flowers are purple or magenta, some are powder blue. They are beautiful and malign, yet more parasites for this over-leeched land. The rivers will never flush away these tokens of infection. The rain fell hard in the afternoon for two hours, forcing our absurd convoy off the road – one more delay upon many. Soon after the sky cleared one of his aides claimed to have heard the engine of a spotter plane and there was general alarm, but when I looked there was nothing. What does it matter? We have reached the Sankuru. On the other side is safety, and he and Auguste and the others of the inner circle are already across. The air has cooled. These are the bewitching minutes of the red sunball and the palms where the pied crows roost, when the bamboo groans, and homeward lines of workers tread the dusty, pocked roads – how far do these people walk in a single day? Near me, very near, a frog croaks. The cicadas are beginning their chorus. What else should I note here? I am the trained observer. Smells? Yes, there are things to smell. I can smell the fish the women have piled before them like neat mounds of twisted silver nails. I can smell the boiled eggs and the *pilipili* and the fried manioc they have prepared in the hope of

1

passing trade. And I smell the hot oil and exhaust fumes of the soldiers' lorries. On the far side of the river he waits with the old boatman.

The soldiers come among us, or among them, for I am not truly part of this, and because my status, my ever-evasive presence, is manifest – in spite of my visible wounds – I do not have to be afraid in the way I can see the others are afraid. Inès is afraid, though not for herself. She stands by the sky-blue Peugeot in which Pauline and little Roland have been travelling for the last three days. The doors are open, the stifled occupants begging the breezes. In the back, Pauline holds the boy. Inès, like the others of our party, studies the soldiers' movements and glances for clues as to their intentions. So far, they have exhibited signs of a morose but unspecific hostility only: as long as their animus remains general and unexcited we may yet get across to join him. They stalk the cars and passengers. No one says anything. They come to Pauline's car. An officer recognizes her and demands, first in Lingala, then in French: '*Où est t-il? Où est t-il?*' Pauline remains silent. The officer's voice rises, sweat blisters on his forehead. A soldier reaches into the car and jerks Roland from his mother's grasp. A cry. Inès starts forward. Pauline is now out of the car, she sees only her child: the soldiers' guns mean nothing to her. There are high shouted words in one of their languages, interrogatory and uncompromising. A soldier raises his rifle butt and strikes Roland in the face. And now we know.

What should I be looking at? Now that we know lives are at stake. A child's face has been broken but I have seen so much. I have seen bodies and blood. I have heard wailing and terror. I watch as though through a screen, I listen as though to a recording I might interrupt at will: the imprecations and pleas, the threats and the whimpers. I am thinking of the leprosy of politics, of the banality of this country and the low comedy of its calamities. I am thinking, actually, of Ruskin. Yes, *Ruskin*. And all of this makes me angry with Inès, for I should not be here and she should not be here: we neither of us belong to this moment of farce and melodrama. I actually feel impatient, almost embarrassed. I will not be able to confess this to Inès. But I have more than a little justification. There is something worked-up, overheated about this whole business. Even this journey. We could have reached Stanley-ville yesterday – we had a day's head start, the roads are for the most part good. As it is, he – the prize – is out of the soldiers' reach. But had we moved with even the minimum of expedition, they would all be safe: Roland would not be bleeding and crying now, his face would not be smashed. I have cause for my irritation.

Things now are getting worse. The soldiers are jumpy, scuffles are breaking out. Someone says they are Baluba tribesmen. I cannot tell, but if this is true the situation is serious for the Baluba have scores to settle. I go to be with Inès. She is so small and frail. I put my arm around her, partly in an act of reassurance, partly to restrain her; I do not trust her temper. There is something proprietorial in my motives, I cannot deny it. Auguste is watching from the other side of the river. He is watching us, and for once – for the first time in a long time – I am nearer than he. I am beside her again, and perhaps I will be able to stay beside her.

It is like trying to hold a bird. She moves restlessly this way and that, struggling to follow the wheeling eddies of the affray. I do not know if she is aware of me or my touch or my careful intentions. She does not meet my gaze but beats the cage of my arms and struggles towards the makeshift jetty where, as though marshalled by a command only I have not heard, our party and the soldiers have thronged. I let her go, and she glances at me for the briefest moment, a look between alarm and accusation: she has news of impending tragedy, and again I have not heard. She is off, away from me, running to join the others. The mêlée has been suddenly quenched, there are no human sounds. I follow her, and as I approach I discover the cause of this sudden respite. We gaze across the river.

He already has one foot on the *barque*. The crude wooden raft can take one vehicle and its passengers at a time. Mungul and the others had insisted he go first. Even then they had dawdled. I can see Mungul now, and Mulele and Kemishanga, pleading with him not to go back. They keep a nervous watch on the soldiers; even now they are slipping away into the bush, leaving words of farewell to hang in the air behind them, apology for their essential desertion. Auguste – he looks distressed, near to tears – embraces his leader. Then Auguste too is gone. Now there is only the boatman.

The pole pierces the waterfilm, the muscle balls in the boatman's arm, the veins swell . . . and they are launched. I see Inès close her eyes. Some of our party, distrait and grieving, break from the jetty like the first mourners retiring from a burial. My irritation rises, I feel like reminding them of all the avoidable delays which have led to this.

He stands towards the front of the *barque*, tall and thin, glasses glinting in the last of the sun. What is he thinking? He will have seen the soldier hit his two-year-old son, and certainly he will be concerned about Pauline's safety. Perhaps this gesture is for her, repayment for his innumerable adventures. (Inès, whom I accuse of having a touch of the puritan in her, has complained many times since our arrival here: 'The men of this country!') I do not believe he is convinced that he is crossing to his death. Probably he is counting on being able to talk our way out of this problem, as he talked his way out of the last, and the one before that. This is not heroic self-sacrifice. It is, as ever with him, political calculation and self-belief.

4

When they are twenty feet from the jetty, a small plane appears and swoops down over the *barque*. It follows the course of the river, then banks sharply and climbs to circle above. Once again the atmosphere alters abruptly. Disbelief and resignation give way to high tension, the apprehension is palpable. I hear a voice cry out, clogged with emotion, 'No!' It is Inès. 'Patrice, no!'

Pauline clutches Roland and stares in bewilderment. I have only ever seen her in stylish European clothes and high heels, but now she is a young village girl: she looks needfully from face to face – can someone explain this to her? What will it mean for her? For her child? The wood of craft and jetty connect with a listless clump. The soldiers come forward for their prisoner. I move away to stand alone, apart, removed from the people and things of this unnecessary moment. The cicadas chirp, the frogs croak.

As the Baluba soldiers take him, a look of alarm crosses his face; he now understands the nature of his position. I am thinking of Ruskin, of his injunction: *Does a man die at your feet, your business is not to help him, but to note the colour of his lips.* On the far bank, Auguste has reappeared for a wordless leave-taking. Inès looks up through her tears to raise a hand, a soldier rushes over to take aim, and Auguste backs away into the bush.

This is a story of failure.

part one

Léopoldville, November 1959

1

THE PITTED SPONGE of jungle gives way to scrub and sand. The sun is red in the east.

I am here to be with Inès, I am here for her, though I do not know what my welcome will be. No one who knows me would say I am a sentimental man, but I have a letter in my hand from the first weeks of our affair. A man my age should know better than to read and re-read such a thing, again and again. The lines in which I had thought to trace a way back to her have already faded. Each time I look I just get more lost.

The plane comes in over the brown slur of the river. The wheels skim the runway with a short screech and we have landed.

I want you to know me. I want you to understand how I am to be found, and where. I want you – very selfish! – to be part of a world that I feel belongs to me. Oh, this is getting complicated, but I have to say it. Ti amo, ti amo, sempre – *Inès.* I fold the words from another time and put the letter away. I am embarrassed by my own melodrama, but I am here because I know – know profoundly – that this is the last chance I have to make love work for me, and I am frightened that I will fail.

The stewardess points the way and I fall in with the returning settlers and their families, with the businessmen, the priests and the nuns, the students and administrators and the army officers. We pass a parked military helicopter and a Piper Cub. The concrete and glass of the terminal building is ahead of us, and behind, in a distant screen of banana trees and palms, a small boy stands with his goats.

A porter holds open the glass door and gives me a sudden

smile. I produce my passport for an official who speaks first in Flemish, then in French. The arrivals hall is ornamented with broad-leafed pot plants and wrought-iron grills. Our luggage is lined up in a hushed operation performed by many black hands.

Inès waits, a small, gauche figure in a sleeveless blue polka-dot frock. She signals her presence to me with a wave and I smile carefully back, as though she were little more than an acquaintance and as though there were nothing at stake for me; I am surrounded – always – by my own distance. I must not ruin my chances by pressing my case; I must be patient if I am to take her home again. And if she says no, she will not hear me complain. This is what I tell myself.

The customs man asks a few routine questions, then I go to her.

'You are here,' she says. She kisses me on both cheeks. 'I am so happy to see you.'

I say nothing, trying to gauge the feeling behind this.

'You are not happy?' she asks.

Her English is good, apart from a few stubborn idiosyncrasies of preposition and tense, but these are music to me, sung solecisms – how else to describe 'I am already loving you', her first declaration of feeling for me, now two years old? Her accent, however, is strong: *You are not 'appy?*

'I am 'appy,' I say.

'You don't look.'

I don't look because I am the lover on the losing side. I am remanded, awaiting her verdict. I cannot make myself look happy, though I know melancholy to be tiresome.

I rally a smile. 'Of course I'm happy – just a bit tired.'

She pinches my cheek and hugs me and there, in her embrace, my heart aches. I don't yet know what the circle of her arms means, for she is naturally demonstrative. The words I need are out of reach. I push her gently back to take her in. She has lost weight in the Congo, in the weeks we have been apart, and her spareness now makes me feel fleshy, sleek and overfed, though I do not think that I am, really, any of these things. Her shoulders are skinny and slightly hunched, her back a little rounded. Her skin is flushed and clear.

I put a thumb to her hairline.

'I know,' she says, rolling her eyes, 'soon – bald.'

She worries about her hair. So do I. Since I have known her it has been getting thinner and duller.

She is with someone, a man. She introduces me to Zoubir Smail. Though I would put his age at fifty, Smail has a freshness that makes me feel worn and shabby. He is tall and trim, with silver-washed straight dark hair. The whites of his green-brown eyes are very clear. My own eyes are burning and sore. They are in any case my weak spot, prone to tiredness. I cannot compete. I try hard to look him in the face as I shake his hand and tell him that I am very pleased to meet him.

'Zoubir brought me to the airport,' Inès explains.

What has she been doing for sex? The same as me? Smail gives her an affectionate smile, which she returns. She has friends here already, she is liked. She is not above letting me know of her little triumphs.

'Your first time in the Congo, James?' he asks pleasantly.

He has that Mediterranean ease and style which the English and the Irish – and those like me in between – admire and begrudge.

'My first time in Africa,' I reply in my poor French.

He helps me with my bags and we walk to the exit. In the sunshine and heat Inès links her arm in mine the way she used to do.

'So, what do you think?' she asks.

'About that?'

'This.'

'Toytown,' I say.

11

My observation pleases her. And it is true: the affluence, the order, the newness of things and their perfect maintenance are not real. Something has been made in a place where it has no place, even I can see this.

Smail has to make a detour to see someone. We leave the paved road after a few minutes to turn on to a track of compacted dirt and I get my first glimpse of the native world. In a clearing of round, windowless mud huts with low doors, chickens peck at the dirt, a goat stands skittishly atop a termite mound, a young girl washes clothes in a zinc tub. Two older women sit like sisters in knowing silence. It seems oddly familiar, even to one who has never trespassed here before. The women sit motionless, staring irreducibly back – it is not the way of Europeans, but neither is it new to me. I have seen the newsreels.

At an isolated reed shack, in exchange for a thin wad of francs, Smail receives a dirty folded cloth from a man he calls Harry who looks like he might be Indian or Pakistani.

'What is it?' I ask Inès.

'A bit of smuggling,' she says in the tone that women use when boys will insist on being boys. 'Zoubir has a small diamond business.'

'How did you get to know him?'

'He is in the Party. The Sûreté are always watching him. He is a brilliant person, isn't he?'

She tells me how exciting it is to be in the Congo at this time, how things are happening, how she wants to introduce me to more brilliant people like Smail, how she knows I will want to write about all this. I remind her I have my book to finish and she says I won't be able to stop myself. She leans forward and kisses my cheek. She searches my eyes.

'Why are you not happy?'

'I'm getting happier,' I say.

She gives me a big kiss. I *am* getting happier. There are things to discuss, but the way she has been with me makes me think our problems can be resolved. I long to be in bed with her, to make her mine again, to start again.

Smail rejoins us and we set off back the way we came. Newly expansive, newly generous and bright, I ask Smail about himself. He replies in English, to my relief. He came to the Congo from the Lebanon before the war. He 'learned diamonds' in Brussels and Antwerp. The real diamond mines are in the south, in Katanga.

'On the big stones the benefit is good. On small ones like these' – he taps the cloth parcel in his shirt pocket – 'it is about five per cent. It's not easy.'

There is a thud and a crack. The car swerves a little. Smail pulls to a halt.

'What is it?' I ask.

Had we hit something? The road had seemed clear. Smail gets out of the car. I turn to Inès who is staring out the back window.

'What happened?' I ask again.

She has seen something.

'Probably just a stone that came up from the road,' she says with an evasive shrug.

She gets out of the car. I do the same.

'It didn't come up from the road, someone threw it,' Smail says, inspecting his windscreen. The glass is chipped and there is a lightning fork of splintered lines; the damage is not serious. A smile plays in the corner of his eyes. He is a light-hearted and amused man. I am beginning to like him, in spite of his familiarity with Inès.

He starts walking down the way we came, a desultory search for the culprit. The car's engine thrums and the air is still. There are some far-off noises from the jungle. Monkeys?

A guess – what would I know? I stare into the trees and the foliage. The jungle is dense, undivided, but it does not seem virulent or vengeful. There are pretty wild flowers fringing the roadside and at the soft edges of the rain-pools small violet and yellow butterflies sap the mineral mud. This is not *An Outpost of Progress.* The sky above is clear now, and only the sun is implacable.

'You saw something,' I say.

'No, nothing,' she replies.

I look at her with plain sight, but she resists my gaze. Her demeanour has changed quite suddenly. She is away from me, in her own thoughts. I try coaxing her with small talk and news of our friends in London, but she won't come back.

The suburbs are pleasant and spacious. The bungalows are whitewashed and the rust on the iron roofs has been tamped down with years of paint – deep red and olive green – and the thin metal now has texture and substance, like canvas worked in oils. Over the walls and spiked fences giant flowering shrubs lie in brilliant mantles. Gardeners in blue boiler suits and Wellington boots are already at work. The air smells summery, of cut grass and the diesel of lawnmowers.

A long, wide, tree-lined avenue cuts the heart of the city, Boulevard Albert I. On traffic islands white-gloved police-men in pith helmets control the flow. The cars are new and shiny, luxury European models and expensive American convertibles, chromed and extravagantly finned. There are flat-backed trucks and delivery vans and taxis and buses, and a silver-black stream of bicycles ridden by the Congolese. At the pavement cafés Europeans read their papers over coffee and croissants. There are boutiques, jewellers, delicatessens, patisseries, ice-cream parlours and hotels. The doors of the Banque Belge d'Afrique are just opening.

Smail drops us outside a new seven-storey apartment block, one of a small cluster at this end of the double boulevard. Inès has borrowed the flat from someone who has gone to Uganda for a year. I thank Smail for the lift. He suggests dinner tonight at the Zoo. The owners are French and the cuisine is the best in Léopoldville.

I yawn and stretch happily. The welcome has been good.

2

THERE ARE TWO smooth depressions, little dips, at the small of her back, above her hips. She lies in my arms and I touch them with my fingertips. I am falling in and out of sleep.

She talks – how I love her song – of things I can only half-follow. She pauses from time to time to kiss my chest and squeeze me. In the gloom of the long flight from London I could find reason only for pessimism, but I had overlooked one thing: her need for me. She enjoys *me*, she is attracted to the physical me, to this body, these arms. She told me once of a lover whose fingers she had almost to unclaw before he touched her. My hands at least are not like that. She likes these fingers, where they go, what they do to her. I close my eyes and soak in the pouring words.

It is a story to do with the war when she was small and the Germans were in Bologna. She remembers a soldier who rode a white horse every day in the Piazza Maggiore, an officer, though *not a big officer*. One morning as usual the German went out to ride his horse. He was never seen again. There were rumours that he had deserted and run off with his lover, an Italian, a married woman; others said the partisans had captured and killed him. No one knew for certain. When she was reunited with her father, after his partisan band came down from the mountains in the last days of the town's occupation, she plied him with questions about what happened to the horse, for even as a child she loved horses. But he had heard nothing and could find out nothing. I am not sure if there is a point to her story or even if I have understood everything: her accent and grammar tear at narrative. We lie still and I see the little girl, big-eyed and hopeful, waiting in the shaded galleries for the day the German soldier's horse will canter riderless into the square looking for her so that she can take him home.

I feel the blink of lashes on my shoulder and close my eyes to sleep.

I smell coffee. She is sitting on the end of the bed. I feel it peevishly, as a form of rejection, that she is already dressed. She puts a hand in my hair and messes it. I rub my eyes.

'What time is it?'

'Almost nine.'

Night? Morning? I have no idea.

She passes me the cup. 'Drink this.'

'Why are you dressed?' I ask.

'For dinner. But we don't have to go if you don't want.'

She makes coffee very sweet.

'What was going on there, on the road?' I ask. 'I know you saw something.'

She shrugs and turns down the corners of her mouth. 'It was only a small boy, twelve or thirteen. He was hiding in the trees.'

'You saw him throw the stone?'

'Yes.'

'Why did you say you hadn't seen anything?'

A shrug. She will not be drawn. But I already know. It was not that she was frightened, rather that she had been caught on the wrong side – a white woman in a white man's car – and was ashamed.

'Is there a lot of stone-throwing?' I ask.

'No. The opposite in fact. This is a controlled place. The

Belgians are very efficient policemen, the Flemish in particular. As soon as they think someone is a troublemaker they arrest him. Like they did with Patrice.'

'I've been reading a lot about Patrice.'

'That's because I have been writing a lot about him.'

'I know, but he's mentioned in the British press now as well.'

She makes a little noise of disdain. Others might now acknowledge Lumumba's importance but she had recognized him first. She came to the Congo for him, for the hopes he inspired and embodied. The first interview appeared in *L'Unità* only days after her arrival. I read it in London and my heart sank. She wrote to me afterwards in a thrill of commitment and dedication. *You must understand,* the letter said, *that my life now can never be the same.* What was she saying with that? What about *our* life?

She tells me: 'Patrice used to work at the post office in Stanleyville. As soon as he was making a name for himself in the independence movement, the Belgians framed him for taking money. Now they can say Patrice Lumumba is nothing more than a convicted thief.'

'Did he steal the money?'

Steal. I opt for *steal.* She pretends not to have heard the distinction.

'Of course not.' She is emphatic. 'You will meet him. He is brilliant.'

Brilliant the way Smail is brilliant. Her language has always been unconditional and absolute. Nothing-everything; never-always; worst-best-brilliant – lots of brilliants. I was brilliant once. 'The years since the war,' I remember her saying one time, 'have been a very omologated period.'

'Omologated?' I said, raising an eyebrow.

'*Omologare?* You don't have this word? It means,' she had explained patiently, 'to accept everything without thinking. It's a very communistic word.'

'Homologate?' I offered. 'But I don't think it's politically loaded.'

'Of course it is.'

'I'm sure it's a legal term.'

She made one of those impatient little sounds of hers, something between a squeak and a grunt. We checked the dictionaries and it was only with reluctance that she accepted *homologate* as a rough approximation, a needy one. She ascribed this dereliction of language to broader deficiencies in the British outlook.

'It is not surprising the British cannot be left – they don't even have the words for a left way of thinking.' She had looked at me with a grin: 'Lucky for me you are Irish.'

'Inès,' I had told her with exaggerated but affectionate weariness – these discussions were frequent and had evolved their own rituals – 'when you find a "left way of thinking" in Ireland you will have the scoop of a lifetime.'

'You have lived too long in London.'

She smacked a kiss to my forehead. It was typical of her way of argument to end with an overplayed generalization, a little barb of criticism and a kiss.

I shower and shave. I give up trying to dry myself. The air is humid, the windows and the walls are sweating.

As I dress she tells me more about the brilliant Patrice Lumumba. She has been to his house in Tshopo, the native quarter of Stanleyville, and to the one here in Léopoldville on Boulevard Albert I, opposite the golf course. She knows his wife Pauline, who is modest and shy. They have four children; one – Roland – is just a little baby and is very beautiful. 'They have practically adopted me,' she says. 'We are so close now.'

We will see Patrice tomorrow because the Mouvement National Congolais is staging a pro-independence rally.

She takes my arm as we walk up to the Zoo. The streets

are well lit and the people take ease as their due. There are no blacks. Talking about Lumumba and tomorrow's rally has animated her. The demonstration will be big. Things in the Congo are moving fast now. I am between waking and sleeping, and I take her word on everything.

3

S MAIL AND HIS friends bid me welcome to Léopoldville. They
are in high spirits and talk noisily over each other. Inès is
shepherded to one end of the table to be with Smail, I to the
other. I find myself between a small, pale man of about sixty
and a handsome, large-boned woman of around my own age.
She has blue eyes and straight, thick, flat flaxen hair.

The man introduces himself: he is Romain de Scheut, the
general manager of a Unilever soap factory in Léopoldville.
His dry face has smoker's lines, the eyes are watery and kind.

'Smail has been telling us about the ambush on the way
from the airport,' he says with a smile.

I am not sure what he is talking about; then I say 'Oh, yes'
as the penny drops. He is not being serious. I am aware that
the flaxen-haired woman is listening.

'It wasn't an ambush, though,' I say for her. 'I'm not even
sure it was deliberate.'

'Of course it was,' the woman says. 'You don't know the
macaques.'

De Scheut chuckles at her vehemence.

'Madeleine has strong views on these matters,' he says.

'What about you?' I ask.

'I am one of Léopoldville's most notorious liberals. It
makes me very unpopular with Madeleine. Isn't that so, my
dear?'

'You should be locked up,' Madeleine replies, meaning it
and not.

Her eyebrows are carefully plucked giving her face, with
its high cheekbones and strong jaw, a lapidary look. The top

21

buttons of her blouse are undone.

De Scheut recommends the chicken cooked in butter or the tilapia or the fondue. There's plenty to choose from. 'The mussels are good too,' he says.

I go for the fish.

'Zoubir tells me you are a writer,' de Scheut says. 'What do you write?'

'Novels,' I say.

'Are you going to write a novel about Africa?'

'I'm one of those writers who likes to stay with what he knows.'

'Which is what?'

'London, I suppose.'

'You are Irish, though, aren't you?'

This always bores me. Irish, English, what's the difference, what does it matter? I have lived in London a long time is all I say.

'Are you a journalist as well, like Inès?'

'I sometimes write for magazines and Sunday newspapers to make ends meet.'

'Novels don't pay?'

'Not mine.'

'Is that why you've come to the Congo – to write for the newspapers?'

'No, I'm here really' – I hesitate to say this in front of a stranger, but there is something about de Scheut I have already taken to – 'because Inès is here.'

'You have made the right decision,' he says, and he pats my forearm. 'She's a very particular young woman, and she's very popular here.'

'She likes to be liked,' I say.

'As we all do.'

He looks at me with sympathy, as though he knows what's going on in my head, the fears I have, the doubts. I have always had a weakness for father figures.

The food arrives, course after course, and so does the drink. When the dinner plates are removed the waiters set before us a selection of cheeses – Camembert, Brie and – a concession to Flemish tastes – Hervese. They bring us liqueurs and spirits; then a bottle of champagne, another, another.

My eyes keep being drawn back to Inès and her light-hearted group. I might have begun to resent my exclusion from the ribbons of her laughter had I not enjoyed seeing again her social display – the flash of the eyes, the gestures, the pantomimic swiftness of the change in tone and look: someone says something and her disagreement is transparent and unmitigated; seconds later she is in full and extravagant accord with the same person. She happens to glance in my direction and gives me a bold wink, then turns back to her friends. She always has friends, she is always with others. In the two years we have been lovers I do not recall ever having seen her alone. I exaggerate. Moments, yes, the small, inevitable domestic moments: when I would return to the flat to find her preparing food or performing some other chore. Images jump into my mind. Of her lying on her stomach on the bed, a pillow under her shoulders and a book propped open before her, wearing only a vest. Or that awful afternoon when unexpectedly I glimpsed her from the upper deck of a bus as she returned from the doctor's appointment. How frail she seemed as she trudged along Kentish Town Road in the miserable January slush. I almost didn't recognize the small, slow figure. But that was not Inès – vital, subversive, impatient, and always part of others' lives.

'You look older than Inès.'

It is Madeleine.

'I am.'

23

'By how much?'

I do not want to appear defensive, but I am unused to direct personal questions of any kind.

'By thirteen years,' I say as evenly as I can.

She studies me closely before taking a cigarette from its packet.

'Hardly anything,' she says. 'My husband is twenty-seven years older than me. He's a farmer.'

I light her cigarette. She holds up a champagne bottle, a mimed query to me. I nod and she pours.

'Are you here like Inès to write about the great Patrice Lumumba?'

She crosses her legs and leans towards me a little.

'Is he great?'

'Ha!'

She drinks from her glass. A bead of sweat trickles by her ear; her hair is tied stringently back.

'Are you going to Bernard Houthhoofd's tomorrow?' she asks.

'Where?'

'Bernard Houthhoofd has people over on Saturdays to his house in Brazzaville.'

'I don't know if we have an invitation,' I say.

'Inès has been before. You should come.'

She says it like a challenge. Her throat is shiny with more of her sweat. She turns back to her companions.

Inès decides it's time to go home. Smail and de Scheut leave with us. Madeleine, busy with someone else, doesn't notice my departure.

Beyond the Zoo, where the streets are darker and the houses meaner, a pair of gendarmes stand guard at a checkpoint.

'The *cité indigène*, where the blacks live,' she says.

24

We are walking the other way.

'The Congolese must be out of the European quarter before dark unless they have a special permission from the police,' Smail tells me; he adds with light sarcasm: 'It makes us settlers feel safe.'

'Not all settlers are the same,' De Scheut puts in amiably. 'Really there are two kinds. The first is born here or has lived here a long time. He understands the African mind, he speaks Lingala or Swahili or Kikongo or one of the other languages, if not several. He loves the country, it is his home. He wants to die and be buried here.'

'And the second kind?' I ask.

'Sees himself as Belgian. He wears a jacket and tie and looks down on the white whose shoes are not shined. He imports frozen butter and cheese, lobster and chicken rather than eat locally produced food, which is better and cheaper. In the middle of the most exotic fruit garden in the world, he imports tinned peaches and pears – at great expense. He is forever complaining about the heat, the water and the Congolese; he is obsessed with malaria, sleeping sickness, bilharzia, river blindness, blackwater fever and gonorrhoea. He knows someone who has had them all. He is here to make money and go home.'

From somewhere not too far off we hear raised voices. We turn and look back to the boundary of the cité where three or four white men stand with the gendarmes in a watchful, wary attitude.

A party of police hurries to the top of the street. There is the sound of breaking glass and more shouting.

'What's going on?' De Scheut shouts to the gendarmes.

'It's the *macaques*,' one of them shouts back.

'I keep hearing that – *macaque*,' I say.

'You know what a *macaque* is,' Smail explains. 'It's a monkey.'

People have left their tables and come out from the restaurants and clubs. They peer towards the darkness of the cité, puzzled and tipsy.

We follow the gendarmes to the cité's boundary, where a small group of settlers have gathered. Confronting them is a crowd of blacks. I can't tell whether there are tens or hundreds. Faces and limbs catch the light for a second and disappear again, rippling the dark. A window beside me explodes.

'Not more stones!' Smail grumbles in mock complaint. 'Will someone tell them please we are friends of Patrice!'

We duck for cover. All except Inès, who stands in the middle of the street as the stones fall round her, caught, once again, on the wrong side of the lines. I run to her and pull her behind a parked car.

The gendarmes seem to be in a state of shock, they cannot believe this is happening. No one moves.

Inès is distant, away from me again, working through her contradictions.

The blacks set up a vibrating and sonorous chant: *Depanda, depanda, depanda!*

'What are they shouting?' I ask.

There is another volley of stones. More windows break. The crowd advances. The gendarmes continue paralysed, moving only to dodge the stones.

Depanda, depanda!

Inès is suddenly bright. The chant means something to her. She turns to me, eyes wide.

A gendarme curses. He has had enough. Without warning, without thinking, he dashes out alone, baton raised, and runs yelling directly at the crowd. As though on some unspoken order his comrades leap forward and charge into the penumbra. The rioters disappear in a hectic scatter.

'*Depanda,*' Inès repeats in a reverend whisper.

26

'What is that?'

'Independence!' she says. 'They are shouting for independence.'

She hugs me so tightly.

I wake when she gets up to go to the bathroom. She urinates,
then pads sleepily flat-footed back to bed. She yawns and lets out
a small noise as she stretches. She breathes deeply, settling again
under the sheet. I am lying with my back to her and do not move.
I am drifting off to sleep when I hear the rasp of fingers on pubic
hair; then, after some moments' silence, there is something
softer, slower: moist flesh palpated. The movement of the sheet
is very slight. I hear something in her breath, a catch, a small cry
suppressed, and though no part of us is joined I can feel her
muscles tense and then relax. I am not the cause of her excitement, not tonight, but I do not feel excluded or diminished or
insecure about this. I am filled with desire.

I turn to her and she smiles guiltily.

'Were you awake?'

'Yes,' I say.

'Why didn't you do something?'

She tastes salty and metallic, she is coming on.

Later she says, 'I suppose you have been with other
women.'

'I haven't.'

It is a lie.

'You know I am a very jealous person.' She pronounces it
yellous.

I say nothing.

'I love you,' she says.

'Still?' I am not sure.

'*Ti amo*,' she says; and she adds the way she used to:
'Don't forget.'

We kiss suddenly and deeply.

She is above me now. I reach up, take hold of her hair and pull her head down to my shoulder, I am not gentle. I shiver beneath her and I say things to her – promise her, threaten her with things I have never done to her. Inès is stimulated by my abandon. She comes with the breath of my hot threat-promises in her ear. She flops on top of me and noisily draws air into her lungs.

She kisses me and says, 'I like you when you are ardent.'

I have forgotten everything. All that exists for me is the lover's state – the bed, the sheets, and the arms and breath of her. These days I am confused about where my emotions lie – they are in the wind, I can never catch them. It was not always like this. Once I was more like her, open and friendly and funny and hopeful. Along the way I have turned into someone I do not like. But tonight at least there is no contradiction between heat and sterility.

4

SHE IS NOT an early riser, but this morning is different. The air tastes of imminence, there are patterns to the clouds and she can see things. I sit on the bed, silent, feet on the floor. She is behind me, playfully, naked, on hands and knees. Her excitement boils and the hairs on the back of my neck bristle with her kisses. She goes to shower and I become the sole object of my own gaze. I bunch the white cotton sheet in my lap. Where this leaves me I do not know.

Her talk is high and fast over the drone of the water. It is of the slaving centuries when Europeans and Arabs hunted down the Congolese in their millions. It is of Léopold and Stanley and the millions more sacrificed to propitiate the accountants and ledgers of the Congo Free State. It is of the old colonial plantations, and the chain gangs, floggings, mutilations and rapes. It is of the lands and factories and mines of the Union Minière, Brufina, Unilever and the Banque Empain.

She comes out of the shower and drops her towel to the floor. The ends of her hair are wet and coiled. She stands with her back to me, still talking, and stoops to recover yesterday's knickers. As she steps into them she notices something about her inner thigh – an insect bite, some red little mark. She splays her feet, bends in a sort of half-squat and pulls the flesh to inspect the irritation. Her underwear is stretched just below the knees. She is telling me now about the Société Générale de Belgique, a fabulous, malevolent giant with interests in cotton, coffee, sugar, beer, palm oil, pharmaceuticals, insurance, railways, airlines, automobiles, diamonds, cattle, shipping. At last she pulls up her knickers, the elastic snaps and she looks about for her dress.

What gives her the right to be like this, so sublimely unselfconscious? She really doesn't see my gaze, or herself. Her figure, in unclothed harshness, is angular and bony. I don't know, even after two years, what she thinks of her own shape and appearance. She spends no time attempting their improvement; I have heard neither delight nor despair nor coy encouragement to compliment . . . A memory comes to me and I smile inwardly. It is from the early days of our affair. Soon after she moved to be with me in London we went to see *Love in the Afternoon*. Walking home that night, she judged the film pretty slight but at least it had Audrey Hepburn.

'She looks like me,' she had remarked matter-of-factly.

She glanced up at me to see how I had taken this.

'Yes,' she said with a little more emphasis, 'she is very like me.'

There are conventions about this kind of thing, there are devices to shelter the speaker's modesty. She might have said that a friend of hers once told her she bore a resemblance to the actress though she couldn't see it and what did I think? But no. Audrey Hepburn looked like her. Inès had stated it as a simple fact and in such a way as to suggest the actress was the copy. I could not think of it as vanity; it was too innocent for that.

We pass a wall daubed with freshly painted slogans.

NO MORE COLONIAL MINISTERS, NO MORE
GOVERNOR-GENERALS!

1959 LAST COLONIAL GOVERNMENT!

INDEPENDENCE OR DEATH!

She notes them with approval and says with a certain friendly provocation, 'You know, Roger Casement wrote a famous report about the rubber plantations. It was because of him that Léopold's crimes were exposed to the world.'

'Yes, but that was a long time ago, I think.'

'Casement was Irish.'

'At the time he wrote the report he was the British consul. He got a knighthood for his services.'

'That's not important. The British hanged him.'

She thinks me a poor Irishman, hardly one at all. I travel on a British passport and I couldn't care less about Orange or Green, about the Six or the Twenty-six, the border she thinks so important. I have tired of trying to explain that the line on the map may have been significant once but it is not so now, and never will be again.

'You could write something like Casement about today's situation,' she suggests.

Her sense of perspective is very particular to her. I smile, amused and touched by her loyally inflated opinion of my stature as a writer; she is forever urging me to put my pen at the service of this or that cause. What cause would benefit? And if by chance it did, what would be the cost? When has involvement with a cause – any cause – ever been good for a writer?

'Why are you not angry about this?' she demands good-humouredly.

'What good would my anger do anybody?'

'It might do you some good.'

On another occasion my detachment might be the subject of a long discussion, but after last night's momentous events it is this morning an irrelevance. The Congo will be free and Lumumba will be a great African leader, as great as Nkrumah – even greater, for the Ghanaians have been forced into compromises by Nkrumah's recent errors of judgement.

31

In some, this kind of talk, with its vocabulary of certitude and supererogation and its premise of limitless commitment, would sound strident or naïve or irritating; in Inès, it always seems yet more evidence of her sunny optimism. I put an arm around her and kiss the top of her head. Her black, brittle hair is hot in the sun. I rest my cheek against it and squeeze her. She tells me she is so happy.

The damage, in the light of day, is not great – some dented car bodywork and a few broken windows, already in the process of repair. People are still drinking coffee at the pavement cafés and buying their bread and meat, but even I – newest of arrivals – can devise in the town something sobered and alert. A military jeep passes and there are patrols of soldiers as well as gendarmes. Inès talks briefly to shop-keepers and traders, to policemen and passers-by. This is not her side, these are not the people she really wants to interview, but even so, she treats them respectfully, solicitously; she does not stalk potential interviewees as though they were a species from another planet. I feel proud of her, and protective: I desperately do not want her to be disheartened.

The roads into the cité are sealed by soldiers and gendarmes and they turn us away – for our own safety, they insist. She argues but they are implacable at first and unpleasant soon after. She tries to find out from the house-boys and workers trickling through the checkpoints if the MNC rally is still going ahead. No one knows anything for certain, or possibly no one is willing to say. The MNC office in town is closed, there is no one around. Her spirits begin to slide. She is anxious not just about her story but about the loss of momentum for Patrice and his party.

I persuade her to have a late breakfast. She picks at her food, then goes to make some calls. She can't get through to Lumumba or any of the other MNC leaders. The morning wears on, nothing happens. Under the brightly coloured umbrella shading our table we have a cold beer.

The sun climbs higher and my heat-sapped mind day-dreams its way back to last night, to the bed, to Inès and the touch of her little breasts on my chest as she collapsed on top of me, breathless and laughing.

Two men make their way to a table nearby. Inès recognises a British reporter called Grant and comically shades her face with the menu. She despises journalists personally and professionally and avoids them when at all possible. It is nothing to do with rivalry. She simply cannot stand the self-regard, the camouflaged allegiances, the humbling generosity of their claims to neutrality. Grant, whom I would put at under thirty, is lanky and slow-moving. His brown hair, which he touches frequently, has a foppish cut; he has the studied languor of the old public schoolboy about him.

Inès surveys the street like a sunbather whose beloved little beach is becoming polluted by crowds and noise. She finishes her beer and decides we should, after all, go to Bernard Houthhoofd's for the afternoon. Most of the people there, she says, will be unpleasant types, but she might be able to pick up some useful information.

We walk down to the public docks, past the Palace Hotel on the left and the GB Ollivant depot opposite. The waterfront is busy – tugs, cargo boats, *vedettes*, canoes, dugouts, river transports; as far as the eye can see there are piers, warehouses, cranes, petrol tanks, dry docks, shipyards. A four-decked, stern-wheeled passenger steamer, painted white and blue, barges lashed to its sides, makes its way upriver, bound for Stanleyville.

'Bernard Houthhoofd is one of the richest men in the Congo,' Inès tells me, 'and one of the most influential. Nothing happens without him.'

'Does that include independence?'

'No,' she replies at once. 'Not even Houthhoofd can stop independence.'

Jostled by the laughing women on their way to market, we board the ferry to Brazzaville.

5

A CROSS THE RIVER and we are in another country. The French colony is different; it is haphazard and scruffy. Whites and blacks mix; they share restaurant tables and queues. We spend a little time ambling through the untidy streets and browsing in the market, threading our way through the women and their mounds of tapioca and cassava, sugar cane and bananas, avocados, tangerines, coconuts and peanuts. We find a taxi near the bus station – Inès hates the extravagance of this but Houthhoofd's house is ten kilometres out of town. The lulling rumble of the cataracts at Livingstone Falls gets louder as we proceed.

A servant opens the gates to the walled villa. To our right is a clay tennis court. Madeleine is one of the players. She wears a short white dress and her limbs are long and strong and tanned.

At the back of the house a wide garden inclines gently down to the river, where a pair of speedboats pull girls on water-skis. Away to our left on the far bank the long, low profile of Léopoldville stretches out. Directly opposite, perhaps a mile distant, is a cluster of dusty brick buildings with tin roofs – some black quarter or other, no one seems sure of its name.

There are about sixty guests standing around in small groups with drinks in their hands; there is a swimming pool and a gazebo.

A fat, soft, goitrous-throated man with bulging eyes approaches us. Inès introduces me to Bernard Houthhoofd.

Our host signals to a houseboy, one of a dozen or so lined up and waiting – almost straining – for summons. He brings us drinks from the little wooden bar by the shade of a mango tree.

'Did you hear about the disturbances last night?' Houthhoofd asks Inès.

'We were there, we saw it.'

'The Force Publique must be firmer next time.'

'They can be as firm as they like,' Inès replies, 'it won't do any good. There are a hundred thousand Europeans who don't want independence and fourteen million blacks who do. The outcome is inevitable.'

Houthhoofd grins tolerantly.

'There are other numbers that matter,' he says equably.

'What are they?' I ask.

'Money,' he says, his grin widening.

There is nothing ostentatious about Bernard Houthhoofd's dress or appearance, but still he has the look of a very rich man: it is in his self-possession and his manners – courtly yet at the same time somehow ominous. His smiling gaze is full of cool appraisals. He is the lord in his castle. We chat politely for a few minutes before he excuses himself.

De Scheut is playing croquet with another man and a boy and a girl in their early teens. They are healthy, shining, handsome children and they call de Scheut *papa*. Inès and I gaze at them and say nothing. My chest tightens momentarily. We cannot speak about this subject. I am again on the bus travelling up Kentish Town Road as Inès walks damp-footed through the grey snow after her appointment with the doctor. I had avoided going back to the flat that afternoon, avoided being there when she got home, for I knew from her expression, from the way she was walking, from the size of her, what she had been told. She cried, of course, but not for long. Inès bears misfortune bravely and I assured her it made no difference to me. At the time I believed this; now I am not so sure. What will the absence of children mean for us? For different reasons – hers to do with politics, mine with doubt – we have so far refused the disciplines and dreams of a conventional life together. We have never spoken seriously of marriage, we have never looked for an ideal home. But both of us feel the tug of domesticity, are aware of what it gives as much as what it takes away, and at moments like this, looking at de Scheut's children, our thoughts cannot but help turn to what we know we shall never have. Two tattered African Greys perch forlornly in their small cage, looking out at nothing.

We fall in with a group of guests by the gazebo. They seem well-meaning, polite, even a little diffident. They ask for our impressions, advise on health precautions, recommend res-taurants and sights to see. We should take the steamer to Stanleyville. We should go to Goma, a nice city with a pleasant climate. From there we can explore the Virunga national park. We should climb the Ruwenzori mountains.

As the conversation broadens I begin to pick up the miscel-laneous little navigational tips the newcomer anywhere requires for his social and political map. How the diplomats tend to look down on the commercial people and rarely invite them to embassy parties. How the British generally are trusted in business matters. How the Belgians are not good at mixing with the other nationalities, and the Flemish even worse – Houthhoofd is the exception. How the Walloons tend to be on the trading side, the Flemish more in administration and security. How the African mind differs from the European.

'The African mind?' I say. 'What is that?'

When it comes to the blacks the first thing I am to understand is that they are like children.

'Naughty children,' a Portuguese trader elaborates.

'Mischievous,' a Swedish dentist adds.

'You can take the black out of the jungle but you can't

take the jungle out of the black,' someone else says. 'Never show weakness in front of them – you're either the predator or the prey.'

The man who had been playing croquet with de Scheut stands on the fringes of our group. He has been silent throughout. He is not tall, he is not physically imposing in that way, but his presence makes itself felt. Even though this is only my second day in the country – my second day in Africa – I have seen enough to understand that white men's frames take on contours and conditions that imply compromise of varying degrees with their new environment. The way this man carries himself proclaims him inviolate, immune. He wears a short-sleeved shirt complete with tie. I assume he is de Scheut's second kind of settler: he looks every inch the parodic *colon*. He seems to be trying to catch my eye.

'One afternoon, a couple of months ago,' the Portuguese trader says for my instruction, 'I got my driver to take a friend home. His farm is on the way to Kikwit and it's a good road. The journey should have taken two hours at most. That night no sign of my driver. Next morning I found him four miles outside town asleep in the back seat without a care in the world. I said to the fellow, "What do you think you're doing?" He hadn't a clue what I was talking about. What was the problem? He knew I'd come along eventually and sort it out.'

'What was the problem?' I ask.

Inès is bridling. I am surprised she has held her tongue so long.

'He'd run out of petrol.'

There is some shaking of heads to indicate shared experience.

'Your driver's behaviour seems perfectly logical to me.'

It is not Inès but the man in the shirt and tie. He speaks with an American accent.

'Treat a grown man like a child,' he continues, 'and he'll

behave like a child. Your child did what any child would do and he looked after your property into the bargain. I don't see you have anything to complain about.'

For a man so powerfully made and for so abrupt an intervention, the voice is disconcertingly gracious.

'I don't think he was complaining,' Roger, a British doctor, says quietly. He is a ginger-sandy man of about my age. The face is faintly freckled and the moustache is of the kind popularized by RAF officers during the war; it tends to go with a pipe and a phlegmatic spirit. He pokes diffidently at an anthill with the toe of his shoe.

'Wasn't he?' the American says. 'My mistake.'

From further down the garden Houthhoofd shouts a summons: something across the river deserves our attention. The group breaks up, thankful to get away.

The American puts out his hand.

'Mark Stipe.'

'How do you do?' I say. 'I'm James Gillespie. This is Inès Sabiani.'

I am very aware that I am looking at what I am not. His eyes are brown and frank and go some way to mitigate the stamp of barely-tethered aggression implied by the large, round head and the close-cropped blond-grey hair. His face is open, and his broad, high brow divided in the middle by a thick, beating vein: for a moment I experience a bizarre urge to press my thumb to that violent pulse, as if in some way touching him there, where his blood runs nearest the surface, would enable me to get the measure of the man, to under-stand, even share, the sources of his authority. I came across men like this in the army, and I have written about them since, pretending – as the writer does – to know them or to know more than they do. I am never easy in their company.

Stipe looks down the garden at our companions.

'When are these people going to see they have a problem

here and they're going to have to do something about it?'

I say nothing, unwilling to collude in something I know so little about.

'James Gillespie,' Stipe says slowly, turning the name over, wondering aloud. 'How do I know that name? You're not the writer, are you?'

I say that I am.

'I've read something of yours. A novel? Set in London, wasn't it?'

'It's possible.'

'I have a bad memory. Remind me of the title.'

I give him three alternatives. He selects my second novel.

'You know, I liked that book a lot.'

I am deeply flattered, more than I pretend to be. My books are not widely read.

'Are you a writer as well, Inès?'

'No,' she replies.

There is a short, rude silence which I try to cover by explaining that Inès is the correspondent for *L'Unità*.

'The communist paper of Italy,' she declares.

This addition, given Stipe's determined amiability, hardly seems called for, and it is uttered with unmistakable truculence. I look at her, surprised. I had thought that after Stipe's intervention she might have found an ally. Her throat has flushed red. She has taken against him. I see it at once. So does he.

'I'm more of a *Wall Street Journal* man myself,' Stipe says.

'I wouldn't expect anything different.'

'Nor I of you, Inès.'

Her whole face now is red; she doesn't have the temperament or a sufficiently ironic grasp of English to deal with Stipe's careful insouciance.

'You're not a journalist then?' I say to get us out of the awkward moment.

'I work at the consulate. I was in the London embassy for

two years before I got this posting,' he says, and he smiles to show he has not taken offence. 'We must have a long talk over tall, cold drinks some evening. Leo has its merits, but culture isn't one of them.'

Inès squints down to the lower end of the garden where Houthhoofd's guests are gathering.

'There's something happening across the river,' she says and she walks down to join them.

Watching her as she goes, Stipe says with an amused sympathy I slightly resent, 'I like a woman who knows her own mind.'

I do not respond to this; he is a stranger. We peer over to the far bank.

'I've got a pair of binoculars in my car,' Stipe says, and, excusing himself, he strides away up the garden.

I go down to the crowd and find myself next to Madeleine. The water-skiers weave and circle, a pied kingfisher hovers twenty feet above the water. There are men in military uniform on the far bank.

'What's going on?'

'You see?' Madeleine says, pointing across the river at the buildings of the native quarter.

There is some ragged movement, people running this way and that. The sounds coming to us from the far bank are muted and flat.

'This will show them who's boss,' Madeleine says with relish.

'It was inevitable,' I hear Houthhoofd announce. 'If we do nothing, they'll get it into their heads that they'd got away with it and next time it will be a lot worse than a few broken windows.'

'You're only stoking up more trouble for yourself, Bernard,' de Scheut says.

'Romain,' Houthhoofd begins in an indulgent tone, 'what is your alternative?'

41

'There is always an alternative to force,' de Scheut replies. 'Talk to them, talk to their leaders, make them feel part of the set-up.'

'How can you talk to those people?' Madeleine breaks in vehemently. 'They can barely speak enough French to understand when you tell them to clean the house.'

Stipe rejoins us. He has a pair of field glasses.

'Looks pretty serious,' he says after a while, handing me the glasses.

I am confronted by a turbid blur – the magnified foliage of the bush, the muddy water of the river or the grey sky above, it could be any of these. Something passes before me, accelerating fast. One of the speedboats. I adjust the focus and trail it. The boat starts to slow down, the girl on the skis slews gently into the river like a landing water-bird, the boat circles and picks her up. I move the glasses and find the kingfisher, its hammer-shaped head cocked for movement below. It folds its wings and drops into the water.

A new image: a small, sudden cloud of dust kicked up on a wall, then another next to it. I am puzzled; then I hear the first of a series of distant dry cracks.

The gunfire is clearly audible now. I realize I was looking at the strike of bullets.

'My God,' de Scheut whispers.

Stipe takes back the glasses.

'I can see one man down,' he says. 'Two.'

The shooting continues intermittently for four or five minutes more. I look around at the faces of the guests. It is strange but there is no trace of emotion. People are being shot and there is no visible reaction. But then . . . why should there be? This is a garden party, after all. There is the tennis and the croquet lawn and the children, there are the water-skiers and the kingfisher and all the innocence and play this implies. Shots have been fired, but injury and death in this arrangement still seem incongruous, mistimed. No one – least of all I – can be sure of our connection with the fuzzy events across the wide river.

The murmuring onlookers start to drift off, back to the swimming pool, back to the gazebo. Madeleine rejoins her tennis partner. A houseboy comes up and offers to replenish our glasses. I search the man's eyes for something, anything. A response of some sort. Resentment, anger, hate. But there's nothing. He fills my glass and smoothly turns to another guest.

Stipe hands me the binoculars again and this time directs my line of sight.

'You see that big floating island of green? The one over by the little jetty?'

I focus on a tangle of vegetation. Amid the trailing roots and the broad, fleshy leaves are mud-flecked flowers of pale blue.

'Water-hyacinth,' Stipe explains. 'It's an exotic. Some fool brought it over from South America because he thought it would look pretty in his garden pond. The damn thing spread like a plague.'

'It does look pretty.'

'It's a parasite,' de Scheut says vaguely. 'It eats the oxygen and kills the river.'

I see something more than flowers. I am not aware of making any reaction, but Stipe picks up on some minuscule betrayal in my attitude, or in my breath, in my smell.

'You see now?' Stipe says.

I see.

It is a human body, half-submerged, half-supported in the chaotic lattice of the drifting island. I move my field of vision up to the jetty where a group of black soldiers, directed by a white officer, are heaving a second dead man into the water. More corpses – four, five, six – are being brought to them for disposal.

The shooting has stopped. Now there is only the noise of Madeleine's tennis game and the gentle roar of the cataracts, many miles away.

'I must take my children home,' de Scheut says.

He puts a hand on my shoulder.

'*Du calme, du calme,*' he says. '*Adieu.*'

He clasps his children to his sides. They trudge up the garden.

I go to Inès. I can see the fury in her, she is absorbed in rage and grief. I saw some things in the army, but have never been witness to anything like what has happened here today. I long ago gave up the search for anger in myself. As I look at her, my thoughts splinter and in their disorder my mind turns to my mother. I am thinking about love – fierce love – and loyalty, and the intent of these things. My mother loved, passionately and unselfishly. She loved the man she once idolized, loved him even after he deserted her and her children. Inès would deny it, but she no longer loves me, not the way she once did. I know it. I can see it. In spite of my welcome, in spite of last night. I am for now replaced by other things. Dramatic, involving – they will take her. But I will not give up hope. The politics of idealism go hand in hand with disillusion, and when disillusion sets in I will still be here for her.

Out on the river the speedboats have started up again. The water-skiers detour towards the jetty. Like the drivers at the scene of an accident, they slow down as they pass the water-hyacinth and its bleeding litter. Then they accelerate and head out to uncontaminated waters to continue their sport.

In the tropics one must before everything keep calm. Of course. Behind, from the tennis court, someone shouts 'Well played, Madeleine.'

Du calme, du calme. Of course. Always.

6

SHE DIVIDES ME. Her words divide me. Her language refuses the disciplines of the eye, of history, of the world as it is. Her imagination turns on symbol and myth. She lives in the rush of all-embracing sympathies, and sometimes, listening to her song, my lulled emotions slip their noose and follow in the blind career of her allegiance; but then a word, a single word, a note so obviously wrong, interrupts and I am filled with resentment of her and her histrionic lexicon. She said to me once – it was during my first visit to Bologna, when she was showing me the plaques which commemorate the city's fallen partisans – 'I often think I am so fortunate to have had the *experience* of the Party, to know there is something to support you always, that you aren't alone in the world. I can't imagine to be without this.' We'd had a nice day: we had got up late, had coffee and *bigné* and *canolo* for breakfast, drunk wine at lunch and strolled through the galleries in the afternoon. She had laced our time with excited talk, but I looked at her when she said this and brutal thoughts hit me like stones: *Who do you think I am? What have I ever said or written to give you the impression I have anything to do with what you're talking about?*

I should have told her then, 'Inès, I know myself too well. This isn't going to work.' But I didn't, I couldn't; I loved the spirit behind the hopeful, spinning monologues. I am in love with it still.

She has left the apartment to file her story from the little office near the Marché Indigène which she shares with the

ABC correspondent. Why did I react so strongly? So savagely?

She had sat at the little table before the window overlooking the street and stabbed at the keys of the typewriter. A wind came up and the late afternoon light gave way to a brooding, luminous gloom. A sudden grey rain swept the street, there was a stunning clap of thunder and the downpour began. She passed me the pages as they came off the roller, translating the words I did not know.

'Well,' she said, her head bent over the typescript, 'what do you think?'

'I think you should take an hour to cool down.'

Her head jerked up and her eyes flashed fiercely: 'What?'

I shrugged; she'd heard. She was on her feet in an instant.

'What are you saying?'

I had no time for this. She clutched at my arm.

'What are you saying?' she demanded again.

I shook her off.

'All right,' I said with heat, 'feel angry about what you saw. But you are a journalist. At least keep a sense of proportion, at least try to keep some distance.'

'And how would you write about this?'

'You don't have to shout to be heard.'

'People have been murdered.'

'People have been shot,' I corrected her, 'and you weren't the only one who saw that.'

'Have I said that I was? Where have I said anything like that?'

Her jaw was set, her face flushed.

'Where?'

It was in every word. The rage of her writing made her the exclusive witness, banned, disqualified the rest of us. This empathetic one-upmanship always infuriates me.

'To write about injustice without anger,' she shouted at

my stiff back, 'is another injustice.'

'I feel confident I could make a strong case for exactly the opposite proposition,' I replied with the disdainful calm I know incenses her.

She snatched up her pages and left.

Why did I react so acerbically? The answer is not hard to find. I am being squeezed out of her orbit. I have come a thousand miles to pin her down, but I see there is no chance of that in these crowded, coursing times. I am bitter. There is no place for me.

But it is also to do with words. The implications go deep: it is about the way we see the world. I know there are inner things, below, beneath, from the dominion of hesitation, and that these, in some degree, count. But not for much, not for as much as Inès thinks. It may not all take place on the outside but there is still much on the surface. What is real to me is what can be seen; I understand above all else the evidence of the eyes. She is moved by things that cannot be described, that are only half-glimpsed, and when she writes – is this allowable in a journalist? – it is not primarily to inform her audience, but to touch them. I object to this; I find it embarrassing, unprofessional, and I object to the implication that those of us who cannot or will not produce in our writing so ostentatious a display of outrage are in some way at fault, that we are at worst collaborators with the enemy, at best heartless, selfish, trivial. Words, real words with real meanings, matter to me. I have never taken strong beliefs seriously; in my first career I was an historian.

She is gone and I feel suddenly very alone. I drink what whisky I can find. I want to shake her and tell her to hurry up and grow up and get disillusioned like the rest of us; and I want her not to change, ever, for I need her to be like this: I have been stimulated, I have found things I otherwise would not have found. I live in the tension of our disparities. But where is this going, this strange affair?

The storm has passed. I pour the last of the whisky, swallow it in one gulp and go outside; I have to walk off my anger. I stride away, careless of direction. The light is fading fast. I walk and walk until I find myself in one of the residential districts. The streets are deserted; most of the houses are locked up. I walk on, further and further from the city. The houses become fewer, the tarmac gives out, the night comes in. I visit bitter retaliations on Inès, I do not keep track of my route. After a while I am completely lost.

Eventually, I flag down a car and ask for directions from a man who is at first wary, then, once I explain the situation, concerned about my safety. After what happened today, he says, who knows what the blacks will do. There are rumours of more disturbances and some property somewhere is already burning. I can taste the smoke and also something sharp – tear gas perhaps. He offers me a lift but I thank him and decline. He is hesitant about leaving me, but I insist I will be all right. I need more time to myself.

I follow his directions but get nowhere. The night is sticky, the shirt is plastered to my back, my hair is flat with sweat. Soon I wish I had accepted the lift.

In the distance I see lights, and, as I approach, I hear the high, heedless voices of people at a party. The poison of the things I said to Inès still courses in my veins and the sound of friends and lovers enjoying themselves only adds to my rancour. When I am close to the bungalow I stop and shut my eyes. I really do not want to face anyone now, not even to ask for directions. What am I doing here? What am I doing in this country? Why did I come here? The heat has drained me, the drink has made me self-pitying.

I have to take stock, Inès, I have to think and I have to be honest. I have to be honest for once in my life.

I open my eyes to see two young women come out on to the bungalow's brightly lit veranda. They wear strapless evening dresses and talk with an animation that is intimate and knowing and innocent. In the darkness I have not been noticed. The smell of smoke is stronger now and there are embers in the air. A gust of wind comes up and the glowing cinders glide like ragged fireflies. The women, with skin exposed, shriek in playful alarm. The younger of the two, a tall girl with short dark hair, takes courage and blows at the invaders, as at bubbles, to the applause of her merry companion. The commotion stirs their friends, and the men come out, gallant and laughing, to perform mock heroics. I watch this cheerful little war, fascinated by the high spirits I cannot be part of. I look. I look too long. What forms in front of my eyes is the disdain and envy in my own face – the compound that is the habitual onlooker's most unappealing property. How many times have I caught myself looking at Inès like this, wondering at the secrets of her optimism and her easy friendships, then waspishly questioning their authenticity and congratulating myself on my own distant self-sufficiency?

I have to be honest. Self-sufficiency has its limits. I have spent too much time in the cheerless solitude of my own ego. In Inès's absence over the last few weeks it has been more than I could stand.

There is a woman in London. Her name is Margaret. I am not proud of this. Some days before I left for Léopoldville I rang her. I had not seen her for several weeks and had not slept with her since Inès. We met that evening in the pub near my flat in Camden. I started, as I am prone to, tentatively, even shyly, not speaking much and tending to avoid her gaze. After a few failed attempts to draw me out, Margaret asked if at that moment I was where I wanted to be. I made some vague sound of affirmation. She asked about Inès and how she was getting on in the Congo. I said she was doing fine and left it at that. Margaret regarded me for a moment, weighing up my silences, speculating on the likely course of the night should she decide to spend it with me.

'James,' she said simply, 'whenever we meet it's as though you have to spend the first hour deciding whether you like me or not.'

It might have been more hurtful to Margaret to get up and walk out. But that is not why I stayed. I desperately needed company and I wanted to forget Inès, to forget her hold on me, to announce my independence to myself. All very banal. I was aware of it at the time, but this did not stop me.

So I told her that I was really, really happy to see her again. She was not convinced. I was acutely aware of my lack of credibility. I was banking on time and the drink to establish my case for me. Sure enough, glass by glass, I began to relax. I encouraged her to talk, which Margaret always does well. I let her fast, salty chatter mask my evasions. I started to remember why I liked her, why I enjoyed her hearty presence. She always made me laugh. She told me stories from the set of her new film, and of how when she had gone for the insurance medical the doctor had asked what height she was. Five-eight, she had replied, only to be told she was in fact five-five.

'Are you sure?' she had demanded, lofty and offended. 'Is that measuring thing right?'

She shrieked with laughter.

'I've lied so often about it, James, I couldn't remember what height I really was.'

Margaret was permanently amused – by life, by others, by me, by her own ripe physicality. Her fine hair fell loosely around her shoulders. She employed the little tricks of seduction with gusto – an occasional flutter of the eyelids, leaning forward to show her cleavage, a casual readjustment of skirt which could not but call attention to her legs. She enjoyed to the full the happy accident of her sensuality.

At closing time she asked again if I was sure. By then the alcohol had done its work for me. Fortunately, in the company of women, I am a happy and flirtatious drunk. Margaret always used to say I should drink more often.

Afterwards, did I feel guilty? I imagined an argument with Inès in which I defended myself from her jealous indictment of my infidelity with *You left me, you went away and left me! What did you expect?* Then I thought of something worse. That her feelings had changed to such an extent that she might not care now at all.

I walk on. It gets lonelier with every step. The pulsing throb of the frogs and cicadas is my only reassurance and whenever it stops I stand still, cautioned and vigilant like some nervous forest animal. I cannot see to put one foot in front of the other. I stumble and fall on the track. An insect I cannot see crawls over my hand and I brush it quickly away.

A car approaches, sweeping me with the headlight beam. I get to my feet and wave it down. I suppose I must look quite frantic and I am surprised when it slows to a halt. The driver reaches across and opens the passenger door. I climb in, muttering a thank you in French.

'It's dangerous to be on foot,' the driver says with a mixture of sternness and solicitude.

'Yes, I know,' I reply contritely. 'I got lost.'

'Tonight the blacks are going crazy.'

7

I FIND A bar still open on Avenue Vangele, the Colibri. I am already aware that white Léopoldville is a small town. The settlers go to each other's houses and parties, they frequent the same restaurants and clubs. So I am not particularly surprised when among the half-dozen or so inside I find Stipe. He is standing alone at the bar, throwing down the last of a drink. He spots me the moment I enter. When I first saw him in Houthhoofd's garden I thought he had the look of a man permanently on call for stern and enigmatic duties, but tonight his expression is compassionate, sheltering.

Though he had seemed to be on his way out when I arrived, he leads me to a table by the window. The interior is small and painted a deep red. The wood of the furniture is dark, there is a brass footrail at the bar, behind which, in a shallow, frosted-mirror alcove, liquor bottles stand on glass shelves. A tape recorder is playing the music of Charles Trenet.

'You look like someone who needs to talk,' he says.

Here is someone who understands. I already know that when I walk out of here we will be friends. He orders cognacs from the elderly Walloon proprietress, whom he calls Anna. His manner with her is flirtatious and jaunty. He tastes his drink.

'Wherever I'm posted I try to find a bar like this,' he says, 'somewhere I can call home, where the people know me and do little things for me, little courtesies, like start mixing my favourite cocktail as soon as I walk in the door, or if there's a crowd serve me first. That way, if you've had a bad day, you always know you have a friendly place to go. It's not much I know, but life can be lonely and by my age you've learned to appreciate the small favours people do for you.'

He pauses and looks at me. His brown eyes are set quite close together, and there is the slightest suggestion of a squint. When he leans forward like this – arms on the table, ankles crossed under his chair, drenching you in his attention – it gives his expression a special and irresistible candour.

'So,' he says with a sympathetic grin, 'how has your day been?'

This is not like me. My closest friends do not know any of this. Maybe it's because he's a stranger and the embarrassment is less and there is no version of my own history and my history with Inès that I have to keep to for consistency's sake, for pride's sake; maybe it's just a kind of exhaustion on my part, as though I no longer have the strength to keep my true words dammed up. I tell him everything. I tell him especially one thing, that after six months of trying Inès had not conceived.

I have as little to do with doctors as I can manage and I would have been happy to leave it for another six months, for a year or longer. For ever. There is value in ignorance, don't let anyone persuade you otherwise: the blind eye serves a function. But her attitude was different. She wanted tests, she wanted to know. She may, I thought afterwards, have already suspected the truth. We went for the tests. The problem, they discovered, was not with my sperm, but with her chlamydia-scarred tubes. It was pure chance I saw her the day of the doctor's appointment. It was about three in the afternoon. The morning had been gloomy, it had never really got light. The people on the streets made their way without spirit, thinking only of home. I glanced out the window of the bus and happened to notice, from the back, a schoolgirl walking along with the aimless, dreamy preoccupation of girls of that age. Alone among the pedestrians she seemed oblivious of the sludge and the cold and the bitter drive of the wind. She looked about, saw nothing, saw no one. She reminded me of the girls from St Dominic's and Fortwilliam, their skinny bare legs in the winter and their touching self-absorption. This one had not yet filled out as a woman, but within six months, or a year, she would be transformed.

As the bus drew level I still did not recognize the pale, cold face. It was abandoned, alone, so very near defeat. In shock I recognized Inès and I bowed my head in instant understanding. My first thought was to get off and go to her; I was already grasping the cold metal rail of the seat in front. And then I let my grip relax. I knew I could not face her unhappiness. Not very noble, but very easy. The bus accelerated. The stops went by, including my own. I did not move.

I don't recall where I got off, but I do remember wandering down Charing Cross Road and browsing in the book shops. I bought a second-hand copy of Henry James's criticism. I walked over Waterloo Bridge and along the Embankment. I was not like Inès, I felt the cold. The sludge seeped into my shoes, my socks became damp. I knew she would be in the flat, waiting with her news. So I walked on, my feet like ice, and on.

Eventually I re-crossed the river and made my way home, slowly and on foot. I got in around eleven. She was already in bed, silent.

'I had a drink with Alan,' I told her as I undressed. 'Sorry. I should have rung.'

She murmured something, that it was okay. If she had seen my face she would have known at once that I knew, but she was on her side, turned away from me.

I got in beside her and kissed the back of her neck. In those days we made love every night. She did not respond and I am not the kind of man to insist. Yet that night I did, I did insist. I should have known better. I thought it would be kind of ecstatic reaffirmation, a defiance, of nature, of failure, of fate; instead it was desolate. In the morning she told me. She cried, only a little. I told her it didn't matter, and we never mentioned it again.

Inès's love is like heated air. It cannot stand to be confined. It must expand. At that point in her life it needed a child, and not finding one, it turned elsewhere.

Stipe listens like a good priest. And in return he gives bits of himself away. Not much, no great detail. But enough. I learn that like me he barely knew his father. Like me, he watched a mother struggle. And, like me, he loves someone more than she loves him. Enough. Enough to know there are things between us.

He looks at his watch. The bar is empty. Anna yawns, encouraging us to go. He stares at me. I can see some calculation behind his eyes.

'Where are you going now?' he asks.

'Home, I suppose.'

'Why don't you come along with me?' he says after a pause. 'I might have something to interest you.'

On Boulevard Albert I there are only military vehicles. The settlers are in their houses.

We pass the cemetery, the golf course and, directly oppo-site on the other side of the avenue, standing in a walled garden, a solid, two-storey, red-brick house that reminds me vaguely of the kind of middle-class homes you find in Crouch End or Muswell Hill. Soldiers and police mill around the closed iron gate. They turn to stare as we pass.

'Lumumba's house,' Stipe explains. 'He was one of the

first blacks to be allowed to live in the European quarter. There are still very few. The Belgians will arrest him the minute he shows up. I got word to him to go to my driver's house. He'll be safe there for a while.'

'How many were killed today?' I ask.

'Could be tens, could be hundreds. African death has a habit of defying accurate quantification.'

'What exactly happened?'

'The MNC held their rally. Patrice's speech was pretty high, as you can imagine, and inspirational.' He gives me a grin. 'It inspired the young hotheads to some stone-throwing and shop-breaking. After last night's little display, the Belgians were in no mood to give them a free hand, so they sent in a platoon of regular Belgian soldiers and the Force Publique. The rest you know.'

'What's the Force Publique?'

'It's not really an army – even though contingents served with the allies during the last war: they were involved in the Abyssinian campaign and I think I heard they sent a field hospital unit to the India-Burma front – but really it's more like an internal security force. Twenty-four thousand men – sort of part-soldiers, part-gendarmerie – with just over a thousand Belgian officers.'

From somewhere in the distance there is the sound of an explosion.

'That's not what I think it is?' I say.

We listen. The sound we are waiting for comes thirty or forty seconds later. A second explosion. Like the first, the sound is muffled rather than sharp or reverberating.

'That's a mortar, isn't it?' I say.

'What a mess,' he says, shaking his head. 'What a Godawful mess.'

We have turned off the boulevard and are approaching a checkpoint at the cité's boundary. A black sergeant waves us down. Stipe reaches into his jacket and takes out his papers, and also a second document to which he draws the soldier's attention. The soldier goes to consult a white officer who, after inspection of the documents, comes over. There is another exchange. The officer withdraws.

Stipe, gazing after the soldiers, says, 'The highest ranking Congolese in the Force Publique are NCOs. As you can imagine, they're not entirely happy about the set-up. Not that it bothers the commander, General Janssens. He's an officer of the old school. A bonehead, and not exactly what you would call forward-thinking on the race issue.'

He hooks his arm through the open window and drums his fingers on the metal.

'This may take a little time,' he says. 'The Sûreté have given me permission to move about, but the soldiers will want to do their own checking.'

He offers me a cigarette. There is a third explosion, followed about a minute later by a fourth. What are they bombing? I try to picture the soldiers and their mortars and the missiles lobbed incomprehensibly into the vast dark slums of the cité. What were they firing at? What did they expect to happen?

'How long would you say the Belgians can hold on here?' Stipe asks idly.

'They seem to be doing pretty well.'

'I don't agree,' he says evenly. 'The shooting this after-noon, the mortars – it's their last gasp. The Belgians are about to give in.'

'Give in to what?' I ask.

'Independence.'

'Yes, in ten or twenty years.'

'More like six months.'

He draws slowly on his cigarette. He knows he has my attention.

'That's not the official position,' I remind him.

The official position, which Inès damns in every angry article, was set out in the *Déclaration Gouvernementale* in Brussels earlier in the year. The Belgians had decided that since the colony would not be ready for self-government for a long time to come, the Congolese people would have to be led to independence *graduellement et progressivement.*

'The *Déclaration Gouvernementale* isn't worth the paper it's written on. They're preparing to pull out as we speak.'

'Is the country ready for independence?' I ask.

'What do you think?'

'I arrived yesterday.'

'Even so, have you seen anything resembling a black professional class so far?'

I make a small laugh in acknowledgement of his point. Five minutes in Léopoldville was all it took to see how and by whom the day-to-day affairs of the colony were managed.

'There isn't a single black soldier above the rank of sergeant,' Stipe says. 'There isn't a single civil servant above junior clerk grade, there isn't a single black doctor, or engineer, or banker. Rumour has it there's one lawyer – the journalists are taking bets on who finds him first. The point is: who's going to run the country when the Belgians go?'

'Does that mean you're against independence?'

The officer comes over to the car and returns the papers to Stipe.

'There are gangs of thugs everywhere,' the officer announces gravely. 'I can arrange an escort if you want.'

'Thank you, but that won't be necessary,' Stipe replies cheerily, putting the engine in drive.

'You are armed?'

'Absolutely.'

I hadn't thought about the possibility that Stipe would be carrying a gun. In our present surroundings the knowledge is reassuring, but it also raises questions about the man, who he is and what he does.

The officer waves to the soldiers at the barrier and gives Stipe a stiff salute. Stipe seems to accept it as his due. I look at him. I look at the fat vein in his forehead and the long, curved lashes over his soft brown eyes. In the distance there is the dull crash of another mortar bomb. As we proceed through the checkpoint, as the officer holds his salute, as the soldiers scuttle to swing the barrier aside and clear our way into the cité, I see again what I saw in Houthhoofd's garden earlier in the day, the authority, the confidence, the self-belief. Even when I remind myself that this is no more than a dark corner of a colonial city most people have never heard of, I cannot help the way my thoughts run. I cannot help but think about power, about authenticity, and the uselessness of being a writer.

8

Sewage runs in the open channels of the cité's narrow and unpaved streets. The low, crude, cube housing is arranged in small, densely packed, alley-scarred blocks. There is little lighting in this squalid labyrinth. There are no other cars, there is no one to be seen.

'You didn't tell me where you stand on independence?' I remind Stipe.

'My government has always had a sympathetic interest in the decolonization of Africa. The US is one of the few Western nations with no selfish strategic or economic interests in the Congo.'

'There are American companies here though, aren't there?' I say.

He is beginning to sound a little disingenuous, even to me.

'Sure, but US economic interests are relatively minor. Mobil Oil is one of the biggest US corporations operating here. They have a $12 million investment in service stations, but when you compare that to a total Western investment of four to five billion, you couldn't say Mobil is one of the Congo's big players.'

'What about you personally, how do you feel about independence?'

'Perhaps I'm making large assumptions here, James,' he says, 'but I'm no more of a *believer* than you are. If I believe in anything, it's government as management – good management. Balanced budget, fiscal probity, low taxes, proper defence preparedness – that's my philosophy, such as it is. I'd be happy with an independent Congo as long as it were stable and well-run. I'd be happy with a continuation of the present set-up, as long as you could prove to me that it would be stable and well-run. But what I think is irrelevant. The fact is the Belgians are going in six months and that's the situation we have to deal with.'

He turns into an alley. The only illumination comes from the car's headlights. He counts off the shacks as we trundle past. They are not numbered. He stops and cuts the engine and lights.

'Can you imagine what's going to happen when the settlers find out?' he says as we get out of the car. 'Most of them right now are burying their heads in the sand. They won't admit even to themselves what's going on. The men are out there on the links boasting about their cars and their pensions and the women sit in each other's houses talking about curtains and kitchens. They think their colony is going on forever, that they're going to live like lords and ladies for the rest of their lives. But real soon they're going to have to make some very big mental and material adjustments. It's going to be difficult for them.'

My thoughts turn to Madeleine. I can see that the required adjustments might not be easy for her.

Stipe leads me to the anonymous door of a dingy shack. He doesn't have to knock, our arrival has been noted. A black man of medium height appears to greet us. He wears sharply pressed maroon trousers and a bright, violently patterned yellow and green shirt which has the sheen of synthetic silk. The ridiculously huge buckles on his patent shoes gleam in the half-light. He has a heavy fake-gold necklace and several rings set with red and amber glass.

Stipe puts an arm around the man's shoulders.

'James, this is my driver Auguste,' he says in French.

Auguste is handsome, with a high-domed forehead, good

cheekbones and a strong jaw, and he would have appeared intimidating, or at least serious, had he not smiled as we entered. The smile spoiled the face; his look then was almost comically craven.

'This is a great kid,' Stipe says, looking at Auguste like a father at a son and shaking him with rough affection. 'You didn't get caught up in the shooting?'

'I was there, but I'm okay,' Auguste replies.

'You shouldn't have gone.' Stipe's voice is full of tender remonstration. 'I told you there was going to be trouble.'

Auguste closes the door behind us. The small, windowless room is bare except for an iron bedstead – no mattress – and a long plank of grey, splintering lumber, raised by mud bricks to about a foot from the floor to serve as a bench. An old hurricane lamp gives out what little light there is. On Auguste's brusque command, two young men shift from the bench to the relative discomfort of the bedstead. The black paint on the iron frame is bubbled and flaking. The air is close with the smell of damp earth and sweat. A grubby kitten plays on the raffia mat laid over the dirt floor. Auguste and his two companions sit opposite us like bored children, watching in a distracted sort of way but saying nothing.

Stipe asks for more details about the afternoon's events. Auguste's French is slow but the accent, cadences and phrasing are too unfamiliar for me to be able to follow easily. I do, however, pick up the mention of 'Patrice'.

'Is Patrice all right?' Stipe asks. His own French is heavily accented but fluent.

Auguste nods to the far wall where an old bedcover hangs over what looks like the entrance to an adjoining room, from where I can hear several voices. We settle down to wait.

'Why would the Belgians want to give up their colony?' I ask Stipe after a while.

'When you ask the Belgians why they're in the Congo they

tell you, *dominer pour servir*. Dominate to serve. To serve and civilize. That, they say, is the sole excuse for colonialism, and its complete justification. It's bullshit of course. The excuse is profit. Once the profits go, so do the excuses.'

'Have the profits gone?'

'Gone and goodbye. The colony's economy is shot.'

'It doesn't look it.'

'It's a disaster zone,' he says flatly; then he adds: 'If you wanted to write an article about this, I could help you.'

The suggestion catches me by surprise.

'Why?'

'The sooner the settlers know what's going on, the longer they'll have to get used to the idea.'

'No, I meant why me?'

'What can I say? You get a feeling about someone.'

He shrugs and puts out his hands in an open gesture to acknowledge the plain fact of our instinctive liking for each other.

'I have the documentation,' he continues, 'all the facts, all the figures.'

Someone pushes aside the hanging bedcover.

I see a tall, thin bespectacled young man with a head that seems too small for his wide shoulders. He is wearing light grey trousers and an open-necked, short-sleeved white shirt. He has a scraggy goatee beard, his arms are long and rangy. I recognize Patrice Lumumba from the newspaper photo-graphs. He looks over at Stipe, then at me. He holds my gaze for a moment, no expression on his face. He is joined by two other men.

'Mark, my friend.'

Stipe goes over and shakes hands warmly with Lumumba.

'Patrice, how are you?'

'It has not been a good day. So many are dead.'

'We have to get you out,' Stipe says, 'get you somewhere

safe. Brazzaville first, then maybe Accra.'

Lumumba considers for a moment. He says, 'Is it right for the leader to run and leave his followers to their fate?'

'Is it right for the leader to allow his enemies to put him in jail? The movement will fall apart without you.'

Lumumba says nothing. His gaze reaches me.

Stipe says, 'Patrice, this is James Gillespie. I think you know his friend – Inès Sabiani.'

'Of course we know Inès,' Lumumba says, his voice becoming suddenly animated. He takes my hand in both of his. 'Inès is a good friend to our people and to the cause of the Congo. She is your woman?'

I hear myself say yes quickly and with emphasis, and I see Stipe look at me. I am not used to describing Inès in this way – *my woman* – and the words do something to give me hope, as if their vehemence alone makes the statement true. Stipe drops his gaze for a moment. He knows what is going on in my head and he cares.

Stipe introduces me to the two men with Lumumba – Nendaka and Mungul. They are senior MNC officials. The first is dressed as a more prosperous version of Auguste, with smart shiny well-tailored clothes. His smile is too broad, his handshake too ingratiating to be trustworthy. Mungul is sober, serious and although polite I get the feeling he does not welcome the presence of these strange white men.

Stipe says to me, 'I have some things to discuss with Patrice. I won't be long.'

The four men disappear into the other room.

I sit back down on the bench and check my watch. It is after one. I close my eyes. I become aware of someone standing at my shoulder. Auguste grins at me.

'This man is my brother,' Auguste says in English, pointing to one of the young men sitting on the bed frame.

'What about the other one?' I ask.

'He is my brother also.'

I smile at the other brother. Auguste grimaces obsequiously.

'You speak English very well,' I say.

'*Ad graecas litteras totum animum impuli.*'

'And Latin.'

'Knowledge is essential,' he says as though revealing a hidden truth. 'For the same reason that Erasmus learned Greek, I have learned English.'

I nod, trying my best to match his seriousness.

'English is the language of the new Romans,' he adds confusingly.

'The new Romans?'

'The Americans.'

'Yes, of course.'

'I will go to America to study,' he says.

'What will you study?'

'Psychology, psychiatry, pedagogy, physics . . .'

'That's quite a lot of subjects to study, and they all begin with *p*.'

'Yes,' he says seriously. 'Do you have friends in America?'

'Some.'

'You can give me their addresses?'

I pause. 'I don't have my address book with me now. I'll look out some names for you later and give them to Stipe.'

'Thank you, *nókó*,' he says gravely. 'I think America is a good place.'

'I think so.'

'In America you are respected for what you achieve. The colour of the skin is immaterial.'

I feel torn; to collude in this is both patronizing and dishonest, but at the same time I have no desire to interfere with a fantasy which may, for all I know, be central to making an intolerable life here tolerable.

I ask instead what he intends to do once he has finished his studies in psychology, psychiatry, pedagogy and physics.

'I shall become a lawyer,' he says with a grin.

'I see,' I respond, nodding uncertainly. 'Why do you want to be a lawyer?'

'To defend the poor people against injustice.' He smiles, with a mischievous sparkle this time, and adds: 'And to have an office on Park Avenue with six pretty secretaries.'

He starts laughing. So do his brothers, though I am not certain they have understood. After a while I get the impression they may be laughing at me.

9

THE TIME WILL come when I am no longer engrossed in her idea. That time may be soon, but it has not come yet.

She is on her side facing the wall with her knees drawn up, feet free from the tangle of the sheet. The room is airless and hot. I undress and get in beside her, moulding against the contours of her narrow back and hips. In an automatic movement, she lifts her wing-folded arm to allow me to put a hand on her breast. It's our way of sleeping together. She has solace fingers between her legs.

'Did you file your story?'

I brush aside a strand of hair and kiss the nape of her neck.

'The Sûreté were preventing journalists to use the telex, but I got a boatman to take me to Brazzaville.'

Her voice is remote and wounded, the dregs of the argument lie between us still.

'Where have you been?'

'With Stipe.'

She makes a little grunt. She is not impressed.

'He's not what you think,' I say.

'The Americans and the Belgians are on the same side. They are enemies of the independence movement.'

'Maybe it's more complicated than that,' I suggest.

'That is very naïve.'

Pots and kettles, but I want to placate. I lean over and kiss her ear. She does not move, she does not respond to me. Her eyes are shut.

'Inès,' I say softly. 'I came here for you.'

'Let's not talk about this now.'

'When will we talk about it?'

She makes a little sleepy sound. I squeeze her breast gently and press against her hips. In London – during our first year at least – she would have turned to me, hungry and ready. Tonight she uses sleep.

'Inès,' I whisper.

I listen to her breathe as she settles into her own deep stillness, her refuge where I cannot go. I close my eyes and hold her tightly. Inès . . . Inès . . . You were fast and I was slow. You used to say before we lived together, When can I see you, when can we meet? You used to say, You can't even imagine how much I love you, don't forget. And I answered, Never. I said, *Mai, mai* – the way you taught me. When we first became lovers I had no intention of falling in love. I liked you, I was charmed by you and I wanted you, but I did not want to love you – different reasons, different things. Too complicated, too unsettling. I am slow. It takes time with me. And you – your declaration was fast, it caught me unawares. *I am already loving you.* Mine was, as is my way, slower. It took time – in Belfast and in Donegal, in Rome and Bologna, and finally in London.

You sleep beside me. At this time of night, after the day we've had, all this takes on the self-pitying proportions of a tragedy, but the truth of my situation is banal; it happens every day, to others. Now it's happening to me. It is painful, it is sad. I said, *Mai.* I said it quietly, I meant it. Now you who demanded have forgotten your question, and wait for no answer, want none.

We met at a party at my publisher's house in London. She was on her way to Ireland for *L'Unità* after she failed to persuade the paper to send her to Algiers. Someone had mentioned my name and she asked to be introduced. One of my books had recently come out in Italy. She had not read it, but had seen some notices. Alan brought her over. I took her small hand in mine and was struck immediately. Not by her looks so much as by her vitality, her openness, and also – I have to be honest – by her evident interest in me. Maybe it amounted to no more than a man being flattered by the attentions of a pretty young woman. I could give it this defensive construction – mock myself from my own mouth to forestall the ridicule – but I know in my heart it was more than this.

The following day we met for lunch in Soho and spent the afternoon and evening together. I did not press her, and I think this disconcerted her a little. Next morning she rang. She was leaving for Dublin at midday. We talked and talked – this is not usual with me. I felt I had known her a long time and wanted to know her more. After perhaps an hour we were both aware that our tone had altered, that we had arrived at a sort of threshold. Her voice became softer. Little silences crept between us. She gathered her nerve and asked if I would join her in Ireland.

In many ways, I suppose, the week turned out as I'd expected. I went for an adventure and I got one. But that was not all.

I used the opportunity to visit my mother in Belfast, whom I had not seen for two years. Her life is filled with pain and patience; I do not know that my presence provides her with much comfort, but I had to see her of course.

I met Inès off the train at the GNR – she was coming up from Dublin. I was, as usual, too reserved, too cautious (what if she had changed her mind?) to greet her the way I would have liked. I took her bag and we got her booked into Robinson's in Donegall Street.

We took the Greencastle trolley-bus as far as the terminus, then walked to Whitehouse and along the shore of the lough where my sister and I used to bring our dog when we were children. She talked and talked – she laughed and said talking was a fault of hers. But she could not be quiet; nor did I want her to be.

She told me how much she loved Ireland. She told me about a holiday she had taken here as a child with her father. She told me excitedly about the interviews she had had with the IRA in Dublin. She had been to Carrickmore, where the people were brilliant, and to Edentubber, where the terrible bomb had gone off the month before. I held my tongue. The peculiar enthusiasms of the political believer have always left me unmoved; and political anger – of all things – provokes in me, depending on the circumstances, mirth or contempt. There would be time enough for correctives, time enough to set her right on Ireland, and in the meantime her idealistic pronouncements gave me the opportunity to be older, wry and amused.

I caught her looking at me once or twice as we walked – it was a look I recognized from other lovers: she did not know if she was going to be petted or pushed away. It had nothing to do with desire or lack of it, but with my internal argument. What was I getting into? And at the same time wanting, wanting . . . desperately wanting . . . I was not feeling all that strong.

The sky was cloudy and sad. It began to rain and we took shelter under the railway bridge at Whitehouse Park. There we kissed for the first time. She kissed me with her mouth wide, with licks and flicks of her tongue. It is not my style of kissing but I was terribly aroused. The rain eased to a drizzle and we moved on in search of a more private place. We went behind a wall under some trees where we kissed again and I pulled up her sweater and kissed her breasts and stomach. She said we could make love. She undid my trousers and her little fingers gripped me. But I stopped it there, confusing her more I think. I held her and she said, 'What if I fall in love?' I said, 'You won't.' She pinched my cheek. 'I am already loving you. *Ti amo.*'

She felt me slide away. I did not have to say anything, she *felt* it. There was the evidence. I could not help myself; it was worse than embarrassing, it was cruel. We fell silent while it sunk in for her that there were limits to this. My heart was low, I felt empty and weak.

We walked slowly back to the terminus. There were few words. It was cold and damp on the trolley-bus and I put my arm around her. Her spirits could not be tamped down for long. She pointed to a notice – *No Spitting* – and said she had never seen this before on a bus. She thought it very funny and was amused by my embarrassment. She said I should be proud of my home town. But what's there to be proud of in this bitter, hard place? I asked her about Italy, where I had never been but about which I had read much. I asked her about Florence and the Palazzo Vecchio, about Venice and St Mark's Square. She told me about the foundation of the Communist Party of Italy, about Gramsci, Togliatti, the partisans and the *svolta di Salerno*. She talked as though I had knowledge of these people, these events. On my return to London I went to St Pancras library.

The following morning I left my mother's house in St James's and went to meet her at the Abercorn in Castle Lane. She was not there when I arrived. I waited, and I began to get nervous. Forty minutes later I paid the bill and was on my way out to go round to the hotel when she entered. She beamed a broad smile, embraced me and sighed.

'Where do you want to go?' I asked softly.

'I don't care.'

As long as she was with me she didn't care. I was filled up with happiness and confidence. I could see brightness in the grey wash of the day.

We hired a car and set off west. It was drizzling and cold

and filthy. We came out of the fog on the Glenshane Pass to see the sky, blue and slate, bending dramatically over Lough Foyle. We stopped in Derry. I have family in the city, but for reasons to do with family I did not go to see them. Instead we went to a pub in Shipquay street, where we sat among the shoppers at a rough wooden table and had a bowl of stew, white pan bread and a glass of stout. The atmosphere between us was warm and intimate and funny. I surprised myself by being relaxed and talkative.

We crossed the border and arrived in Carrigart, not by any design; we were going where the fancy took us. We parked by the strand and walked and kissed. There was a piercing veer to the December wind, my uncovered head felt the squeeze of its vice. Her long nose was red and wet and cold. She told me she loved camping, that if she'd brought her tent we could have pitched it here. I said I was too old for that. She was twenty-six.

We found a hotel. Before we entered she produced from her pocket – she never carried a handbag – a thin gold band. She grinned as she slipped it on her finger. Her preparedness set up sudden doubts in me. Who is she? How often does she do this? She took my arm gaily and we marched up to the desk. I forget what name we used.

In the room we took off our clothes almost at once. She had a small, slight body; it was not so bony then. She came by getting me to be still and holding me tightly by the waist or buttocks and rubbing herself against me. She came quickly and, it seemed, easily. She made little noise. The pattern was quickly established. After wildness and abandon she would slow me down with a whisper to be still. The sex would continue afterwards, though the first time she whispered to me she was coming I came with her. But once I got used to her I let her come in her own manner and stayed hard inside her afterwards.

We had sandwiches and then went to the pub where I heard more of her likes and dislikes, and their vital declaration. Milan had too many banks and the people spoke with arrogant accents; Turin's buildings were too big and in any case fascist, though they were not as bad as the university in Rome – a true monstrosity of 'the fascism'; Naples, where the red of the traffic light was only an opinion, was brilliant, and the people of the south were like the Irish – warm and always hospitable.

We returned to the hotel at midnight. I lay on my back while she kissed me. She turned around and presented herself to me. I worked on her with my mouth, and she on me. Later we made love again. She talked and I fell asleep thinking, *Do her eyes never close?* I always seemed to be the sleepier. Whenever I looked at her during the night, her eyes would be open, big and bright and gazing into mine.

'Why do you not sleep?' I asked.

'Because I love you more than you love me.'

I could have said something, perhaps even convincingly. I rested my hand on her tight, flat stomach and pushed my fingertips into the spring and curl of her hair. I was confused, struggling; the words had come too soon, too soon – I wasn't sure I believed her. But I could not deny it to myself: I liked what I had heard. A need came up from somewhere deep and unknown, rushing as though to the promise of light. I shut my eyes to keep within the darkness and turned away from her.

We had four more days together.

I drove her to Dublin airport. She talked hardly at all. We sat in the lounge drinking coffee and reading the papers, Inès not interested in anything very much, and still quiet. When we parted she was crying. I can't say I felt as strongly as she did. Our adventure was over, our time together had ended. I had accepted the inevitable trajectory of this affair and kept part of myself in reserve to deal with any sudden surges of emotion. I kissed her goodbye and made lame jokes about the tears in her eyes.

With me, emotional reactions are delayed, but by the time I was back in London I was aware of being without something I had had. I felt jaded and lethargic; my mood was inward. When Margaret rang I made some excuse.

Inès wrote to me from Rome.

'I feel lost,' she said in her letter. 'In Italian the word is *perso*, but I think it has a different meaning. I don't know how else to say it. My eyes are lost and my voice is lost. I am *persa*.'

A month later I went to Rome, and some time after that she managed to arrange with the paper that she could come to London.

I fell in love with Inès in bed. I fell in love with her in the street, and in bars, and in the company of others, watching the expressions on her face as she talked and argued, listening to the little grunts and sighs and sharp inhalations of breath. Most of all, I believe, I fell in love because she was promising me a way out of myself.

I look at her now asleep beside me, foetal, guarded. I am angry, tense and doubtful, but I am not yet emancipated from my need for her. Our disagreements are fundamental, our minds dispar, but I live in our differences: my blankness draws on her vitality. She exists me.

We start out in these things from the same place, the fast and the slow. We pass along the same stages: excitement, enchantment, dispute, anger, reconciliation, love. And the end of love. We pass these same stages, unevenly paced, until at last, everything exhausted, we arrive at a place marked *I just don't care anymore.*

How I hate this. She got there before me.

But soon I will be able to see the funny side. These things happen, they happen every day. Usually to others, now to me. Already I am laughing.

74

10

A T A TABLE on the other side of the swimming pool a small party comes down for a late breakfast – a Sabena crew by the looks of them, enjoying some free time before their next flight out. A man and a woman dive in and swim a length underwater. They come up at the far end, spluttering and laughing.

I sip my coffee and turn the pages of Stipe's file – cuttings from the *Economist, Le Monde,* the *Wall Street Journal;* extracts from a British naval intelligence report, marked 'for official use only'; financial and banking reports; and confidential projections by State Department analysts and US consulate officials, several of which bear Stipe's signature. There are assessments of the current political situation and profiles of the most prominent black leaders – Lumumba, Kasavubu and Gizenga, among others.

Lumumba is described as 'Most likely to succeed to leadership post-independence. Earnest, energetic, hot-headed, charismatic, tough, can be ruthless. A republican and a reformer. His hero is Ghana's Kwame Nkrumah. Like Nkrumah, believes a young state must have strong, visible powers. Believes in firm, modern central government for independent Congo, rejects plans for federation, opposes authority of tribal chiefs. Lines up alongside Nyerere in Tanganyika and Sékou Touré in Guinea. But raised by devout Catholic parents and outlook has always been pro-Western in spite of occasional socialistic outbursts.'

Kasavubu, leader of the Abako party and chief of the Bakongo people, is summarized as 'lethargic, inward-looking, suspicious, unforthcoming and serious. Closest adviser is A.J.J. van Bilsen, Belgian liberal and staunch Catholic. Highly regarded by Belgians as one of their 'trusties'. Essentially conservative and middle-class, but also stubborn and proud. Stands more for creation of the ancient Bakongo kingdom – the territory now covered by northern Angola, Bas Congo and Brazzaville – than for independence of a united Congo. A federalist.'

Gizenga, leader of the Parti Solidaire Africain, which controls the Kwango and Kwilo regions of Léopoldville, is 'an undiluted extremist. After visit to Eastern Europe earlier this year, returned a convinced doctrinaire communist. Anti-Western, pro-Moscow. Believed to hold racist views. PSA is small, but Gizenga appears to have dangerous and growing influence on Lumumba.'

The bulk of the file, however, is concerned with economics. There are figures for the volume and value of shipping in and out of Matadi, for net and gross profits from palm oil and copper and diamonds and cattle, for budgetary receipts, Treasury holdings and the public debt.

I order another coffee and light a cigarette. I check the time. Stipe is late. I turn to a section headed *Katanga/Union Minière*. The southern province accounts for three-quarters of the colony's mining production and almost all its foreign earnings. The Union Minière's impressive profits – 4.5 billion francs last year, mainly from copper but also from tin, silver, zinc, manganese, cobalt, platinum, radium, uranium, tantalum, germanium and other metals and minerals of which I've never heard – allow it to function almost as a state within a state. The company has built up a close relationship with a local black leader, Moise Tshombe and his tribal party Conakat. Bernard Houthhoofd gets several mentions as a figure of extreme wealth and behind-the-scenes political influence.

I glance up to see a long-legged, blonde woman in dark glasses and a towelling robe approach the next table. She sets down her room key, bag and towel.

'Hello,' I say.

'Hello.'

'Are you staying at the hotel?'

'I'm going back to the farm tomorrow. I felt like a little pampering before I left Leo.'

'Will you join me?'

I pull out a chair for Madeleine. She takes up her things and comes over.

She orders orange juice, coffee, toast and scrambled eggs. I offer her a cigarette and light it for her. She leans back in her chair and crosses her tanned legs. She is wearing a black one-piece swimsuit under her robe. She draws on her cigarette and exhales a jet of smoke. I can't see her eyes behind the shades.

'How often do you come to Léopoldville?' I ask.

'Whenever I can.'

'You don't like your farm?'

'I love my farm.'

She taps the room key abstractedly on the table-top as she looks over the pool and scans the Sabena crew.

'What about your husband?' I ask.

'Do I love my husband?'

'I meant, doesn't he mind you coming here, leaving him at the farm?'

'I never ask him.'

'Do you have children?'

'A daughter. What about you?'

'No children.'

'But you want children,' she says in a half-question, half-guess.

I should have known when I asked her that she might

turn the question on me. She senses my discomfort and, being the kind of woman she is, presses her advantage.

'Don't you want them?'

'It's not an issue,' I say curtly.

'For someone your age it has to be an issue. What about Inès?'

How I dislike her, this froward, vain, silly, empty woman. I glance at my watch and wish Stipe would hurry up. The waiter brings her order.

'They're all at it,' she says.

'Sorry?'

She is looking across at the Sabena crew.

'The pilots and hostesses – they're all screwing each other. Part of the job, I suppose.'

She stubs out her cigarette. I say nothing.

'I'm not puritanical about these things,' she continues. 'It's just that it's all so obvious. I prefer a little more discretion.'

'I suppose so.'

'Are you puritanical about these things?'

She lifts the coffee cup to her lips.

'No.'

She makes a small sound of appreciation. It could be the coffee but I'm sure it's something else, and I'm sure she intends me to understand it's something else.

'I didn't think so,' she says. 'You have that look about you.'

'What look is that?'

She shrugs. 'You know it when you see it.'

Her cup shivers in the saucer as she puts it down.

'People tell me I have it too,' she says, and waits.

She lifts her knife and fork when I make no reply. Her hand is trembling slightly, she is not quite as composed about this as she would like, and to my surprise I find her nervousness touching.

'I was talking to someone,' I say, only partly to change the subject, 'who told me the Congo would be independent within six months.'

She lets out a snort of forced hilarity.

'You don't think it's possible?'

'It's absurd. Not even the *indigènes* think they'll get independence in six months. Most of them don't want it, you know. They have a good life under us, better than anywhere else on the continent. You've heard about the railways?'

'No.'

'Our drivers and firemen are *indigènes*, but when the main train arrives at the border of Northern Rhodesia the black driver has to be replaced by a white. It's the same with the firemen and the waiters in the restaurant cars. Our blacks can go to the theatre and cinema if they want, they can sit at European cafés and restaurants.'

'They can't enter the European quarter after dark.'

'And there's a law against Europeans being in the cité after dark as well,' she replies tartly. 'It works both ways.'

'But if it were true that in six months—'

'It's not true,' she says sharply, and throws her knife and fork on the plate.

A little crumb of scrambled egg sticks just below her fat bottom lip. I have to stop myself from leaning across to lick it off.

'The blacks are children,' she says. 'What use have children for elections? They don't want democracy. They don't understand it. They need a father, a chief.'

'A white chief?'

' "How can he get wisdom that holdeth the plough, and that glorieth in the goad; that driveth oxen; and is occupied in their labours; and whose talk is of bullocks?" '

'I was educated in Catholic schools. We didn't read Scripture much.'

'I am the daughter of a Lutheran pastor,' she says. 'Time doesn't matter to these people. In Lingala, *lobi* means both yesterday and tomorrow. How can you run a government without the concept of time? How can you plan ahead?'

'Is it possible you're exaggerating?'

She pushes away her plate, her meal barely touched, and stands up before me. I assume she is going to walk away to brood alone on her settled prejudices. Instead she removes her dark glasses and puts them on the table. Then she takes off her robe. There are small bruises on her arms and thighs. They make me think of sex.

She is a strongly-built, mature woman with a broad back and full breasts. There is a bit of extra weight around her stomach – she has that little ridge that women get – and the skin of her chest and throat and upper arms is no longer taut. Few women I have known would have the confidence to stand before a virtual stranger like this, even those whose bodies are younger, suppler. She holds my gaze. I can't decide whether like some mad diva she thinks she is still young and irresistible, or whether she is saying this is what women my age look like and I look better than most, take it or leave it.

'Hold this.'

She drops the robe into my hands, takes her towel, walks to the edge of the pool and dives in. She crawls for a length, breathing correctly, her arms making clean, effortless cuts in the water. She reaches the end, tumbles smoothly under the surface and launches into the butterfly. I watch, admiring the steady, confident rhythm of her propulsion and the power in her back and shoulders.

I turn to the file and consider what I've read. The figures show the extent of the Belgians' success but, though the great concessionary companies are making billions of francs of profits every year, the colony is on the verge of bankruptcy. I check the figures again: according to an unnamed State

Department analyst, the Congo's current deficit is running at approximately $40 million. I have no idea what a figure of this size represents in relative terms, but by any measure it seems substantial.

'Monsieur Gillespie?'

A black bows his head and hands me a folded piece of paper, then steps deferentially back.

The note is from Stipe: 'Lumumba's house, opposite golf course. Quick as you can.'

I look again at the black. He rubs his hands humbly and gives me a dazzling grin.

'Mister Stipe asked me to take you,' he says in English.

I know him now – our Erasmus-quoting host from last night.

'Auguste?'

'Yes, sir.'

He is wearing the same maroon pants but has changed his shirt. It's an unforgivable shade of purple.

'What's this about?'

'Mr Stipe asks for you to come, sir. To the house of Mr Lumumba.'

I reach for my cigarettes and the file and get to my feet. Madeleine is climbing out of the pool. She brushes off the water from her arms and legs and comes over, patting her hair with the towel.

'I have to go,' I say, handing her the robe.

She gives me a curt nod, but her eyes are fixed on Auguste. He responds to her hard stare with a servile bow and a shuffling retreat of several paces.

'I will get the car, *nókó*,' Auguste says quickly, already scuttling across the patio towards the lobby and the exit.

'What did he call me?' I ask Madeleine. '*Nókó?*'

'It's Lingala for uncle. To these people the uncle is the provider,' she says, pulling on her robe. 'The Congo is a

81

miracle. It was jungle, it was swamp and scrub before we came. Now there are towns and plantations and farms and the blacks have good jobs and homes, they have medical care and education. We are their providers and they know it. You hear them say all the time, *Les Belges sont nos oncles.* Next time you see your friend who spun you this fantasy about independence tell him he doesn't know what he's talking about.'

'I will.'

She drops into her seat.

'If the *macaques* ever get their beloved independence, it will be a catastrophe.'

'I'm sorry we couldn't talk more about this,' I say.

'Outsiders never seem to have the time to listen to our side of the story.'

Her imagination is irredeemably belligerent. We do not like each other, we have nothing in common except the difference between man and woman. We are flirting with each other.

'Perhaps another time,' I suggest.

'If you can find the time,' she says in a bored challenge.

11

I STEP OUT of the Regina into the white sun and shade my eyes. Sweat erupts at once on my back. A horn sounds and I look across the street where Auguste is waving anxiously from Stipe's Chevrolet. Behind, the angry driver of a second car blares his horn again. Auguste, flustered, manoeuvres to give the vehicle behind enough room to pass. Instead of taking the opportunity, the driver gets out, strides up to Auguste and starts shouting.

'Can I help you?' I say.

The man is young, barely into his twenties; the Flemish face is bland and boyish and stolid.

'Is this your driver?' he demands of me.

'Yes.'

Auguste's eyes are penitent and downcast.

'Then teach your dirty monkey not to block other people's way.'

The young man quickly turns and goes back to his car. He roars up as I get in beside Auguste, leaning on his horn, and shouts something unintelligible before screeching around the corner. Auguste raises his eyes and glances at me carefully before making a small, tentative laugh. I know enough to understand there is a little test of the boundaries here: can he get away with giggling at the rage of the European in front of this particular European?

'I'm sorry, sir,' he says in a silky voice.

'Sorry for what?'

'For making the young *nókó* angry.'

He is pushing the test. I stare straight ahead.

'Don't call me sir, don't call me *nókó*. My name is James.'

'I'm sorry, James.'

His spirit is nowhere near as deferential as the show he puts on suggests. He is like the servant whose little joke is to abase himself before his master while behind his back he drinks his brandy and sleeps with his daughters. He puts the car in drive and pulls away.

On Boulevard Albert I most of the shops and restaurants are closed, the streets are empty. Things have not yet returned to normal. By a military checkpoint at the cité's boundaries there is the tangled wreckage of burned-out cars.

'Where did you learn to speak English?' I ask.

'In the beginning I learned English empirically,' he replies.

'Empirically?'

'From meeting British businessmen here in Leo. Then I was in Bristol.'

'You've been to England?'

'Correct. I was sent to study at Louvain, in Belgium. After four years I went to visit my brother who lives in Bristol. He is a seaman.'

This information is conveyed in a casual tone, but then his voice changes; something respectful and slow comes into it.

'Mr Stipe says you are a writer.'

'Yes, I am.'

He seems terribly impressed and looks me over carefully.

'I like writers very much,' he says earnestly. 'Plato, Socrates, Tom Paine, John Stuart Mill.'

'I write a different kind of book.'

'Yes?'

He looks at me expectantly, as though waiting for me to elaborate on the difference between Plato's work and my own.

'Are you involved with Lumumba?' I ask, keen to change the subject. 'Are you a member of his party?'

'No, James. I am not a member of the MNC.'

'But you obviously know Lumumba.'

'When Patrice came to Léopoldville he went to work with Bracongo, the brewery where I was also working. Mr de Scheut and his friends in the Cercle Libéral found him this job. Bracongo makes Polar beer. Have you seen the advertisements?'

'I don't think so.'

'Polar is good beer, but Primus is better,' he says with a mock-guilty giggle. 'They are rivals, but even when I was working for Polar I used to drink Primus. Patrice was sales manager for Polar beer. He was a very good salesman because he always loves talking to people, even though he did not know Lingala when he came first from Stanleyville. Patrice is Batetela tribe from Sankuru district of Kasai. Here, in Léopoldville the people are Bakongo.'

'Are you Bakongo?'

'Correct, James. But I am *évolué.*'

'Evolved? What do you mean by that?'

'I am detribalized,' he says gravely. 'I am African, but I am educated and my thinking is Western. I want to study in America and I love Plato and Socrates very much. I am also a member of the *Association des Classes Moyennes Africaines.*'

He reaches into his pocket and draws out a card which he passes to me, pride beaming from his eyes.

'What's this?'

'This is my *carte d'immatriculation.*'

The buff-coloured card contains a passport-sized photograph of Auguste in a dark jacket, white shirt and tie. For the occasion the student of Plato has forced his features into an expression of sublime high-mindedness.

'With this card,' he explains, 'I can sit in European

restaurants. I can go into hotels like the Regina and, if I can afford it, I can send my children to a European school.'

'How many children do you have?'

'I am not yet married, James,' he replies with a hint of evasion.

'That doesn't mean you don't have children.'

He erupts into bashful giggles.

'How many?'

He giggles again. I make as if to hand back his card but when he attempts to retrieve it I snatch it away and hold it out the window in playful threat.

'Tell me how many.'

Panic sweeps his face. He tries to concentrate on the driving but his eyes are glued to the card. The car swerves.

'Here.'

I give him back his card. He takes it quickly.

'I was only teasing, Auguste.'

'Yes, James. I am sorry.'

We drive on.

'Most Bakongo people do not support Patrice,' he declares after a while, to fill the silence. 'When he first came to Léopoldville they said he was just a provincial *évolué*, a man less *évolué* than themselves. The Bakongo people support King Kasa, chief of the Bakongo tribe.'

'King Kasa?' I say, trying to remember the names I have been reading in the file. 'Is that Kasavubu? The Abako leader?'

'Correct, James. Mr Kasavubu. Abako is a tribal party and wants to make a separate state of the Lower Congo, the same as Tshombe wants in Katanga.'

'Moise Tshombe?'

'Yes, James. Tshombe is the puppet of the Union Minière in Katanga, the richest province of the Congo, which he wants to rule by himself. His party is Conakat and his tribe is the

Balunda tribe, friends of the Baluba people.'

'I'm getting confused. There seem to be a lot of tribes.'

'Correct. Many tribes,' he says, and he adds mischievously: 'All beginning with *b*.'

'Yes,' I say.

'Patrice says you can have tribes without tribalism, that
the Congo is one country and the people are one people.'

'Do you think Patrice would be a good leader of an
independent Congo?'

'With the help of our American friends, yes, I think
Patrice will be a good leader.'

Our American friends? Stipe's influence runs deep.

Ahead, at a traffic circle, a white-gloved gendarme is
diverting cars off the boulevard. Beyond, several military
lorries are blocking the road. A crowd has gathered. Auguste
goes round the circle into Avenue Crespel.

'How do you know Stipe?' I ask as he selects a place to
park.

'I am Mr Stipe's driver. I have been with him since I left
my work at Bracongo.'

'What kind of work does Stipe do at the consulate?' I ask
innocently.

I have been thinking a lot about the nature of Stipe's
work.

'He is in the political office.'

'The political office?'

'Yes,' he replies, parking the car.

He does not seem inclined to continue. I can't tell
whether this is the full extent of Auguste's knowledge or
whether he is being loyal and discreet.

'Do you know what exactly he does in the political office?'

'Mr Stipe talks to people. He loves to talk.'

'Like Patrice.'

'Yes,' Auguste says. 'Mr Stipe and Patrice are very big

87

friends. They are excellent friends.'

'Is Stipe good to work for?' I ask.

'Oh, yes. Mr Stipe is a very good man,' he says. 'Mr Stipe understands.'

'What does he understand?'

'Everything. Mr Stipe understands everything and he understands everybody.'

The devotion is unmistakable.

As he locks the car he says, 'I'm sorry, James.'

He holds up his silly card in explanation.

'We are fourteen million in the Congo. One hundred and twenty have the *carte d'immatriculation*.'

'I had no idea,' I tell him.

The proud member of the Association of the African Middle Classes beams a broad smile at me.

'I wish one day to be a writer like you, James,' he says.

'I thought you were going to be a lawyer.'

'No, now I want to be a writer.'

'What for? There's no money in it.'

It is one of those flip responses you make without thinking to someone you are at best not taking seriously and at worst patronizing. He gives me a wounded look.

'The money is not important and Mr Stipe pays me very well,' he says.

'Why do you want to be a writer?' I ask, chastened and cheapened.

'So I can look upon things calmly and show that I am wise.'

'Yes, yes,' I say. 'That's very important, of course.'

'Do you have an office, James?'

'A sort of an office.'

'And six secretaries?'

'No secretaries at all, I'm afraid.'

He looks momentarily downhearted.

'It's not important,' he says, grinning brightly. 'I will bring you three secretaries from my law office.'

'Why am I getting the feeling you're not being serious?'

'I am always serious,' he replies, still grinning.

'Not with me you're not.'

'I am as serious with you, James, as you are with me.'

He holds the grin fixed on his face. My response is to feel offended, until I see the truth of what he is saying. We walk on.

Up on the boulevard something is happening for us to look upon.

12

THERE ARE TWO crowds. The whites, fewer but more confident, have gathered in small knots on the grass verge on
the northern side of the road. They seem in good humour,
like theatre-goers about to resume their seats for the second
act of a play they have enjoyed so far. By contrast, there is an
ominous neutrality about the blacks. They are massed in front
of the golf course on the cité side of the boulevard facing
Lumumba's house, from which they are separated by a line of
soldiers with rifles at the ready and bayonets fixed. Two
golfers stroll nonchalantly up the fairway, their black caddies
in tow.

Flitting between the crowds is the busy figure of Inès. I
also spot Smail, and Grant, the British journalist, as well as a
number of other reporters. Unlike them, Inès does not have
a notebook. She never does. Her refusal to carry one – she
insists they set up barriers between her and the people of
the story – is only one of several idiosyncrasies I would have
thought a handicap in her profession. There is also her
chronic lack of punctuality, her wayward sense of direction,
her forgetfulness – to say nothing of her unabashed parti-
sanship. But of course, as I know well, Inès is an unusual
journalist. She hates government palaces and ministerial
offices, and the hotels and bars and restaurants frequented
by journalists and their sources. She is never interested in
interviewing the big people – the ambassadors, the ministers
and generals – and rarely bothers to go to press conferences
('all they ever say is lies'). What she covets is not contacts
with the high-placed and the respect of her colleagues

('more interested in their careers than in what is going on around them'), but the friendship of ordinary people; she will hang around the stall of a market vendor for hours, listening to talk of everyday things; she will eat and drink beer in the homes of day labourers and street sweepers; she will sleep on their floors when it is too late to get home. She pours her love into these people and their causes, a river that will not be dammed.

I go up to her.

'Hello,' I say.

'Oh, hello,' she says quickly and with no indication that she is pleased to see me.

'You'd already gone when I woke up.'

'You needed to sleep.'

Not waking me had been a calculated aggression, and her thin effort to pass it off as in my interests annoys me.

'I would have liked to talk to you.'

'About what?'

'About what we're going to do,' I say.

She turns away. I can't tell whether she is angry or upset or – more wounding – simply bored. I feel the stab of bitter pride in my chest. Is this really it? Are we really coming to an end?

I let out a heavy sigh. 'Inès, we're going to have to sort this out.'

'I don't think this is the time or the place for that,' she says. 'In case you hadn't noticed there is something important going on – they are arresting Patrice.'

'When can we talk then?'

She shrugs.

I look at her with the whole fetch of our story behind my eyes, but she will not yield, she will not soften. Why is she being like this? She used to love me.

'I have to talk to the people,' she says.

'Why don't you interview Auguste?' I say, pulling Stipe's driver forward: he should meet her criteria for an authentic interviewee. 'He's a one of the people, and he's a friend of Lumumba's to boot. Isn't that right, Auguste?'

'Correct, James.'

His eyes drop so he can adopt the overly respectful demeanour I have noticed he likes to put on for first meetings with whites.

'Inès is a journalist,' I explain. 'She's sympathetic to Lumumba.'

'It's a bit more than "sympathetic",' she says with some asperity.

'Of course it is.'

'Were you at the demonstration yesterday?' she asks Auguste.

He seems bashful in front of her. He is polite, his words lavishly humble. He tells her about the shootings.

Stipe has seen me and nods for me to meet him at the cordon. I leave Inès with Auguste and push my way through to a soldier standing guard at a lorry. Stipe comes out to greet me.

'Sorry I couldn't get to the Regina, James,' he says, 'but as you can see things have gotten a little out of hand. The Belgians have been rounding up everyone connected with the independence movement they can find. They even arrested Kasavubu this morning. Up until a few days ago they liked to show him off as a "good African". He's a bad African now. They all are. I didn't think Patrice would risk coming back to his own house.'

'He knew they were looking for him, didn't he?'

'Sure, but Patrice is a family man. He can't be without his wife and kids.'

'What's going to happen now?'

'Kasavubu's already at the police station at Avenue

Lippers, so my guess is they'll take him there and then to the Central Prison.'

'Why is it taking so long?'

'The Belgians are worried about the crowd.'

There must be four or five hundred blacks, with more streaming down from the cité every minute. Too many for what looks to me like much less than a full-strength company of soldiers to contain.

'The authorities want to keep temperatures down today,' Stipe says. 'Lumumba says he'll get them to disperse quietly if he can make a speech. The Belgians aren't crazy about the idea, but I suggested they give it a shot.'

'Why do they listen to you?' I ask mischievously.

He may work in the political office, but it is obvious Stipe is a spy, a conspirator of some sort. Just what is the nature of his power?

'They don't like it,' Stipe answers with a grin, 'but they're hardly in a position to object. Didn't you read the file? As we speak, the Belgians are in New York looking for loans to try to keep the place afloat. If they want the Yankee dollar they have to listen to the Yankee advice.'

'What I can't work out is why the colony is in such trouble, given all the resources.'

'A Marxist like Inès would understand the way the Belgians have developed the Congo,' Stipe says. 'It's the Soviet NEP all over again – rapid industrialization of a primitive rural economy. They've had some success, you can't take that away from them. But taxes are high, the average national income level is low, expansion is lagging behind population growth, and the Belgians just doesn't have the capital for more investment – and the situation's getting worse because with all the political uncertainty the banks and investors are taking their money out.'

'How bad is it – in a nutshell?'

'In a nutshell bad, real bad. The Congo Central Bank can't meet its obligations so the Belgians have agreed to guarantee its operations but only on condition that the colony's gold and dollar reserves go to the vaults of the National Bank in Brussels. But these loans . . . it's crazy. You don't meet current and past deficits by raising long-term loans – it's like mortgaging your house to pay last month's grocery bills.'

'Not that crazy,' I say. 'When they hand over the country presumably they'll be handing over the debts as well.'

'Absolutely right. Patrice doesn't know it yet, but the day he walks into the prime minister's office to take a look at the books he's going to see that not only is the country broke, but he owes Brussels over two billion francs. That's one hell of a tab to pick up, isn't it? Who says Belgians don't have a sense of humour?'

'I don't suppose he'll be picking up the profits.'

Stipe lets out a short, sarcastic laugh.

'Say you're Bernard Houthhoofd, or any other big shareholder in the Union Minière or the Société Général,' he begins, 'and you have a piece of the twelve-billion-franc investment in Katanga alone. Your copper industry is the second biggest in Africa. Last year your mines produce three hundred thousand tons of copper at $100 a ton which you sell on the world market for $250. Are you going to allow some jumped-up local politician to take away your business? Are you hell!'

From the black crowd come sudden shouts of *Patrice, Patrice!* Their gaze is fixed on the balcony, where Lumumba, flanked by a Belgian officer, stands, his hands resting on the concrete balustrade.

'Who's the soldier?' I ask Stipe.

'That's Lieutenant-General Émile Janssens. I told you about him. He's the commander of the Force Publique.'

Janssens has the barrel-chested aggression of the middle-aged soldier who prides himself on his continuing hardness and regards scornfully the widening hams and girths of his pampered civilian peers; he looks like the kind of man who takes cold showers and throws medicine balls on the beach.

'Janssens is tough,' Stipe says, 'a real disciplinarian.'

There are a few isolated jeers and catcalls from the whites.

'What do you think of Lumumba,' I ask, 'as a politician?'

'Outstanding,' Stipe replies without hesitation. 'Really. As a politician and as a man. Here's a guy, very little formal education, nothing more than a dirty *macaque*, everything stacked against him. And by pure effort of will, by refusing to be put down, he transforms himself into a figure of genuine power. He has charisma, oratory, real moral authority. His only flaw is that he can be a little impetuous sometimes, but he's still only thirty-five years old. With the right help, the right advice, Patrice could shape up to be one of Africa's great leaders.'

'That's what Inès says.'

'So we agree on something,' he says brightly; then, more seriously: 'How are things with you two this morning? Any better?'

'Not really.'

'I'm sorry,' he says, putting a comradely hand on my back. 'Do you want some Yankee advice?'

'Is there a price tag?'

'This is for free,' he says with a grin. His teeth are small and even and white. The lips go far back over the gums. 'Is Inès the woman you really want? I mean is this the one?'

'Yes.'

'Then don't give up. Don't be discouraged. Do whatever you have to do – even if there's another man.'

'Do what you have to do, even if there's another man? What does that mean?'

95

'Kill him, of course.' He laughs. 'Is there another man?'

The thought unnerves me. 'I don't think so,' I say uncertainly.

Stipe considers for a moment.

'All I'm saying is stick in there, James, however long it takes. I haven't found a woman yet who doesn't secretly like a siege. That's my recommendation. Take it – I know what I'm talking about.'

'I don't know,' I say, 'it sounds like it could be pretty humiliating.'

He makes a gesture as though to say he's tried his best.

'It always beats me when people don't listen to things that are for their own good.'

'Is your advice always for their good?'

'Without exception.'

'Yankee advice is never wrong?'

'I can't think of a time it ever has been – no.'

We become aware of a thin, high-pitched voice speaking in French and turn to look up at the balcony. The voice does not carry well and I miss the first few words. I hear 'crisis'; I hear, I think, 'many wrongs have been perpetrated'.

A white man next to me cups his hands and shouts hoarsely up at the balcony. His friends take up the chorus. Lumumba stops speaking and looks down at us. He remains still in that position for some moments in an effort to design for himself a kind of sculpted dignity. It seems a little laboured and contrived to me, but the catcalls begin to die down.

'Today is not the day,' Lumumba goes on, 'and these streets are not the place for the wrongs we have suffered to be redressed.'

He speaks slowly, like Auguste, like most of the Africans I have heard so far.

'Inquiries have been promised,' he continues. 'We must

trust that those charged with finding the truth will conduct their inquiries without regard to the colour of the person's skin, that they respect the rights of all persons guaranteed in the law of the land and in natural law. We must trust that those charged with finding the truth tell the truth when they find it. If their version differs from what the people know to be true, if it differs from what they saw with their own eyes and heard with their own ears, the inquiry will be damned by the people and the reputations of the officials who put their name to it will be dishonoured for ever.'

The whites start heckling again. Whistles and jeers go up. This time Lumumba speaks through it, goaded, his words coming faster.

'We have suffered like beasts for a thousand years. Our ashes have been strewn to the wind that roams the desert. They had the right to the whip, we had the right to die, but the hard torch of the sun will shine for us again.'

Stipe grimaces. 'Oh-oh. This wasn't in the script. Janssens isn't going to like this.'

There is real anger in Lumumba's posture now. Janssens tenses as if preparing himself to drag him physically from the balcony. Lumumba scans his audience. Then his gaze seems to bump into Stipe, and stop there. Glancing at Stipe, I see his eyes are fixed on Lumumba. His head makes a barely discernible movement. A signal to Lumumba to rein himself in?

There is a long, tense silence, everyone hanging on the next words from the balcony.

Turning to the black crowd, Lumumba says at last in a low voice, 'Go home now. Go quietly. Do not give the soldiers an excuse to hurt you. Go home and remember that I promise you this: the evil, cruel times will go, never to come again.'

There is no cheering from the blacks, nothing at all.

Perhaps the end has come too abruptly, perhaps cheering and clapping are not their way. Perhaps it is simply because they feel the extent of this their most recent defeat.

Lumumba disappears into the house, escorted by Janssens. It all seems terribly anticlimatic. The whites relax and resume their idle chattering while I wonder again about the extent of Stipe's influence: with Auguste, with Janssens, with the Sûreté, with Lumumba. It seems to go far, and in all directions.

We stand in the avenue, midway between the two crowds. Stipe surveys the scene. The blacks wait where they are; I can't tell whether Lumumba's speech has calmed or inflamed their feelings. The whites start drifting away, the play over, though I get the feeling they are disappointed with the denouement.

'So, what do you think?' Stipe asks. 'Are you interested in writing something?'

'You're certain the Belgians are going to capitulate on independence?'

'Within six months.'

It is a good story. I think of Alan, my publisher in London. He likes to see my by-line. I also think of the fee and the possibility of more work, and I think of Inès. She will take notice. At the very least it will give us something to talk about.

'I'll write something,' I say.

'Need any help getting it placed?'

'No.'

'If you want anything else, facts or figures, give me a call. I know you'll be careful how you source it.'

A great cheer suddenly goes up from the blacks. Lumumba has appeared at the gates of the house with Janssens and a party of soldiers. His hands are chained behind his back. The crowd starts chanting: *Depanda, depanda!* Janssens leads his prisoner to a military lorry. The soldiers haul him up and push him into a seat between two armed guards.

The blacks send up a deafening cheer, one of triumph almost. The chant changes to *Patrice, Patrice!*

'It's so predictable, but no one ever seems to learn,' Stipe says, waving a hand over the black crowd. 'Half these people weren't even MNC supporters this morning. The more demonstrators you shoot down, the more leaders you lock up, the more people flock to the cause. But I hardly have to tell you that.'

Puzzled, I look to him for an explanation.

'Isn't that what happened in Ireland after your Easter Rising?'

'It wasn't my Rising,' I say tightly, hoping Stipe isn't going to turn out to be one of those maudlin Americans who has discovered he has Irish ancestors who arrived in the New World on the famine ships, 'and anyway, the situations are hardly comparable.'

He responds to my defensiveness with a chuckle and gives my back a parting slap. 'That's what every colonial power always says: "you don't understand – things are different here, the situation's more complicated".'

Looking for Inès I bump into Smail. The handsome diamond trader shakes hands warmly.

'I suppose you will want to write something about this?'

'About what?' I ask abruptly.

He is a little taken aback by my harshness.

'The arrest of Patrice, what happened at the river yester-day.'

'I don't think so,' I say, again in a rather uncompromising tone; then, seeing his look of puzzlement, I add: 'Inès will write about it, and she does that kind of thing so much better.'

He wishes me well and says he hopes we will be able to have a drink soon.

I pick Inès out on the other side of the boulevard, the black side. I start to cross the road. Then I see that she is crying. Next to her is Auguste. She looks at him and sniffs. He puts a thumb to the corner of his eye and carefully rubs away a tear of his own.

My presence would be an intrusion. I leave them to their sore tears and clotted grief and drift away with the last of the whites.

13

I WORK ON the novel every morning after Inès has left, and again for a couple of hours in the early evening, but I like to sit out the electric afternoons of the rainy season at the Colibri, where I have become friendly with Anna, the owner. She is a tough old woman who pretends to be more cynical about men than she really is. Why she likes me I do not know. She says I make a change from her usual clientele – Sabena pilots and Otraco employees, lawyers and officials. She even defended me after *Courrier d'Afrique* and *L'Avenir* picked up my article. Their editorials were not friendly and they commented with withering sarcasm on my newness to my subject and to the colony. I had not expected anything like the hostility I was to encounter, in print and in person.

Had I known what I was letting myself in for I doubt I would have agreed to write the piece. At the Sabena Guest House, having oysters one night with Stipe and de Scheut, a Flemish woman spat in my face and pummelled my chest with fat and ineffectual fists. She accused me of wanting to see the Congo destroyed, she screamed that I was advocating a communist takeover. I replied coldly that I was an advocate of nothing, precisely nothing, that I was neutral in this, that I was merely painting the picture as I saw it. De Scheut, unflappable, genial and unassuming, remonstrated with her in his fatherly way and led her struggling and shouting back to her husband.

'Handled with admirable aplomb,' Stipe said to me, topping up my wine.

'*I want to remind you I am quite detached from this, and so can look on it calmly,*' I replied with a smile.

I do not normally pull quotations out like this, but I'd had a little to drink and was over-compensating to cover up what I have to admit was my shock. The truth is that though writers like to think their words have meaning and importance in the world beyond the printed page we are not used to being held so directly and emphatically accountable. I had not experienced anything like this before. But then I asked myself if the woman's display of outrage was really so unforgivable. If the pen is mightier than the sword, as we tell ourselves every day, can the wielder of the pen complain when one he has struck retaliates with her fists – a much inferior weapon by our own account?

'Joseph K.,' Stipe said, identifying the quotation, 'very good.'

We had by then spent many evenings over tall drinks talking of books and writers. We had discussed Flaubert and Sand, we had discussed Jonson's masques and the irony in *Mansfield Park,* but he had not mentioned Kafka as a favourite; nor – to a disappointment I tried my best to conceal – had he raised again the novel of mine he had read. I began to wonder if he had read it at all. But if he hadn't, how had he known about it? And why would he have mentioned it?

The woman continued to fire salvos from her table, turning heads throughout the restaurant.

'The Liberals and Socialists in Brussels have no use for us,' she shouted. 'We're an embarrassment. But if they try anything, we'll fight them. We have the guns. We'll show them what we think of independence!'

Stipe grinned. 'Some people take things very seriously.'

'Not us,' I said, raising my drink.

Stipe clinked my glass with his.

'When people like this good lady start talking about taking up the gun you know the revolution is in trouble,'

Stipe said. 'You've read *A Sentimental Education?* And Baudelaire – "Mon coeur mis à nu"?'

'The revolution *was charming only because of the very excess of its ridiculousness.*'

'The middle-class has many talents but insurrection isn't one of them.'

De Scheut, when he rejoined us, was embarrassed and full of apologies for the behaviour of his fellow-countrywoman. He and Stipe, and also, to my surprise, Bernard Houthhoofd, were my principal defenders in the controversy the piece provoked. Their varied influences helped keep the bad feeling from spilling over into anything nastier and after a week or so the stir died away. I must not exaggerate. The story was moving and soon left me and my article behind. The Belgians had inaugurated a round-table conference in Brussels to which all the independence leaders – except Lumumba, who was in jail for his part in the disturbances – were invited. In the pages of *L'Unità* Inès asked sarcastically what kind of settlement was possible when the most prominent figure in the independence movement was denied a place at the talks?

I wrote a second piece for the *Observer* when a leaked copy of the colonial administration's report into the shootings at the river was delivered anonymously to the apartment. I assumed Stipe was responsible, and though he did not confirm my suspicion, neither did he do much to deny it. The report absolved the Force Publique, though it said that the actions of one or two soldiers had 'bordered on the reckless'. Responsibility for the deaths was fixed squarely on Lumumba and the organizers of the illegal march and on the demonstrators themselves. The pockets of several of those killed were found, on examination by the soldiers, to contain stones. The Force Publique had acted with restraint against the determined provocations of a riotous mob.

I know Inès read my articles, but she never talked to me about them.

I find her working at the little table when I arrive back after a long afternoon at the Colibri with Stipe. She is not often home so early. I ask her how her day went and she says fine. I cannot get her to say anything more. The typewriter clacks, she gets on with her work. This is not unusual. Today – I don't know why, perhaps because I have drunk an extra couple of glasses – it is more than I can stand.

'Talk to me!' I scream.

'About what?' she says in a bored voice without looking up.

'You know about what.'

She continues her typing.

'Inès, I can't go on like this any more.'

There is no break in the rhythm of the keys. In fury, I spin her round and pull her up, holding her wrists fast.

'Can you hear me? I can't go on like this.'

Does she care? She looks at me without tenderness.

'You are going through a confused period in your life,' is all she says.

And I want to hit her. Hatred boils up inside me. I am not much, but I have been her lover for two years and I deserve better than this. I am on the verge of tears of rage and self-pity.

'I'm not confused,' I shout at her. 'I am clear. I want to be with you. It's that simple. I want to be with you, Inès. With *you*. Forever. There's nothing confused about that.'

'I can't talk about this now, there's too much happening.'

'So you keep saying.'

She does not respond to me. I let her out of my grip.

'What's happening?' I ask in a tone of spite and pettiness.

'What's happening here that's so important? It's a grubby little squabble about which bunch of power-hungry, corrupt, venal, little men will end up being in the most advantageous position to line their own pockets.'

'Are you saying Patrice is power-hungry and corrupt?'

'I'm saying that politics stinks. I'm saying that it's not important. I'm saying it's a spectacle, a farce we've seen a thousand times. The set varies, the actors change, the plot twists in different ways, but it's always the same story and you always know the ending. And who cares anymore? Politics is boring. Who cares?'

'I do, for one. I care, and if you can't see what's happening here with your own eyes, then there is nothing more to say.'

'Come back to London with me,' I say as calmly as I can, 'please.'

She says nothing.

'Inès, I love you. I have waited all my life to love the way I love you. I'm afraid I will never love like this again.'

'You will,' she announces matter-of-factly. 'I don't believe there is ever just one person in the world for us.'

'I don't want to hear that!' I scream. 'Don't you know what it does to me hearing you say that?'

'Things have changed.'

'Don't say that!'

'They have changed.'

'For you maybe, but not for me. They haven't changed for me and it's tearing me apart.'

I bow my head and close my eyes to collect myself. I take deep breaths. I hadn't meant to get into this, but I can't stop myself. I hadn't exaggerated: I can't go on like this. It is more than I can bear.

I let some moments pass. At least the keys are not hammering, at least she has not gone back to work.

When I look up she is staring at me, and now there is tenderness. At last she sees my hurt. We stand together in silence. I put a hand out to her, not knowing if she will let me touch her. How that stabs at me! When once I could at any time have put my fingers to her breast, to her arse, between her legs and she would have been yearning for my touch. Now I cannot even be sure she will allow my hand to touch her face. I am shaking. She smiles hopelessly and sadly, as though looking at the victim of an accident who lies on the roadside and will not survive. I stroke her hair. It seems to be getting thinner and more brittle every day. I can see the grey of her scalp.

'You look so tired,' I say. 'You are out running around all day, you never eat, you come home so late. You have to look after yourself.'

'I'm fine,' she says. 'You're the one who needs to look after yourself, especially with Stipe.'

She doesn't understand anything about Stipe and me. I laugh scornfully. She springs at me. I brace myself as if for an assault. Instead she takes my hands in hers and pumps my arms.

'Listen to me,' she says urgently. 'Stipe is an enemy. All you have to do is look at him to see this. The way he is, the way his body is. Everything about him hates this country and the people in it. You can see it in his eyes, in the way he moves.'

It's preposterous, so absurd.

'You're wrong, Inès.'

'Just because that day in Houthhoofd's garden he said he liked your book you trust him.'

'Oh come on, Inès. Give me some credit.'

But of course there is truth in what she says. I feel pathetic, my craving for praise exposed. The minor writer – the very minor writer – is always susceptible; he can be bought and sold with a single line of flattery.

'He probably hasn't even read your books. De Scheut probably mentioned to him that you're a writer.'

It's horribly plausible.

'Don't be ridiculous,' I say.

I have an awful headache. The drink, the anger, the hurt, the heat.

'Stipe is working against Patrice,' she goes on. 'Don't trust him.'

'If he's working against Patrice why did he give me the information for the article?'

'The Belgians aren't going to give independence. They murdered the demonstrators and lied about it. They've arrested the leaders and thrown Patrice into the Central Prison. Stipe knows everything in the article was a lie.'

'What did he have to gain from it if it was a lie?'

'It was to undermine support for Patrice and the MNC.'

'Stipe is Lumumba's friend. He's doing all he can to help. I was there when he tried to persuade Lumumba to go across to Brazzaville after the demonstration.'

'The article Stipe manipulated you to write was saying to the people the Belgians are going to give in anyway so you don't have to be mobilated.'

Mobilated. I smile but I don't correct her.

She pulls gently at my arms. We are holding each other, our foreheads touching. She puts a hand to my face.

'You look tired too,' she says quietly and kisses me on the cheek.

We take our clothes off and go to bed. We kiss, we caress, but we cannot make love. It is my fault. I wish I could say it was the whisky, but it is worse than that. There is no hunger in her, no passion. Her dryness withers me. The last thing I had for her – the physical me – is gone.

When first we met she saw my silence as something she would penetrate. She believed she would find hidden meaning in my blankness. I tried to tell her, many times, but it only deepened my mystery for her. There once was a time when she admired me. I am not all bad, and sometimes in my writing I come close to showing something good. In the evenings, in the Camden flat, she would read the pages I had written that day and she would say, 'Don't hold back, don't hold back. Be honest. Let your true feelings come into your words.' But my third eye, my writer's eye, monitors every word and gesture. It makes me fearful of my own censure. I can only hold back.

She once admired me. She once believed in me and was intrigued by me. Not now. She penetrated, and found nothing.

This thing is dying. Soon I will have to accept it. I feel so sad.

14

I AM STILL here, though I will leave soon. We share even less than before. Stipe advised me to hang on, but being around her and receiving nothing has discouraged me. It has worn me down. It has overthrown my self-esteem, sapped my pride. She is indifferent to my presence. I can take no more.

She has not been well. Out of habit, I suppose, I badger her about not eating properly. When she goes out on her tours with Smail and Auguste – who now seems to drive for her as much as for Stipe – she makes do with *fufu*, plantain and cassava. What's good enough for the people is good enough for her. She is so thin and worn. Her big blue eyes seem bigger now; there are black-brown smudges beneath them and they are disturbingly bright.

There is a funny side to this. Though she would deny it, Inès has a competitive sense – not about esteem or earnings or proficiency with languages or anything like that, but about health and stamina. During our first winter in London I came down with a bad cold. She brought me endless hot whiskies and whispered comforts, and informed me – a little boastfully – that she never got colds. When a few days later she took to her bed *dying* of one I teased her, but she of course could not remember having said anything of the sort. She doesn't play fair: she gives you pieces of the jigsaw and snatches them away again. Little details, the things that make up the whole.

I do not tease her now. I am too worried. When Lumumba was unexpectedly freed to attend the Brussels conference – something she is convinced her campaign in *L'Unità* was instrumental in bringing about – she could not find the strength to get out of the apartment. She insisted she would be fine and was adamant about not seeing a doctor. Doctors are panickers, she says. But the truth is she does not want to be reminded of London, of what the doctors told her there. There are days when she is fine, and days when she is not.

I am writing at the table when I first hear it. The noise is low, indistinct, faintly like the air being sliced, a sound you think you have heard, then decide is inside your head. Inès is in the bedroom, reading, dozing. Today is one of the bad days.

'Can you hear that?' she calls out weakly.

The sound is louder now. I become conscious of something odd, something missing. I look at my watch. It is just after four. There should be traffic and there isn't any. Not a single car.

'Can you hear that?' Inès calls again from the bedroom.

'Yes.'

'What is it?'

I get up and look out the window.

'What's happening?'

Inès comes into the living room pulling a dress over her head. I glimpse her white stomach and breasts and feel a sudden sharp pang of loss. The beautiful things that were mine and are no longer. This proximity is killing me. I have to go, if I am to survive. I have to go, but I don't want to.

The phone rings.

'I can't see anything,' I say to her. 'But have you noticed? There's no traffic.'

She comes to the window and stands beside me. Her skin smells of sleep and milk and sweat. I go to answer the phone.

'Heard the news?'

110

It is Stipe.

'No.'

'You must be the only man in Leo who hasn't. What the hell do you writers do all day?'

'Write.'

'Try to get out a little more. Or at least listen to the radio.'

'What is the news?'

'Remember your article – six months?'

'And?'

'You weren't out by much. June 30th. It's just been announced from the round-table conference. Congratulations. Let's have a drink at the Colibri soon to celebrate.'

He hangs up. Inès is looking at me.

'Well?'

'Stipe.'

She makes a noise of disapproval and turns back to the window. Nothing Stipe has to say could possibly be of interest.

'The Belgians have set the date for independence – June 30th.'

She turns back at once.

'Jesus,' she says quietly. 'Is he joking?'

'I don't think so.'

I have never seen her look so astonished. She hurries into the bedroom to finish dressing.

I check the date: February 27th.

'Four months,' I say to myself. 'Four months to independence.'

Only now do I realize that I hadn't believed Stipe when I'd written the article. I'd been a proxy floating something speculative and provocative. I had claimed – the way journalists do – to be painting the picture I had seen before me. Inès has no time for this defence. What colours do you use? How do you mix them? Where do you stand? What factors influence your choice of perspective? But in this case the defence was especially spurious. I had painted a picture I hadn't even seen. It was Stipe's picture.

She re-emerges clutching a pair of scuffed old shoes and leans against me as she slips them on.

A middle-aged Belgian woman in a pale blue floral dress tugs at my arm. She clutches a white handbag to her breast. She has a desperate look.

'*Nous nous trouvons devant l'inconnu complet,*' she mutters. '*L'inconnu complet, l'inconnu complet.*'

She wanders off with the distracted air and unseeing eye of someone who has just been told that their child has been killed in an accident. She is not alone. Every white face betrays loss, and utter bewilderment. At the corner of Lambermont a small group of white office workers have come out to confirm with their own eyes what they have been told on the radio. They are speechless, blank, horrified.

'Come on,' Inès says urgently and she starts down Avenue des Aviateurs, where the blacks are marching. I follow, pushing past the benumbed white spectators.

'Where is the army? Why are they letting this happen?' I hear a man say to his companion as I pass.

Something about this jars. Not the words. Not that. Something else. It is not until I have gone another ten or twenty paces that it hits me: the man was whispering, he was speaking under his breath. I have often heard whites being defensive and wary, but this is the first time I have ever heard a *colon* keep his voice down. In that instant I grasp the extent of what we are witnessing. I stop to look back at the speaker. I have to see him, I have to fix the image of this moment. He notices me, and so do his companions; they see me and unite against me in paranoia and aggression.

I hurry after Inès. All around is suppression and silence. There is only the steady, foreboding swish.

Towards the bottom of the avenue, near Place de la Poste, we come upon the marchers. They are in their thousands. They walk at a deliberate step, their eyes straight and implacably ahead, expressions set with a confidence I have not seen before on black faces: it is mixed with ostentation, borders on hostility. They whip the air with palm fronds to make the violent hiss I first heard in the apartment. The sound sends shivers down my spine.

A frightened white woman at the post office gathers up her daughter, an infant too big to carry, and hastens away, staggering bow-legged under her load like some comic female impersonator. The gendarmes stand around, resentful, frustrated, humiliated, leaderless.

Inès and I follow the marchers as they turn up towards the boulevard, where we bump into Grant among the growing crowd of onlookers. He puts a hand to his floppy brown fringe and brushes it from his forehead. As far as I can tell from the snatched conversation I have overheard at the Colibri or the Regina he is a man entirely devoid of enthusiasm. Inès says it was trained out of him at whatever public school or university he was educated. Today is no exception. The news to him is nothing special. He casts a languid eye over us and from his much superior height – he is at least six foot four – condescends to speak to me.

'Congratulations,' he says with a politeness so tight it conveys no congratulations at all. 'Your piece turns out to have been rather prophetic in the end.'

'Thank you,' I reply.

Inès walks ahead. Her dislike is for the type as much as the man.

'Did you know this was coming?' he asks.

'I had no idea,' I say.

'I thought your CIA chum might have told you.'

'I really had no idea,' I repeat.

He seems to read this as a competitor's rebuff. Part of me tingles with the satisfaction of the outside chance who has won the race against a stronger and more fancied opponent, and without even trying. Some of the other correspondents gravitate over. They gaze at me expectantly. One of them is trying to catch my eye. When, out of mere politeness, I nod at him he smiles as though favoured.

'You'll be in demand now,' Grant says.

Further down the boulevard one of the marchers has broken from the demonstration and run up to Inès.

'Auguste!' Inès cries out in delight.

They rush to embrace.

'It is coming,' Auguste says, his voice high and thrilled. 'Freedom is coming. Just like Patrice said.'

I hadn't realized Auguste was so ardent a Lumumbist and wonder if Stipe knows. Inès hugs him again.

'I am so happy,' I hear her say.

I watch as, arm-in-arm, gabbling excitedly, they fall in with the demonstrators. Their friendship has grown steadily over the weeks since I introduced them. Neither notices how shocking their display is to the white crowd. Grant is going on to me about the inevitable offers of work that will come from the London papers, about word-rates and expenses. I hardly hear him. My gaze is fixed on a thick-armed, stocky man who has started after Inès and Auguste. I cannot see his face, but the outrage and anger building up in him are clear from the way he moves.

'Perhaps you'd like a drink later?' Grant says.

'Excuse me,' I reply quickly and start after Inès and Auguste.

It is too late. The stocky man has exploded. He lunges from behind, throwing them apart with a violent shove.

'You like black cock, is that it, you fucking bald whore? You stinking whore! You have to get it from niggers because no real man would touch you.'

Inès shouts something back in Italian, too fast for me to understand. The white crowd hovers, tense and unpredictable. The stocky man spins round and pushes his face into Auguste's.

'Get out of here you ugly monkey or I'll kill now with my bare hands. Go on, you dirty black monkey.'

Inès shouts at their antagonist, but Auguste glances warily around him. He does not want to leave Inès, but the anger of the other whites, the men and the women, is getting up. He takes a cautious step backwards. Someone lunges from the crowd and punches him in the chest.

Auguste stumbles. The whites close in. How big his eyes are now, how manifest his fear. He is like a silent movie nigger, a joke to those who cannot know the reach of his terrors. Someone kicks at his legs. He knows he must not go down. He begins to retreat, backing off carefully, trying to find a way back to the safety of the march. The demonstrators are becoming aware of what is going on but seem uncertain about what to do.

'Leave him alone!' Inès shouts.

I try to push through the clotting crowd. They are shouting insults at Inès – *Salop, salop!*

'Let me through,' I shout. 'Let me through.'

Hearing my accent they eye me suspiciously and become slow to budge. I am not one of them; they have associated me with Inès and Auguste.

'Get out of my way!'

Someone smacks the back of my head. A glob of spit lands on my nose. I push ahead, someone grabs my arm.

The stocky man is confronting Inès. She is not intimidated and gives as good as she gets.

'Shut up, you filthy whore!'

He bumps her with his fat chest, pushing her off the pavement on to the road. She pushes back. The man raises his hand and slaps her across the face. She is taken by surprise but rallies immediately, fire in her eyes, and throws a tiny fist back at him.

I am in the grip of someone who will not let go. I lash out and, without knowing who I have hit, find myself released. I think I have just seen a face I know. Smail? I turn back. It is Smail. The diamond trader is fighting with the crowd, pushing them off me, swearing and challenging them. Our eyes meet briefly, just long enough for us to confirm the presence of the other; then I turn and struggle my way through to Inès. I manage to get between her and the stocky man. I am not a fighter. I cannot remember the last time I threw a punch – a very long time ago, at school probably – but there is blood on Inès's mouth.

'Don't touch her,' I tell the stocky man.

I am not shouting, my voice is quiet. I can hear the menace in it myself. Some way behind us I am aware of the scuffle still going on around Auguste.

'You filthy racist!' Inès shouts at the stocky man.

'Be quiet!' I tell her.

I can see that the stocky man is thinking about taking me on. If he does he will beat me. I have to concentrate on not letting him see that. He pauses. There is such contempt in his eyes.

'Keep your fucking woman under control,' he says.

He spits in my face, then turns away. The crowd stares at us but no one seems to want to make the first move.

I take Inès's hand and start to lead her away.

'Auguste!' she cries.

Twenty yards further up the avenue Auguste is on his knees, encircled by the mob. Smail is doing his best to defend him. Someone kicks Auguste savagely in the chest.

It is the signal for the start of the fight proper. The marchers are already breaking ranks and, throwing aside their palm fronds and placards, they dash headlong into the enemy to rescue their comrade. Some of the whites scatter, others run to take them on. Gendarmes rush over.

'Auguste!' Inès shouts.

He staggers to his feet, helped by Smail. The marchers, the crowd and the police join in a fighting swirl.

'Auguste's all right,' I say. 'Smail's with him. He's all right.'

Auguste is not all right. But I have to get her away.

I lead her down the boulevard, back the way we have come. There is fighting all around us. The streets, normally so well kept, have a sudden air of shabbiness, of discouragement: there is a pair of man's underpants lying sodden and grey next to a storm drain (what happened that they should be there?); there are discarded palm fronds and placards; and strewn everywhere is the diamond glass of smashed car windows. An armoured car cruises up behind us, its machine-gun turret swivelling with robotic dispassion. Rioters scatter as it advances.

'Stop,' she shouts suddenly, her voice urgent and weak at the same time.

She bends over and puts her hands on her knees to try to rally her forces. I hold her from behind by the waist. She is a feather.

'Are you all right?'

She does not say anything.

'Inès?'

She makes a little groan. From behind on the boulevard there is a pop. Tear gas.

'I can't move,' she says and tries to sit down on the pavement.

I will not let her free.

'We're going home,' I say.

As I pull her gently up I notice Grant and one of the correspondents looking at us. Grant nods to me and I give him a stiff smile in return. I see a smirk cross his face. He turns to say something to his colleague. I doubt that it's kind. It must please him to see his competitor embroiled in so undignified a situation. I doubt Grant has ever been in the middle of something like this – with temper, anger, passion flaring, with someone's spit trickling from nose to chin. I doubt he has been with a woman like this, a woman who causes fights and flails with her fists. No, Grant would never put himself in such a ridiculous position.

I can see myself and Inès now, the state we're in, from where he's standing.

15

I DAB HER swollen lip with iodine. She demands I telephone Stipe to get him to help Auguste. If Stipe can't, or won't, I am to go to the cité, to the house of Auguste's brother, where there will be people who will know what to do.

I say all in good time, first she must see a doctor. Above her protests I telephone Roger. She hasn't forgotten what Roger's friends said in Houthhoofd's garden all those weeks ago, even though compared with the things whites say every day about blacks their observations seem mild. I have bumped into Roger occasionally at the Regina and the Caravelle. He is a gentle, well-meaning and unimaginative man, thoroughly English, thoroughly decent. He comes over straight away.

He is kindly with her, though she is an irritating patient, interrupting his examination with questions about the Brussels announcement, about Lumumba, the demonstration: what has he heard?

'The radio said there are going to be elections in May for a Chamber of Representatives.'

'Patrice will win easily,' she predicts confidently. 'The MNC is the biggest party.'

'Are you taking your malaria tablets?' he asks.

She seems not to hear the question but muses to herself: 'I will arrange an interview when he comes back.'

'Nivaquine? Paladrine?' Roger presses.

'Paladrine,' I answer for her, though I am not sure how regularly she takes her pills.

'How about your movements?'

119

Inès looks at him, puzzled. I explain. She flushes a little. She is coy about this, engagingly so: it is the one thing about the body that discomfits even her earthy senses. She always used to go to great lengths, adopt all sorts of stratagems, to contrive that I was out of earshot when she went to the bathroom, and sometimes, if she couldn't get me out of the way, she would hum nervous little improvised tunes to cover her distress. She has not been able to keep up this fastidious-ness. Two nights ago I woke to find myself alone in the bed and to hear her vomiting and shitting. I waited for the sound of the toilet to flush, for the tap-water to run, for rinsing and spitting. There was nothing except the dull whirr of the *condi*. I leapt out of the bed and in the semi-darkness of the bathroom found her sitting naked on the toilet, leaning forward in an attitude of complete exhaustion. There was a lumpy grey-brown splatter of vomit on the floor between her feet. I helped her up and got her into the shower. Her skin was cold and damp. She sat in the basin, her back against the tiles while I directed the jets of water. I dried her off and carried her to bed, then went back to clean up the mess.

I leave her with Roger and her modesty and go to the window in the living room. I call the consulate and leave a message for Stipe, telling him about Auguste. The street below is silent. No one is stirring. I glance down at the table, on which my manuscript lies. What do I feel about the novel, if I am honest? It is about a man who has reached a point in his life where, unsure of who or what he is, he becomes convinced that only by finding the father he never knew will he discover the clues to his own identity. When I first told Inès that I was planning to write this book she became very excited. For reasons to do with her interest in my past and my family and my make-up, this was the novel she wanted me to write. It would be different from what I had done before, it would be a departure, it would be *felt*. She plied me with questions, she made endless suggestions, her enthusiasm stoked mine. Every evening, when she came home to the flat, she would ask to see what I'd written. She devoured the pages. *Bravo, complimenti.* She would kiss me. But then, as the work progressed, her attitude began to change. Her reactions were formal. I tried to hide my disappointment, but one night I tackled her about it. She said of course the work had technique and craft. She said she liked some of the descriptive passages (the more practice, the greater the opportunities to perfect the tricks). But the book's heart should be the son's need and this she did not feel. After that, she would turn the pages with the air of one who reads from duty. One evening when she asked to see what I'd written I replied with studied casualness, 'Oh, I don't think I have anything worth showing you tonight. The passage I'm working on isn't ready yet', and she did not ask again. Having been disappointed in the book, it was as though she'd forgotten all about it.

It's true, she's right. Though I write and rewrite, I still cannot seem to make felt what's at stake for the son. Melodrama embarrasses me, raised voices are unnecessary. Whenever I try for emotion, anger, fire, the effects seem false. I will write to Alan to tell him I need a little more time.

Roger comes out of the bedroom.

'She's anaemic,' he says in the bland, matter-of-fact way that doctors have of announcing everything from corns to cancer. 'She's probably got a touch of malaria, and she's almost certainly picked up amoebic dysentery. Probably got it from eating in the street. That's not to be advised. Pretty unhygienic, you know. Actually, manioc has virtually no nutritional value. It's a filler, a bulky starch. You can really feel it in the tummy but it does nothing more than satisfy immediate hunger pangs. It's also thought to contain more than a trace of cyanide.'

'I suppose there's something fitting in that,' I say.

The idea that the staple food of the black Congolese should be poisonous seems all too appropriate but Roger is not a man for whom ironies or metaphors have much meaning.

He runs the side of his finger along the bristle of his short ginger-brown moustache.

'She needs to pay a bit more attention to her diet – plenty of protein, fresh vegetables and fresh fruit. I've left some vitamin supplements and iron tablets. You should see that she takes them.'

'I will.'

'And something for the tummy trouble. I've also taken blood samples and specimens and I've made an appointment at the clinic in Gombé. In the meantime keep her in bed. She needs rest and looking after.'

I ask about her hair. I feel embarrassed doing so, embarrassed for Inès, more so than if we'd been discussing her movements. *Bald whore.* The stocky man's insult rings in my head.

'It is a bit thin,' Roger acknowledges. 'Women occasionally do lose some hair. It's sometimes related to a nervous condition and it's usually only temporary. Diet should help.'

I walk with him to the door.

'What do you think of the news?' I ask.

He sighs. 'When I came out in '49 it was a terrific life. Wonderful standard of living, far better than anything a young bachelor was likely to have back in England. And conditions for the blacks, you know, were actually on the whole jolly reasonable. But it's all started to go a little downhill. It's not the fault of the big companies. Unilever and the Union Minière built really splendid homes for their workers – I mean splendid by African standards: running water, electricity and so on. The trouble is that a lot of the Belgians who came out in the last ten years or so – the *petits colons* – they're not terribly nice or terribly educated people. I think they've done an awful lot to inflame the blacks. I doubt I shall stay on much longer.'

I thank him again and open the door.

'If I were you,' he says, almost as an afterthought, 'I'd think about getting out as well. I suspect what you saw today is a sign of things to come.'

I ask him how much I owe but he won't hear of it.

I go in to see Inès. She is groggy. I sit on the bed.

'Will you phone to Stipe? You must find out about Auguste.'

I bend over and kiss her hot forehead and tell her I have already phoned to Stipe.

'Now that we know Stipe was right about independence,' I say, 'what do you think now about his motive in giving me that story?'

She says nothing.

I tease her. 'You won't admit you got him wrong?'

'I do not know what his motive was, except that it wasn't honest.'

I put my fingers to the side of her face.

'You know I love you,' I tell her.

I feel able to risk this because we have been together again; in the street it had been as though there was nothing wrong between us.

She presses her cheek against my hand, but does not otherwise respond. Her eyes are closed. One thing about Inès – she never lies, not even to spare someone's feelings. She is tactlessly sincere. Her silence now is silence to avoid a lie.

'Roger says we should consider getting out,' I say slowly. 'What do you think?'

I ask the question as though we had a future together.

'Roger is a panicker,' she announces after a minute, 'like all doctors.'

There is no future.

'Of course.'

Doctors are panickers. That's all there is to it. She avoids the other implications.

'Anyway, how can I leave now, with independence coming?'

These are hurrying times; she must not be left behind.

16

Her illness has brought out the best in me, or what little there is I might reasonably claim for the best. I like her being sick – this is the truth of it; her weakness now plays to chivalric fantasies which have lurked in me from the day I saw my father raise his angry hand, the day I saw my mother tremble.

But there is more to it. Something is being recovered, slowly, unevenly. At times it almost feels a little like it used to after we had made love. In those minutes – if it had worked, if I had done it right – this restless, tumbling woman was momentarily calm, and in that calm I could glimpse a place for myself. It was when I most felt her need, and she mine. And now there is need again, on both sides. At least I think so, I hope so.

In the mornings I go out to get the papers. Since the Brussels announcement dozens of new journals, magazines and party news-sheets have appeared. I buy a selection for Inès, as well as *Courrier d'Afrique, L'Avenir, Actualités Africaines* and whatever foreign papers I can find. They are costing us a fortune. I come back to the apartment and make coffee for myself and weak lemon tea for her. I sit on the bed and read aloud the headlines. She picks the stories she wants to hear. They are mostly to do with the election campaign, which began the moment Lumumba and the other delegates stepped off the plane from Brussels. I was already familiar with the larger political parties and tribal associations – Lumumba's MNC, Kasavubu's Abako, Tshombe's Conakat – but new parties appear almost daily, as do coalitions, cartels, federations and alliances. These are shifting, to say the least: announced in sacred declarations of eternal fraternity in one issue of a news-sheet, they are dissolved in the next in language of low abuse and high charges of betrayal. There are so many chaotic and clamorous voices, so many names, acronyms, initials: PSA, Cerea, RP, PP, Reko, Mederco, Luka, Puna, RDLK, Unimo, Coaka, Abazi, Cartel MUB, Unebafi, MSM, Balubakat. Not to mention the Parti National du Progrès. Inès calls it Parti des Nègres Payés for the PNP is the Belgians' favourite and its links with the administration's coffers are no secret. Money – its sources and the channels in which it flows – is the subject of endless and vitriolic speculation.

She gets enraged by the bulletins of *Inforcongo*, the government's mouthpiece.

'Look at this,' she howls in protest. '*The only mistake the Belgians may be making is to expect moderation and commonsense from the self-appointed leaders.*'

I tease her by reading the worst of the silliness in *Indépendance*, the MNC newspaper: '*Patrice Lumumba, you are the man we need, you are our hope and the hope of our future . . .*'

'Shut up,' she says, roused to the effort of trying to snatch the paper from my hands.

'No, listen – it gets better. *Martyr of freedom, child of our fatherland, symbol of liberty, protector of our ancestors' rights, valiant soldier, let your agonizing enemies watch your triumph and our glory.*'

She grabs the paper and skims it to the furthest corner of the room.

'It's easy to mock,' she chides, 'but there are important things happening now.'

'Perhaps, but language like this makes important things difficult to take seriously.'

'Maybe for you. But when you think of what has been

done, of all the oppressions and the miseries, words like this are inevitable. Anything less would be an insult to the people who have suffered.'

Suffer is *soffer*. There is always a lot of suffering in Inès's lexicon. She reminds me these people have been *rightless* since the arrival of the first colonists and that only when Lumumba comes to power will their rights be restored.

'*Martyr of freedom? Child of our fatherland?*'

'One day you too will be forced to take this seriously. You won't escape.'

In the early afternoons, instead of going to the Colibri, I sit on the bed and read novels to her.

'He is not there when he is speaking. It is too technical,' she complains half-way through *A Sentimental Education*, which Stipe had lent me. 'If he is not moved, why should I be?'

She had listened with the same kind of withdrawn impatience to *Salammbô* and *St Antony*.

'Just relax,' I say. 'Listen to the descriptions, imagine the pictures in your head. Enjoy them. *Like an architect designing a palace he drew up his plans for his future, full of things dainty and splendid, towering to the skies; and sunk in contemplation of such a rich array he lost all sense of the outside world.*'

'How can anyone lose all sense of the outside world?'

The Realists are not to her taste. She prefers the metaphors of Yeats, prefers his extravagances and symbols and terrible beauties, shares his disdain for peering and peeping persons and the hawkers of stolen goods. I should have remembered before choosing Flaubert that language for her is not about precision, it is not about verisimilitude or the perfect description of person, thing, time, but a burning tessellation of images and instincts, of deeply felt, half-real things. In her world reality, imagination and emotion are

127

indivisible – in deed, in thought. She is never detained by detail.

We have, in a way, made up some lost ground. I have no illusions. Nothing has been settled. We neither of us are certain where we stand with the other or what the future holds. It is just that for the time being there is a different, quieter context in which to be together.

Sometimes when I know she is sleeping I will leave the desk and go to stand in the doorway of the bedroom. I love to look at her. There are times when I can almost convince myself that all I have to do is rush to the bed, fall on my knees and beg her to make everything all right. It would be too absurd. My father was a man of impulsive and transparent gestures, performed intermittently in compensation for other, larger, more fundamental derelictions. After a bolt of his temper, after a hurt he had visited, he would present my mother with flowers he could not afford and she did not want. He always dreamed of making good and as his failures mounted so his attempts to buy his way out of them intensified. More flowers, bits of jewellery, dinners – not expensive, but more than there was money for. I used to see him stand before my mother, the little boy with his head hanging, waiting to be kissed, to have his hair ruffled and patted, but most of all waiting for a forgiveness he knew my mother could not withhold. She was soft and he made promises for the future. I cannot say I knew my father well but I saw enough of him to loathe this courtship by stealth, by trickery, by feint. It seemed cheap to me then and it does so now; I am only amazed that it seems to work.

My father's flowers, my father's flowers . . .

. . .and my words. What worth have they? From my youth I have lived by disguises – and with each disguise a new set of words to please the ear of my new audience. Like Margaret who had forgotten her height, I have forgotten what my real words are. I have lived disguised from myself, in permanent doubt of my own emotional authenticity; and since I am never alone with myself, since I am always watching the character playing my part in the scene, there is no possibility of spontaneity.

And so I leave her to sleep and say nothing.

I am writing at the table one afternoon when she calls to me.

'Do you want something?' I ask from the door.

She looks low.

'What is it?' I ask.

My hopes are up. There is never a chance of anything between us when she is happy, distracted by her commitments. In her sadness there are openings.

'I don't know,' she says wearily.

She looks a little better. Her eyes at least are clear, though her face is still drawn.

'Come here,' she says.

'Do you want me to read to you?' I say, sitting on the bed.

'No,' she says. 'Are you working?'

'It's okay.'

'Are you sure? I don't want to interfere with your work.'

'What's work, Inès? You have interfered with my life.'

She reaches up and kisses me.

With my hand, with my right hand, I stroke her. She whispers for me to get undressed. I hang my head, feeling nervous and uncertain. We have not made love for many weeks. Our last attempt was not a success.

'Come on,' she says gently.

I do as she says and open the sheet. The bed is an

envelope of her smell. She has never been fastidious, there is
no rule about showering every day. I lie beside her and press
my nose into the sourness of her armpit. I breathe in deeply
and kiss the side of her breast. She says nice things to me, that
I am patient, not just in bed, that I am a good man, that I am
kind. It is true, I suppose, I can sometimes be kind. I would
put it no higher than that. But at this moment I do not want
to contest her judgements; I want to feel well about myself.

'Tell me more,' I whisper.

Instead of speaking she gently pushes me on to my back.

'Are you sure you're strong enough?' I say.

'I am very strong.'

She reaches down to take hold of me. We both smile. This
is one of our shared sexual jokes. Once – soon after we
became lovers – I had guided her hand to my cock. She
hesitated and I was surprised because in everything else she
had been abandoned, and I felt a little humiliated, as though
chastised for something unseemly, for greed or perversion.
But she had explained, 'I am no good at this, I have never
known how to do it right.' In my lover's joyful egoism I said I
would teach her. But I never did: patterns formed, self-
consciousness settled, the moment never arrived again.

I do not at once collude in what she is doing, I do not
relax – out of fear she will lose confidence, that she will think
it is taking too long. But she continues, she goes on. Then I
close my eyes and give myself up to it. I caress her back, I
lower my hand to her cheeks and cup her and squeeze her. I
give her small signals that it's working, a clinch of my hand, a
flaw in my breath. She kisses me and I respond.

'I want to be inside you,' I tell her.

She shakes her head. 'I want to do this for you.'

She licks my teeth and lips and moves her mouth to my
chest. She licks my nipples, bites them, flicks them with her
free hand. I say her name over and over and say don't stop,

don't stop and when she makes me come I feel momentarily embarrassed, a weakness exposed. But she does not make the false cooing noises of mistimed or unsatisfying sex. I see that she is excited by what she has done – even that it has made her love me again, and I feel suddenly whole and happy and confident.

She lies quiet, her hand running across my shoulder. After a while she begins to press herself against my thigh. She moves up to the bone and, reaching across my stomach, pulls us closer. I feel the prickle of the hair between her legs, a burn on the smooth skin of my hip and waist. I feel wetness and heat. How I love it that she comes so easily.

I can feel her breath on my stomach. We lie in silence until she tells me she loves me.

'Where is this going?' I say.

'You are . . . I cannot think of the word in English. In Italian it would be *catastrofista* – a catastrophist. Is there this word?'

'I've only ever heard it used in a geological sense.'

'As usual! English is always so poor. The meaning of this word is much bigger. If you are *catastrofista* no problem is small. Nothing can be fixed, it is always the end. Do you recognize this person?'

'A little.'

'Me too.'

'But if the problem is big,' I say, 'if it can't be fixed, the only thing to do is leave it behind.'

'You are *catastrofista*,' she says, putting a hand to my cheek, 'but I don't care.'

She sits up. I regard her from behind. Her vertebrae are clearly visible, there is a slight curvature from left to right. Her little bottom sinks into the mattress and looks as though squashed, pressed.

'I am depressed,' she says.

'Depressed?'

'It's this stupid thing,' she says, reaching down to the floor. She comes up with a newspaper. 'Here,' she says, presenting me with this morning's edition of *Indépendance*. She taps the page. 'It is the *Loi Fundamentale*.'

'You're depressed about this?'

La Loi Fundamentale, the sixteen resolutions passed unanimously by the Brussels conference, will form the basis of the post-independence constitution and the future Congolese government. They were agreed with pronouncements of high sentiment, amity and idealism – the kind that typically are made at the end of long and bitter conflicts when those charged with finding a settlement find first and most praise for their own statesmanship, far-sightedness and generosity. I saw a newspaper photograph of Lumumba shaking hands with Eyskens, the Belgian prime minister, just after the Brussels meeting broke up. Inès thought he looked handsome and dignified; I saw the child in the schoolyard who had at last been allowed to play with the big boys. At the time, *La Loi Fundamentale* was hailed as the beginning of a new era.

'No, not depressed, just . . .' – she trails off and shrugs – 'sad, I suppose, that Patrice agreed to these things.'

Oh, talk about us, please, not the politics of this absurd place, anything but that. What is wrong with us cannot be recomposed so easily, so quickly. It will take more than an afternoon in bed. Talk about us, Inès, and what the future will be.

She talks instead about Patrice. He is too trusting of the Belgians, apparently. Like the other delegates he was thrilled to be in Brussels. He thought he was being treated as an equal, meeting ministers, meeting the King; all the misunderstandings of the past had been cleared up. He and the others were so proud of having won independence, they didn't think about the details – and the details, she insists, are very bad.

'Are they?' I ask without enthusiasm.

'The economic and financial details are terrible. Patrice thinks he will win the elections and probably he will, but he will still not have power because the bankers, the business-men and the mining corporations, they will control the economy. The Belgians are being nice to him now, but does he really think the Union Minière in Katanga and the Société Général will be partners with him in the new Congo, that they will agree to use their wealth for the people?'

'Does he?'

She still doesn't hear the void in my voice.

'Probably,' she continues. 'I will have to talk to him. I can explain to him where he has gone wrong.'

'I'm sure he'll appreciate that.'

'Yes.'

She starts to slip down in the bed, overtaken by tiredness. I kiss her gently on the lips. She raises a hand. I clasp it.

'I am so 'appy,' she whispers.

'Me too.'

She embraces me, pulling me down to the pillows, and with the last of her energy kisses me noisily and playfully – the Italian girl again.

'Don't stay up too late tonight,' she says.

'I won't.'

'Good. I want you to do to me what I did to you.'

Hold up the moon. Who needs daylight? Wrists fast in my grip, ankles at my shoulders. Hold me, don't let me breathe! She is almost doubled, her eyes are screwed shut. There are flinches in her when I push. I pause to pray, to count, to remember.

I want to find a story to tell her. But she knows me. I cannot move her with tales of my past in which I appear well or wounded. There is nothing new I have for her, no secrets with which to fascinate her now. But tonight it doesn't matter. Tonight I am enough.

17

I HAVE COME with Stipe to Mungul's house to see Lumumba. Stipe knew it would be a long wait and he wanted the company. We sit with Auguste on a rough bench in the courtyard. Moths wheel round the hurricane lamp, fireflies blink in the dark corners, and the air smells acrid, of batshit and sewage. A dozen or so young men – guards, officials, cousins, brothers, hangers-on – loll pointlessly around, the usual MNC coterie. No one ever seems to have anything specific to do, no one ever seems to know anything. They can't say whether Lumumba is expected or not, or even if he's here already.

So we wait. Recently, Stipe's air of imperturbable good humour has given way to something more withdrawn. These days his friend Patrice is getting harder to pin down. He hasn't been returning calls, he's been missing appointments. The election campaign is in full swing, there's always an excuse, but Stipe doesn't like it. Lumumba's elusiveness has coincided with a souring of the political atmosphere. For some weeks after the Brussels announcement Patrice seemed to be co-operating with the Belgians, and they, dropping their old favourite Kasavubu, noisily promoted him as the new Good African. Then, for reasons no one is quite sure of, the insults began. The *colons* started calling him nothing better than another Hitler; Lumumba was a Bad African after all, no better than the communist Gizenga with whom he was now cavorting. Kasavubu was discovered to be a Good African after all.

In the glow of the lamp Stipe turns to Auguste and speaks

in a low voice, a mixture of Lingala, English and French. It is always touching to watch them together, even more so by this soft light. Their intimacy is that of brothers, or better – if the thought weren't so comical – sisters. They huddle, they conspire, they read each other's whims and intentions, and laugh together at things outsiders don't think funny. Whatever Inès might think of him, whatever Stipe is doing in Léopoldville, with Auguste at least he is a good man. And a different man. Auguste brings out in him something lighter, younger, carefree. He teases him in a way I could not contemplate, about his lack of height and hair, about his drinking, about his pronunciation of African names. Stipe chuckles at all of it. It is more than simple good-natured patience at being ribbed, more than not wanting to appear defensive. He enjoys it, savours it. Auguste takes him out of himself in a way I cannot.

And in return Stipe is a good friend. De Scheut and I accompanied him the night he went to the police station in Avenue Lippers to demand Auguste's release after the demonstration. He argued and threatened until the jailers produced their prisoner. Auguste was tame and fearful, and Stipe looked him over in angry silence, taking in each cut and bruise as if they were injuries to himself. His broad face filled up with red, his lips paled and pursed. A Flemish gendarme unchained Auguste and pushed him forward and for a moment I was sure Stipe was going to explode. I put a restraining hand on his arm but he shook me curtly off. Somehow he mastered his rage and went instead to embrace Auguste and tell him he was safe now and always would be. I left them outside the station to go back to Inès, but de Scheut told me later that Stipe had driven Auguste to his own apartment where he bathed him and cleaned up his wounds. Then he took him to the Zoo, seated him ostentatiously, glared at the Belgians and ordered the most expensive champagne in the house. Auguste has told me that Stipe gives money to his family, that he paid for medical treatment for his grandmother, that he is putting one of his brothers through school.

Stipe is a loud and a quiet man.

And yet something is changing between them. I can see it even now as the bats flit in their crazed paths around Mungul's house and the bored young men whisper and snigger. Inès has had a hand in it and though Stipe has said nothing to me, I know he is not at all pleased with her intervention.

I first noticed that something was going on when we went to an MNC congress in Léopoldville, one of a series staged throughout the country as the elections neared. The event had culminated in a torch-lit rally in Matongé football stadium. Sweat glistened on every face, spirits were high and the booming chorus of *Depanda!* filled the night. Lumumba had given the most effective speech I had heard him deliver. I had heard many by then, for I had gone for the *Observer* to rallies at Luluabourg, Coquilhatville, Ininongo and Stanleyville. Until that night in Matongé I had thought of Lumumba as a kind of conjurer; I knew there was magic but I knew there was trickery behind it. This performance, however, was special. It had the hairs on the back of my neck bristling, it raised goose bumps on my arms. There were moments when I found myself being swept along in the emotional waves he sent crashing over us. I had to force myself to pull back, to stop, to think, to listen to the words – the habitual words of the politician, all the usual grievances, exaggerations, platitudes, generalizations and promises. I had to fight, to make an effort of will in order to hold on to myself.

I bumped into de Scheut and his children. They had not held on but had been swept along; de Scheut was brimming with sentiment. People were decent, the world was good – and would soon be better. He always sees the best in everyone.

The children, Julie and Cristophe, greeted me a little shyly but with none of the tormented awkwardness of some youngsters.

'Wonderful speech,' de Scheut said, 'wonderful, wasn't it? This really is a momentous time – the first chance people in this divided land have had to find a way to live together in equality and peace, our first chance to compromise.'

'Do you think Lumumba is interested in compromise?'

'Oh, yes, undoubtedly. Don't listen to people who say Patrice is a communist and an extremist – and he's not a racist either. He genuinely wants the whites to be part of the new Congo. He's a fine and honourable man.'

'Patrice used to come to our house,' Julie said shyly.

'And what did you think of him?' I asked.

'He's very nice,' she replied, tightening her hold on her father's arm as the departing crowd swayed this way and that.

'We played football with him,' Cristophe put in. 'He's very good at football.'

De Scheut smiled at his son. The boy's skin was clear and his fair hair was neatly combed across his head. He had sloping little ears.

'It's going to take a lot of effort and goodwill,' de Scheut said, 'but we can make it work if we put our minds to it.'

He said Inès and I must come for dinner soon. He said goodnight and put his arms across the shoulders of his children and I watched him navigate their way through the streaming crowd, an old, good father with a beautiful child on either arm. On the morning Inès told me that she wanted to have a baby – crude as this sounds (and it was deeply confusing to me) – my reactions were centred in my cock: I experienced an erection so strong, so instant it was painful.

When I moved, I felt the wetness on my thigh. Inès discovered my arousal – she was always highly attuned to my sexual state. She laughed and said it was appropriate, in a biological sense.

If there had been a child, the possibility of children . . .?

Stipe and I found Inès talking to Auguste. There was something collusive about their manner, something excluding, which Stipe and I had different reasons for disliking. Inès gave me a particularly hard look – a rebuke for being with Stipe. Auguste was wearing glasses with heavy black frames of the kind Lumumba favours. I had not known he wore glasses and commented on them and said he looked well. He beamed at my compliment.

Stipe did not waste time on pleasantries. He long ago gave up trying to get through to Inès.

He said, 'Come on, Auguste. Let's get the car.'

And then there was something extraordinary. Auguste, standing next to Inès, hesitated. He stood there and he looked at his employer, his friend, his mentor, his master, his provider – but he did not move. It was the first time I had witnessed anything like this between them. In that moment I recalled something Stipe had said to me one afternoon over drinks in the Colibri.

'Are you familiar with the concept of neoteny?' he had asked. 'It's a zoological term.'

'I don't think so.'

'It's about stunted growth, you might say, psychologically and emotionally speaking. The dog is neotenic in that over thousands of years we have bred it from a wild pack animal into something more at home in your yard. We've done it by encouraging the retention of the juvenile characteristics of submission and subservience in the adult. That's why your mutt licks your hand instead of tearing it off the way its wolf ancestor would.'

'Science is always good for metaphors,' I'd said, 'though

they can sometimes be a little obvious.'

'Yeah, but no less true for that,' he'd replied.

In Matongé stadium, in front of the hesitating Auguste, I wondered if Stipe was thinking about neoteny. No amount of intimacy could disguise the obvious bias in their relationship. Stipe seemed to be the only one who couldn't see it. He looked at his driver and worked through the implications. I knew he was thinking Inès was behind this little rebellion and I felt awkward about it.

'Are you coming, Auguste?' Stipe said slowly.

The words were filled with meaning, and also with emotion. This was not simply the insubordination of an employee, but the betrayal of a friend. Stipe's cold fury concealed a deep hurt.

Inès's face was set, she was ready for combat. But the fight was not to be that night. I think Auguste may have seen the anguish behind Stipe's eyes, even if Inès did not. He smiled suddenly – his special huge smile of deference and non-aggression. He was not yet ready to bite, but I knew then he was tired of licking hands.

When they were gone, I asked Inès if she was ready to go home. I did not want to talk about Auguste and Stipe, for I knew her mood. She looked frail and worn. She had of course resumed her schedule as soon as she had risen from her sickbed.

'No, I have some work to do,' she said abruptly.

'What work? It's after midnight.'

She looked at me severely.

'I would hardly discuss this work with you.'

'What are you talking about?'

'So you could tell your spy friend.'

'Inès,' I said softly, putting a gentle hand on her shoulder.

The last thing I wanted was an argument, but she twisted away from me, out of reach.

'What work?' I demanded, annoyed.

'I have been asked,' she began deliberately, 'to do some work for Patrice, and I said I would do it, so I am going to do it.'

'Okay, do your work. What time do you think you'll be home?'

'I don't know.'

She said it aggressively.

'I don't understand why you're so angry,' I said.

'I am angry because of Stipe. Because you should not be with him.'

'He's my friend. Why shouldn't I be with him?'

'You think only of yourself, as usual. It's always about you.'

I had in my right hand a rolled-up newspaper. Without thinking I swung it at her face. I felt brutal and hurt, and this time I was not going to be weak and pleading. My pride would not allow it. I was going to tell her once and for all that sometimes she could be a silly bitch and why didn't she just stop all this nonsense. She jerked her face away, letting out a little cry, but I stayed my hand in time. I did not hit her.

'Oh Inès, I'm sorry.'

She glared at me.

'I'm sorry,' I repeated.

'I have work to do.'

'Inès, is there someone else?' I asked.

'No,' she replied, but there was something in her voice that did not convince me. It wasn't hesitation – it wasn't that, she hadn't hesitated at all; it was more the boredom with which she had said it.

'It that the truth?'

'Yes it's the truth.'

And again I did not feel convinced, again because of the lack of effort she put into her answer.

'I don't know what time I'll be back,' she said, starting off.

141

'Are we going to argue because of Stipe?' I called after her. 'Are we going to lose all the ground we made up because of him?'

She spun round to face me.

'When will you see what he is doing?' she said sharply. 'When will you see what is happening around you?'

I would rather have heard her condemn me as a woman-beater than hear this. At least then it would have been about us. She turned and walked away. Away to do her work for Patrice.

Things have been cold between us since. She is involved with her people, her cause, as never before, staying out all hours, spending more time in the MNC headquarters and Lumumba's house than in her own office. She is frequently with Smail.

The bats continue in their zig-zag flight. The young men are still bored and listless, they drift away and back again, murmuring to each other indifferently. A large flying beetle, the buff-coloured kind that stream in from the river, lands in my hair. I flick it off with a shudder and the young men snigger among themselves. I am getting sleepy. Tomorrow I have a long article to write for the paper. I also have to get back to work on my novel. I have reached the climax. The son has found his father but has not yet found himself, and I have not yet found a way to make his feeling of failure and desperation seem real to the reader. I will have to write again to Alan, there will be another delay in delivery.

I tell Stipe I think I will go home. He has been silent and brooding for the last hour. There is none of the usual banter between him and Auguste, their strained talk has faded away. He says something in Lingala to one of the men lounging around. Lingala is a military-like language and always sounds abrupt. It sounds even more so in Stipe's mouth tonight. I know enough to understand that he has told them to remind Patrice that he is here.

One of the men gets lazily to his feet, spends a little time stretching, yawning, a little time talking to one of his friends. Then he goes inside.

He does not come out again.

Fifteen minutes or so later a man emerges from the house. It is Smail. He seems surprised to see us.

'Hello, James. What are you doing here?'

'Mark's waiting to see Lumumba.'

'Really?' Smail says.

Stipe doesn't like Smail: the communist diamond merchant is as bad an influence on Lumumba as Inès and Gizenga.

'Well, the thing is,' Smail says, a little embarrassed, 'Patrice isn't here. He left.'

'What do you mean he left?' Stipe demands.

'He *was* here, but he left a couple of hours ago.'

Stipe says nothing. He does not move.

Smail, reading Stipe's mood and trying to appease it, says, 'Patrice hasn't a moment these days. He has his work in the College of Commissioners office. When he gets home there's always thirty or forty people waiting to see him. That takes him up to midnight. After that there's party business to see to. He gets to bed around three if he's lucky, then he has to get up at dawn for more appointments before he goes to the office and the whole thing starts again.'

Stipe is not mollified.

Smail wishes us goodnight. To me, he says: 'Give my regards to Inès.'

'You should give her mine. You see much more of her than I do,' I say to the man whose company Inès seems to prefer these days.

143

He smiles tightly, gives a courteous little bow to Stipe and is gone.

In the car Stipe remains silent until we reach the apartment block. As I bid him goodnight he tells me he is thinking about a trip to Katanga to visit Houthhoofd.

A few days later he calls to suggest I come with him. He assures me I will be interested in what Houthhoofd has to say. I ask if he has managed to see Lumumba. He tells me he hasn't in a tone that strains to say he never expected to and it's no big deal that he hasn't, and I know at once that some significant realignment is underway. Advice has been offered and spurned. Stipe won't let that go.

18

Though Auguste is with us, Stipe is driving. He seems to think this a kind of punishment for Auguste; if so, it is one his driver, sprawled in the back seat fiddling with his new glasses, is taking in his stride. Auguste adjusts the spectacles continually and checks his reflection in the window when he thinks we're not looking.

On the road out of Léopoldville towards Kikwit we pass an endless parade of posters, hoardings and painted slogans.

Stipe reels them off in a bored voice: 'Votez MNC, Votez Abako, Votez Puna, Votez Redako . . . Did you know there are over thirty parties fighting this election? Someone should tell people here about the benefits of the two-party system. At the very least it would cut down on the waste of paper.'

'The MNC is the biggest party,' Auguste puts in from nowhere.

Stipe looks at him in the driver's mirror. Auguste, feeling Stipe's soundless censure, turns to stare vacantly out the window. We drive on in endless silence. I am in the middle of another family's row. It is a five- to eight-day drive to Katanga, depending on the state of the roads. We could have flown to Élisabethville in a few hours and gone on to Houthhoofd's estate from there, but Stipe wanted to see how the election campaign was progressing up-country. Stipe's temper would be worse if he knew what I knew, but Inès made me promise not to tell. Auguste has secretly joined the MNC; not only that, he has been elected – it still seems incredible to me – to an important party post.

Shortly after the Matongé rally Auguste came to the

145

apartment. It was late and Inès, who had been out with Smail on party business, had gone to bed. While she got dressed I had to act the host, not something I am good at, the awkwardness made worse by the atmosphere between us. The apartment reeked of our estrangement. I put on a jolly front but I was sure Auguste could sense what was going on. I could see he was bursting with excitement but the exaggerated sense of propriety he reserves for Europeans – at least for the first few minutes he comes into their presence – meant we first had to proceed through the rituals of politeness: he asked elaborately after the progress of my novel, after my health, my mother's health . . . Auguste always gets proportions wrong.

'So?' Inès asked on entering the living room.

She knew something, or wanted something confirmed; the two were in a quiver of conspiracy.

Auguste delivered his news with great solemnity: at a meeting that night he had been elected deputy chairman of the party's newly-created youth wing, the Jeunesse MNC. Inès let out a whoop of delight. She threw up her hands and rushed to embrace him. I could see the pride growing in him. As an *évolué*, as possessor of the *carte d'immatriculation*, as a member of the Association of the African Middle Classes, he was already a man of some account. Now that he was an officer of the colony's largest political party – soon in all probability to be the country's governing party – he had double reason for his *gravitas*. But he did not stay frozen in his seriousness for long. A few bottles of beer and Inès's mischief thawed him out. He quickly relaxed into a more comfortable self and relived for us, in large and scatological detail, his success at the meeting. Inès was overjoyed about this first advance in what she predicted would be one of Africa's great political careers. Her own sense of proportion is much like Auguste's. She sat with feet drawn up, face flushed from the heat and drink, eyes wide while he boasted of the vanquishing of his rivals and the power of his oratory. The night went on a long time. When eventually he took his leave he attempted his new role of political leader; he embraced us with a look that implied we three had accomplished some momentous feat that bound us in the bundle of history and heroism and eternal comradeship. I was willing to bet he was thinking of Horatio at the bridge, or something similar. The Catholic priests who educated him had given Auguste a weakness for melodrama and tales of classical valour. In Belfast the Christian Brothers had tried to do the same for me. Inès was swept up in an historic moment, but all I could see were empty beer bottles – Primus, Auguste's favourite – strewn over the table and floor. I had not seen Inès as happy for a long time. That someone else – a man whom I thought little more than an amiable buffoon – was the source of her joy did not sit well with me. And the minute Auguste was gone, her happiness drained away. The coldness returned and she went to bed without saying a single word.

She told me the next morning Stipe must not find out. But I am beginning to think he already knows. How could they hope to keep something like this secret from Stipe? He finds everything out. It is his job.

'What do you think Lumumba's motivation is?' Stipe says as though thinking aloud. 'I mean his real motivation?'

He is talking to Auguste through me.

'He's a man with a mission,' I reply, ready to go along with it for at least part of the way. What else can I do?

'Is he? I mean, sure, Patrice cultivates the image of a man with a mission. But what really, deep down, makes him tick?'

'Who knows what really makes people tick?'

'You're right there,' he says after a pause, 'you're absolutely right.'

The road runs through the heart of the jungle, through

147

the vines and the wild orchids. The ebony and mahogany and rubber trees are laced with creepers and furred with mosses. Eerie animal noises come from nowhere, barking, howling, screeching. There is very little traffic. Every hour or so a jeep or a truck might pass over-laden with sacks of rice and baskets of manioc and beans, on top of which men and women and children perch in watchful silence.

'Who knows what makes people tick?' Stipe muses aloud.

He goes quiet before continuing.

'When I was at college there was a girl. Rita. She had the most beautiful chestnut hair, she had big dark eyes and a figure straight out of a magazine. She smelled – I'm not kidding you – she smelled of apples. It wasn't synthetic, it wasn't perfume or soap. It was her natural smell. Everybody asked Rita for a date, but no go. Then one day we're in a literature class together, Rita and I, and she starts talking to me and one thing leads to another and before you know it we're going out together. All my friends are green because she's chosen me. I should have been a very happy kid.'

'But you weren't?'

Stipe has all my attention. He rarely gives away any personal details. The few he lets fall I hoard like gold sovereigns.

'I wasn't happy because I couldn't stop wondering why she had chosen me. It was a puzzle because I am not a handsome man.'

I laugh, but I cannot make even the weakest effort to contradict him.

'It's okay,' he says lightly, forgiving me. 'I've come to terms with it. It's not a problem.'

'Was it a problem for Rita?'

'Not at all. In fact, her not finding it a problem *was* the problem,' he continues in the same airy tone. 'I kept asking myself, what is she doing with me? It got to me. After a while it became an obsession. I couldn't sleep, I couldn't eat, I started flunking my exams. I just couldn't handle it. So one day, blunt, straight out, I went to her and I said, "I don't love you any more".'

He falls silent.

'And?'

He sighs, more serious now.

'Rita was devastated, as you'd expect. I can still see her face.'

'So why did you end it?'

'Why did I end it? At the time, I put it down to all sorts of vague but implacable things. It was fate, it was God, it was the need to suffer for redemption. Whatever it was, it was big. It had to be big, I knew that.'

He snorts before continuing, a prelude to frank confession.

'Indoors with Rita, no problem. I was a *lover*. If you could have seen me . . .' His voice trails off, momentarily diverted by memory. 'Outside was different. Outside with friends, going to the movies, to games, I was embarrassed to be with her.'

'Why?'

'You see, Rita . . . This is not easy. I'm a short man, as you can see, and Rita was two-and-one-half inches taller than me. I would see my friends with their girls. They looked great and we didn't. I ask you: can a man two-and-one-half inches shorter than his girl play the part of the romantic lover, which is how I saw myself then? It's not possible.'

He laughs at himself.

'My crisis wasn't to do with anything big,' he says with finality. 'It came down to this: I wanted to feel Rita's tits in my stomach, not in my throat.'

I look at him. I don't believe him.

'You're being too hard on yourself,' I say.

149

'No,' he answers. 'Our instinct is always to dress motivation up. I prefer to strip it bare. Take Lumumba. Patrice is
highly intelligent, no question. He's gifted, original. But he
has a flaw and that flaw is going to be his undoing.'

'What's the flaw?'

'He cannot put the past behind him. In the Belgian
Congo the highest Patrice could hope to be was a clerk. Not
unnaturally he resents this. He's a very talented man. So he
steals from his employers and they, not unnaturally, throw
him in jail. Now he's really angry. Now it's not just about
frustration, it's about revenge, revenge on the white man.
Then along come Smail and his friends with their Marxist
theories and their scientific socialism. It's all bullshit, but
Patrice laps it up because it gives him justification for turning
one individual's resentment into a political crusade.'

In the back Auguste is listening to every word.

'If you accept,' Stipe concludes, 'that Patrice's motivation
is at bottom petty and personal, then you know that all of his
followers have no real cause.'

We are approaching Port Francqui. On the other side of
the river lies the long road south-east to Luluabourg, Bakwanga and Katanga.

I pinch the sticky shirt and tug it from my breast. The air has
no energy, neither do I. I look at the luxuriant water-hyacinth,
the ravenous oxygen-eater, the killer of the river. I look at the
pretty purple flowers.

I think of the road ahead, the endless track that stretches
on and on through the wilderness. Five minutes out of a
town, any town, and there is nothing, only the hot, sweet,
decaying smell of the forest. I used to enjoy long drives. I
could inhabit whatever fiction I was writing at the time. I
could talk to my characters, live in their story. But this

journey is already proving disagreeable. It is not just the heat and discomfort, not just the tension in the car. So far I have managed to avoid thinking about Inès, but during the monotonous hours my thoughts will inevitably turn to her, to our situation. It is worse now than it has ever been. She is out all the time, for the paper, for the MNC; she has thrown herself into this thing completely. I cannot remember the last time we had a meal together. She often does not come home at night and has long since stopped phoning to warn me. I exist for her only as a minor irritation. I wake up every morning feeling empty; I put off going to bed until I think I will collapse from exhaustion. But I never do. I lie in the wrinkled, clammy sheets brooding about her. The drive will be like that. I will invent scenes with her, I will relive arguments, remember the wounds I have received, pick them, infect them. They will darken my imagination, make me short-tempered with Stipe and Auguste . . . Italians often use a *faux ami* when they want to say affairs or relationship. Inès calls it a *story* and it's one of those mistranslations I never corrected because I liked the sound of it. It seems especially appropriate here, now. We can't go on like this. Our narrative has lost its thread. We must recover it and see it to its conclusion. We must provoke the climax to our story.

'This is the Sankuru River, James,' Auguste says.

We are leaning on the rear of the car as the boatman poles the flat raft across the brown water.

'It's a big river,' I say.

'It is not as big as the Congo River, or the Volta River in Ghana. Do you know Ghana, James?'

He pushes the bridge of his glasses up with his forefinger.

'No, I've never been to Ghana,' I say.

'Ghana is a wonderful country.'

'How the hell would you know?'

It is Stipe. He has been listening from the car. He jumps

151

out. The *barque* shudders under his angry stomp. The boat-man does not look up but gets on with his labour.

'What the hell do you know about Ghana?' Stipe demands. 'You don't know anything about it.'

'Mark, take it easy,' I say, surprised by his vehemence.

'He doesn't know anything about it!'

I expect Auguste to go quiet. He always does in the face of Stipe's displeasure. I wait for his smile, but this time it does not come.

'In Ghana,' he continues slowly, 'Dr Nkrumah is building a hydro-electric dam on the Volta River. The dam will trans-form all Ghana. It will bring electricity to every village. It will give power to factories and to smelters and make many new industries possible. This is Kwame Nkrumah's vision. It is a great vision, a true pan-African vision.'

'You know who's building the fucking Volta Dam?' Stipe shouts at him. 'Do you? I'll tell you. The Kaiser Steel Corpo-ration of America.'

'Patrice wants to be friends with the Americans,' Auguste says. 'He knows we need the Americans.'

'Patrice can't be friends with us and be friends with the Soviets at the same time. If he tries he'll get burned.'

Auguste does not respond.

Stipe, calmer, as though regretting his display of temper, says, 'Look, Auguste, I know a lot of this stuff doesn't make sense to you right now, but you have to trust me. I've never let you down yet, have I?'

'Correct, Mark.'

'Correct,' Stipe says, patting him on the shoulder.

We have almost reached the far bank.

'Tell me what you want, Auguste,' Stipe continues in a conciliatory voice.

'What I want?' Auguste replies uncertainly.

'What you want – yes.'

'I want for my country to be—'

Suddenly Stipe is hard again.

'No. I'm talking about you, Auguste. You, the individual you! I'm talking about what you want for you!'

Auguste looks at him levelly, with challenge in his eyes; then some old inclination reaffirms itself and he lowers his head.

Stipe prompts him. 'You want a car, like this one here. Right?'

'Correct, Mark.'

'And you want a nice house. Correct? And you want nice clothes and a sexy, beautiful young wife and a good education for your kids. Am I correct?'

'You are correct, Mark.'

'Then what the hell are you doing with these?'

Stipe snatches Auguste's glasses and throws them in the water.

'Mark . . .!' I protest.

'They're not real,' Stipe shouts back at me. 'He has twenty-twenty vision, for Christ's sake. It's clear glass. He only wears them because he thinks they make him look like Patrice.'

Auguste is browbeaten. He has nothing to say.

'You want goodies?' Stipe continues, his words coming fast and hard. 'You want lots of goodies? Of course you do. Just like everybody else. Just like Gillespie, just like me. And you can have them, Auguste. I can make sure you have them. But mess with those other people and you're not going to get your car or your house or any of it. Do you understand me?'

We have reached the far bank of the Sankuru. Stipe goes to pay the boatman. He gets into the car and, revving up the engine, drives from the *barque* on to the crude wooden jetty.

Auguste and I walk slowly after him. We cross a streaming colony of enormous black ants, crunching them underfoot.

153

'Patrice's vision is a great vision,' Auguste repeats as we near the car, brushing ants from his trouser legs. 'The Americans will support this vision. We need American help to build our country. Like Kaiser Steel in Ghana.'

'American corporations never give anything for free,' I interject, sounding weirdly like Inès; I put it down to the immutable habits of scepticism.

'If the Americans ask too high a price,' Auguste states simply, 'we will go to the Russians.'

'That's a dangerous game,' I say.

'It is the game we are forced to play, James.'

That night at the guesthouse Stipe joins me on the patio to drink gin and listen to the BBC World Service on the short-wave radio. One hundred thousand people have demonstrated in Trafalgar Square in favour of nuclear disarmament. This report is followed by an item on Nyasaland and Sir Roy Welensky, and another on the aftermath of the shootings at Sharpeville. Then comes the Congo's elections. In Léopoldville last night there were three more political murders; in Stanleyville a Belgian engineer accidentally shot and killed a black woman coming out of a shop.

'That story about Rita,' I ask, 'was it true?'

'Yes.'

'What happened to her, do you know?'

'I should do,' he says, slurring the words slightly, 'I married her.'

I look at him, surprised.

'Where is she?' I ask.

'At home. We have a house in Philadelphia. Three kids, two dogs and a cat – at the last count.'

He takes a photograph from his wallet. The picture is pure Americana: husband, wife and children dressed in

154

bright, clean, casual clothes gathered with the family pets around the family car in front of the family home. Smiles and braces and shy grins and crew cuts. Rita is noticeably taller than her husband. Her look in the photograph is not an obviously happy one.

'I'm glad it worked out for you,' I say, returning the picture.

'It didn't work out,' he says. 'Nothing worked out.'

'How can you say that? You're married, you have kids, a family.'

Stipe sighs deeply. 'I begged her, on my knees I begged her to come back to me. She held out a long time. But I wouldn't let go. I knew I had to have this girl, that she was the only one for me. And in the end I wore her down. She gave in. But it wasn't the same. She never forgave me for what I'd done. Oh, she didn't say anything – ever – Rita is not a talker, not about these things anyway. But she never trusted me again. My feelings were the same, they never changed. She's still the only one for me. In my life I've only ever slept with two women – the other one was before Rita. Two women. Can you believe that? It causes my colleagues a great deal of mirth. But I'm just not interested. Maybe I should be interested, but I'm not.'

'I don't see why it should be a reason for mirth,' I say.

He shrugs wearily. 'Rita's feelings changed.'

'Is there another man?'

'No. She says no and I believe her because one thing about Rita, she is an honest person. It's almost like she doesn't know how to tell a lie. Sometimes I think it would be better if there was someone else. At least that way there might be a chance she'd get bored with him and rediscover me, as it were. But it's way worse than that. She just doesn't love me any more and there's nothing as painful in life as love going in one direction only.'

155

We sit in silence, refilling our glasses and looking out at the night.

'I was an asshole with Auguste,' he says after a while.

'Why are you being so hard on him?'

'If he gets mixed up with the wrong people he's going to get hurt. And I don't want that to happen. I care about him.'

He gives me a look that implies I doubt his sincerity.

'I meet a hundred people every day, James, but the fact is I generally don't get along with very many of them,' he says quietly. 'Never have. And people are the same with me – they look at me and they're put on guard. They see beef, aggression. People don't go for that. So when I meet someone and you get along – well, it means a lot to me.'

Suddenly I see Stipe in true light. It makes sense. He has always given the impression of being self-sufficient, utterly and enviably so. Partly – he is right – the impression comes from his build and carriage – the beef he referred to, solid beef, packed, dense, muscular, and the aggression. People look at a man like that and never think him other than anchored. Self-doubt is for the rest of us. But now it makes sense. The endless invitations to drink at the Colibri, the shameless courting of Anna, the trips to the Matongé rally, to Mungul's house, to see Houthhoofd and a hundred other places and people – Stipe is a needy man. He wants to be liked. I cannot feel angry with him in spite of his treatment of Auguste today.

Stipe admits of no higher motives, he is cynical and sometimes bullying, but he is a loyal and true friend, and he is hurt.

19

STIPE'S CHEVROLET RESTS at the side of the road. He has gone to the improvised checkpoint to talk to the soldiers. The jungle is far behind us and we have almost completed our journey across the open country of the Kasai. Ahead are the brown hills of the Katangan copper belt. The air will be cooler on the plateau where the sky is vast and still and clear.

In an open-sided thatched hut beside a water pump children conjugate *donner* in African half-song before their old teacher. They steal glances in my direction and in Stipe's. The two white men who shouldn't be here. The villagers ignore us, but the teacher has, I think, been trying to catch Auguste's eye. He seems shy, or perhaps nervous. He wears a short-sleeved white shirt and a dark blue tie. I am sure he wants to talk to us. To warn us? The people here, even the children, act as if there is something in store: there are rumours in their looks.

I join Stipe at the roadblock. A pregnant woman squats by a termite mound, prising away lumps of woody earth which she proceeds to gnaw. The soldiers are sullen. They have no white officers with whom Stipe might parley. He tries sweetness and flattery, he tries bribery, he tries the barrack-room camaraderie of a man who understands the business of soldiers, who apprehends their orders and the rules – formal and informal – by which they must do their duty. He tries anger. This, especially, does not work. I do not like the look of them, I cannot read them. They flick their eyes from one to another. I hate this: the uncertainty, the anxiety, the powerlessness – and the fact and taint of this confrontation. I may not be a believer, but the starkness of black and white makes me acutely uncomfortable. I want to say, 'I am not a racialist, I am not Belgian,' but I can hear in my head the laughter; and the question: 'What are you then?' – to which I have no answer.

Stipe turns away from the morose men.

'Well?' I ask.

'They won't let us through,' he says. 'No way.'

'What's the problem?'

'There's rioting ahead. The Baluba and the Lulua are at it again.'

Since crossing into the Kasai we have passed a string of burned-out villages, looted shops and houses. Parts of the countryside are deserted, ghostly. There are refugees on the road.

'We're probably only four or five hours from Houthhoofd's place,' Stipe says, 'but the soldiers say they can't let us through – for our own safety.'

I watch the pregnant woman chewing termite earth. Stipe fidgets with the collar of his soiled shirt. My own sweat-hardened collar rasps at the back of my sunburnt neck.

Stipe pays a woman to give us some beer and manioc, flavoured – a small blessing – with a little onion, tomato and hot pepper. We sit under the shade of a baobab and eat hungrily. The teacher has dismissed his students. Auguste has disappeared. We will just have to wait until the soldiers change their mind.

Stipe asks how I am getting on with Inès these days. I tell him. I tell him that her commitment to Lumumba and the MNC doesn't seem to leave any space for the two of us to rebuild our life together.

'*Commitment?*' he says, shaking his head. 'What kind of word is that?'

'Inès's father was a communist partisan. She grew up with commitment.'

158

'There you go,' he says. 'There's the answer.'

'What was the question?'

'Why she is the way she is. Obviously it's a father thing.'

I pick at the food. I've had the same thought many times, then dismissed it as unworthy – of me, of her.

'She's a young woman who wants heroes,' Stipe continues. 'Her father was a hero, you were probably a hero to her once . . .'

The pain of hearing this. Stipe *penetrates*, he has all the gifts necessary for his special line of work. I think of the way Inès used to talk to me, look at me, write to me when we were first in love. Stipe knows what he's saying, he knows what these words are doing. He is taking out his own hurt on me.

'Lumumba's just the latest in a long line of heroes,' he goes on. 'Poor bastard. Having to bear the load of her dreams, her and a million like her. He'll either collapse under the weight or it'll drive him to a martyr's death.'

I have known for some time that Stipe was annoyed with Inès because of Auguste, but he has never before dared voice his feelings in front of me. Now they come tumbling out. But perhaps it's what I need. Perhaps he is being cruel to be kind. I have wallowed in my misery long enough. It's time my idealization of her stopped.

'Come on, Gillespie, don't try to tell me there haven't been times when all those extravagant displays of idealism and solidarity didn't embarrass you just a little. That time outside Lumumba's house when he was arrested, for example? I saw the way you were looking at her.'

'How was that?'

'You were squirming. She was crying her eyes out with Auguste and you were squirming.'

It's true, I know it is true: Inès weeps well. Perhaps I should be defending her, but I can't.

159

The more Stipe talks, the more embarrassments come to mind.

'She was demonstrating to everyone her sensitivity, demonstrating especially to you, so that you could see how deeply moved she was while you, you cold bastard, haven't the heart to feel a thing . . .'

There have been many.

'. . . which is all harmless enough, except that you and I know there's something . . .' – he pauses to select the right words – 'something not entirely authentic about such displays . . .'

One in particular.

'Admit it, Gillespie. She embarrasses you when she's doing her revolutionary grandstanding bit.'

One in particular . . .

After we'd been together a couple of months she'd had to return to Rome to talk to the paper about her contract. We decided that instead of her coming straight back to London we would take a holiday in Ireland and that she would fly to meet me in Dublin. Her plane was late. There'd been fog at Rome and they'd waited on the runway for three hours.

'The pilot was coward,' she complained as she marched into the arrivals hall.

'*A* coward,' I said in a gentle reminder.

I was always in two minds about whether to correct her mistakes – as she insisted I do – or savour them.

'Yes, coward,' she said as though I hadn't understood the first time. 'He could have taken off after just one hour.'

She was so annoyed by the pilot's timidity she forgot to kiss me.

We drove to the west, pursued by rain.

'We are always unlucky with the weather,' she said.

'Ireland's unlucky with the weather.'

It was late April and Mayo was still in the grey wrap of winter. There was sleet and hail, both were fierce, driving the dogs and the sheep to shelter. At Westport the river boiled over the stone bridge and I had trouble getting the car across. *Vai, vai,* she said, kissing me. We found a cottage to rent five miles from the town. The bed-linen was damp. I built a fire and kept it in all night.

Next day out walking we took refuge from a downpour in a warm bar. We got talking to the farmers and labourers and, several rounds into the afternoon, she brought the conversation round to the IRA. In front of outsiders the reaction of country people is rarely marked, but the change in atmosphere was unmistakable. I felt the stiffening of the people around us, their withdrawal. Inès blundered on, misreading silence for licence, the slant of her talk more and more tendentious. She stopped only when I caught her eye.

Back in the cottage I said icily, 'Couldn't you see how embarrassing that was for them?'

'Perhaps it was just embarrassing for you.'

'Yes, it was.'

'Well, it isn't embarrassing for Italians to talk about the partisans,' she snapped back.

'The IRA are not the partisans.'

The outsider with strong but uninformed opinions about Ireland is nothing new, but to hear someone so close to me speak this way was more than I could bear. For the first time I shouted at her.

'They are not partisans. They are foolish seventeen-year-old boys who get shot in some pointless, bungled raid and die alone in a cow-byre on a freezing winter night with their guts hanging out. They're middle-aged bachelors who've lived all their lives with their mothers on some God-forsaken smallholding and then blow themselves and everyone around them to bits with their home-made bombs. They're not fighting Germans, Inès, they're shooting ordinary policemen who have homes and wives and children.'

'The German soldiers in Italy had wives and children as well.'

Her arguments were glib and sentimental. When we returned to London I found myself wondering for the first time if I had made a mistake. And Inès? What did she think of me then? To my surprise she was as soft and loving as she had been before.

'Why?' I asked her. 'What do you see in me?'

Sitting under the baobab tree with Stipe I try hard to remember what she said in answer to my question. Nothing comes to mind. I don't know what she said. I think now she just didn't want to admit she'd made a mistake.

A shadow falls across my legs. I look up to see Auguste. With him is the teacher. He is stick-thin, with wiry grey hairs at his temples and a dry, lined face. Up close, his shirt is shabby, his dark blue tie is frayed and stained. His baggy trousers are the colour of the earth and patched at the knees. His bare feet are splayed and grow out of the dust.

'This is my brother Cleophas,' Auguste says.

'Your brother?' I say. Another brother? How many are there?

'Yes – not my real brother,' he replies as though I'd asked a stupid question.

Cleophas bows uncertainly and asks politely how we are. His French is simple, easy for me to understand, and his tone is deferential. He can barely look us in the eye.

'You must leave here at once,' he says quietly, 'to be safe. Here is not safe.'

He raises a finger and points to something approaching from the same direction we have come. The road is shimmering with mirages. The ocean of yellow elephant grass around the village is limitless and still. I shade my eyes and see an open-topped limousine in which a man stands as though in a chariot. He is dressed in what looks to be black tie and tails, over which is draped a leopard skin. As he comes closer I see he is wearing white gloves. He has a sergeant-major's swagger-stick tucked under his arm and he wears dark glasses. A huge black umbrella held aloft by a tall servant protects him from the sun. Behind the cruising limousine are perhaps thirty or forty followers, armed with spears, machetes, bows and arrows, and stone-age clubs and axes.

The villagers come out from their huts and converge in the open space around the water pump.

'What the hell is going on?' Stipe asks.

'It's an election meeting,' Cleophas explains. 'This gentleman is the MNC candidate. He has come to ask for our votes.'

'It's not how they do it in my country,' Stipe says.

'Isn't' it?' Auguste asks.

He and Stipe regard each other for a moment.

'Maybe he has a point, Mark,' I say reasonably. 'It's not as if you don't have political razzmatazz in America.'

Stipe says nothing. He looks sulky.

'This village is Baluba, but all around is Lulua,' Cleophas explains. 'There has been much fighting.'

The limousine pulls in, followed by the Baluba tribesmen. They jeer at us as they pass and make feinting lunges. One man wearing an army helmet and a loincloth runs up. A small monkey perches on his shoulder. The man jabs his spear to within an inch of Stipe's face and utters a stream of taunts and insults. Stipe doesn't flinch. Cleophas speaks sharply to the warrior who, after another feint, gives up his sport to rejoin his comrades.

'You should leave,' Cleophas says again. 'It is not safe here for you.'

'I'll go talk with the soldiers again,' Stipe says.

The candidate, standing in the limousine, starts to speak. He is a vigorous orator.

'What language is that?' I ask Cleophas after a while.

'It is Tshiluba language, the language of the Baluba people.'

'What's the candidate saying?'

'Bad things, sir.'

'What bad things?'

'He is telling the people that if they vote for him, they will all live in big houses, that they will have the houses of the whites and also the wives of the whites.'

A raucous cheer goes up from the villagers.

'He is telling the people now that if they vote for him their crops will be good . . .'

Another cheer.

'. . . that they will find Belgian money growing in the fields instead of manioc . . .'

'He's really saying that?'

'He is telling the people that when independence has come their dead relatives will rise from their graves and come back to them, their bodies perfect as they were when young.'

'You don't believe what the candidate is promising, do you?'

'What he is promising is impossible, sir.'

'So you won't vote for him?'

Cleophas glances at Auguste.

'Yes, sir. I will vote for Mr Lumumba and the MNC,' he says, almost inaudibly.

'Why on earth would you do that?' I ask, taken aback. 'This man's obviously a charlatan. Why would you vote for him and his party?'

164

I sense Cleophas wants to answer but is afraid of offending me.

'I would like to know,' I say, modifying my tone, making it less strident, 'but only if you want to tell me.'

Cleophas gathers his nerve.

'I will vote for the MNC because Mr Lumumba is the only leader who tells us we do not have to be poor for ever, that if we unite as one nation we can use the riches of the Congo for the people of the Congo.'

From the checkpoint comes a shout. I look over to see two soldiers angrily confronting Stipe. He raises his hands to show he intends no aggression. A soldier pushes him roughly. I start forward.

'No, James,' Auguste says instantly. 'The soldiers are bad men.'

The soldiers shout at Stipe, waving their arms hysterically. He looks over and signals for me to stay put.

'Please get in the car, sir,' Cleophas says, 'and be ready to drive. I will explain to the soldiers.'

Before I can say anything he has set off to the checkpoint. Auguste and I watch as he walks submissively towards the soldiers, his hands open, his arms by his sides. He goes up to the surrounded Stipe and starts to intercede for him.

Auguste and I get into the car. I start the engine. Behind us, the crowd is getting heated, responding to the candidate's oratory.

A soldier raises his rifle butt as though about to strike Cleophas. He lowers his head but does not attempt to defend himself. The soldiers gather round and shout at him. They push him forward and back. He endures everything, he says nothing. Stipe remains still. Cleophas starts to plead again for him, whispered intercessions. From time to time the soldiers threaten him into silence, only for him to begin again.

The candidate's speech continues to cheers and chanting.

Suddenly, the tribesmen rush to surround the car. A warrior with a spear jabs at the headlights as though taunting a chained beast.

'Go, James,' Auguste says. 'We must go.'

I edge slowly forward towards the checkpoint. The warriors bang the bonnet and roof and slap the windscreen with their hands. I press on the accelerator and slowly increase our speed. When they flock in front of us I put my foot down sharply. The warriors spring out of the way.

I accelerate to the roadblock. They give chase and throw a few stones, then jeer and laugh at us.

Cleophas hurries over.

'The soldiers are good men,' he says. 'They are Bamongo people, far from their villages and they are very frightened.'

'Will they let us go now?' I say.

Cleophas looks back at the soldiers. One of them nods tersely.

Auguste calls Stipe to the car, reaching over to open the back door. Behind, the tribesmen seem to be preparing to rush us again.

'What about you?' I ask Cleophas. 'Will you be all right?'

'I will be all right, sir,' he says. 'Thank you.'

His eyes are muddy, without definition; the irises have a kind of greyish bloom around the edges.

'Go, James,' Auguste urges me as Stipe jumps in the back.

The soldiers stand aside. I put my foot down. Auguste waves to Cleophas and we shoot through the checkpoint.

Something flies in through the open window behind me. I look back to see an arrow impaled in the arm rest of the near-side back door an inch or two above Stipe's knees.

'Roll up your window,' Stipe shouts.

More arrows hit us, not from behind, not from the village, but from both sides. Men leap from the elephant grass, hundreds of them. One appears on the road ahead of us and

launches a spear. It skims the bonnet and cracks the windscreen. He jumps out of the way as our speed gets up. There is
a rifle shot.

I turn back to see the soldiers at the roadblock fleeing
towards the village under a shower of arrows and spears.
Cleophas is nowhere in sight.

'It's a Lulua attack,' Stipe says.

I press my foot to the floor. I wish Inès had been here. I
wish she had been here to see the triumph of this her new
cause.

20

I WILL WRITE the article they want me to write. It's a good story, they did not have to work hard to convince me of that. I will write it though I know what it means for Inès and me. I will write it *because* I know.

Stipe and Houthhoofd do not get down to business straight away. First there are long cool drinks on the veranda during which there is an account of our escape from the village. Houthhoofd reacts with a shrug. What can you expect? There will be worse to come unless strong measures are taken. But the government in Brussels has a weak stomach; it's up to the *colons* themselves to bring order out of the looming havoc.

Afterwards, Houthhoofd takes us on a brief tour of the estate. I don't know that I've seen anywhere in the world as beautiful. It is early evening and the sky is red and gold. The views are long and calming. I can imagine an early morning climb to one of the huge boulders on the hills overlooking the valleys where the thorn trees and baobabs rise out of the yellow grass of the savannah. There I might spend the whole day alone, my thoughts going nowhere, the scenery for balm. Noises in this place come softly, unwilling to disturb or clutter. In such a setting I might be free of Inès.

Houthhoofd shows me copper clearings where the mineral is so dense in the ground trees cannot grow, and he tells me that Africa is a poor continent with a handful of extravagantly rich areas. Katanga, the size of Britain, is one of the richest. *The* richest. The mines of the Union Minière and Forminière provide the world with eight per cent of its copper, sixty per cent of its uranium, seventy-three per cent of its cobalt, eighty per cent of its industrial diamonds. Katanga has gold, silver, tin, zinc, manganese, columbium, cadmium, tungsten, tantalum; its supplies will never be exhausted.

At dinner Houthhoofd asks rhetorically, 'Can we trust these riches to a man like Patrice Lumumba?'

Stipe is unusually silent; he lets the Belgians make the running – is he feeling guilty about turning on his old friend? – in tandem with the man I have been brought to meet: Victor Nendaka. Nendaka is one of Lumumba's closest aides, vice-chairman of the party. He made a name for himself when he forced the Belgians to release Lumumba by telling them he would not bring the MNC delegation to Brussels for the Round Table Conference without his leader. I know him. I met him in Auguste's house in the cité, the night I first saw Lumumba. He struck me then as a man of limitless insincerity. He is sleek and self-satisfied and has a specious charm. I have always thought he would make a good pimp. He owns a bar, a travel agency and an insurance company.

I am only half listening. I have already made my decision. I am in any case distracted by another of the guests. Madeleine is here. She is having an affair with Houthhoofd, it is obvious from the extent of their discretion, from the care with which they avoid each other's eyes.

She sits opposite me. Something strange is going on in my head. It is to do with sex. With Inès I enjoyed a sexual life I had not thought possible. Inès's physical preferences are direct. She is not prudish, but I cannot really say she is adventurous. Not like Margaret, who loved to be surprised, demanded it. With Inès, there was very little foreplay – she was easily aroused – and she liked it best with me on top and she wanted that I get there quickly. The variations didn't hold much for her. To begin with, I did not think her simple tastes could sustain my interest. But they did. I found sex with her profoundly, deeply satisfying – moving. I never knew I could feel so good afterwards. I remember looking forward every night to going to bed. Waiting for her to finish what she was doing, telling her to hurry up, sometimes saying all right that's enough and taking her by the wrist. I suppose one reason I loved it so much was because I seemed to be pleasing her so much. (A terrifying thought strikes me: am I over-estimating how much I pleased her? Am I deluding myself, typical man? Perhaps her disillusion with me is no more than the disillusion of the bored sexual partner? If I pleased her so much, would she be so distant? Perhaps, like Bovary, I took her happiness for granted; and perhaps, like Emma, she found happiness elsewhere. I fight down the thought, it makes me sick in my stomach.) I loved it with her. I needed it. I could say that it was more important emotionally than physically – and it is true my emotions were sparked by our intimacy, then soothed and calmed. I could say this and claim for myself a kind of sensitivity. But the truth is I relished her, the squeeze and the smell and the wrap and the fit of her. When I was jammed inside her and could hear her hard breath, could feel her heart pound and the quiver in her leg. Then my body was alight, all my senses. The pleasure of it, the pleasure . . .

It is not until tonight that I realize how much I have missed this part of my life. Since arriving in the Congo, I have almost forgotten about women. I cannot remember the last time Inès and I made love.

The sight of Madeleine arouses me. As Houthhoofd speaks I am entertaining fantasies of fucking his mistress. I let the red wine seep into my imagination, staining it, dirtying it. Her thick blonde-silver hair is tied back as usual, showing off her long, slim neck and little ears. I want to bite them and whisper things to her.

'He's dangerous,' Houthhoofd is saying. 'He's the most dangerous man on the African continent today.'

I suppose I should say something to make it look as if I am interested. I keep a lazy, insolent eye on Madeleine as I remind Stipe that he has many times sung Lumumba's praises. An outstanding man, was his earlier verdict.

Stipe shrugs. 'I tried to keep Patrice on the straight and narrow, so did Bernard, so did everyone else, but Patrice is headstrong.'

'He's unstable,' Houthhoofd interjects. 'I think he may be mentally ill.'

'He uses dope,' Stipe tells me.

I look sceptical.

'It's true, James,' Stipe continues matter-of-factly, without any special emphasis, sure of his case. 'I've seen him in his office smoking weed with his cronies and a couple of pretty secretaries hanging around, who, incidentally, he's balling. In a country of swordsmen, our boy is a veritable D'Artagnan.'

'I have nothing against a black government if it's a government led by responsible men,' Houthhoofd says.

'Do you have a particular responsible man in mind?' I ask without interest.

I am thinking about kissing Madeleine. She has stayed out of the conversation, she has barely looked in my direction, but I know she is aware of my gaze. I lean back in my chair, drain my glass and stretch my legs out straight under the table, crossing my ankles. A houseboy refills my glass.

'In Leo there is Kasavubu,' Houthhoofd continues. 'He used to be a firebrand, very anti-Belgian, and he's an intro-verted and solitary man, but he's become more stable recently. In Katanga there is Tshombe. He's not quite as stable – in fact he's a playboy and a gambler – but he knows

171

enough to listen to good advice from business people.'

In the boldness of my reverie I summon up the image of Madeleine as she stood before me at the Regina's poolside, dressed in her black swimsuit. I remember the heavy breasts and the little ridge of weight on her belly. I remember her nervousness when she tried to pick me up. Why didn't I go along with it? We might even have gone up to her room then and there. I could have pushed her against the wall and pulled down her top and licked her nipples. I could have pushed her knees apart and pressed my cock against her. I could have turned her round and slapped her palms against the wall and pulled her back and tugged the swimsuit over her arse. Why didn't I do it? What did I deny myself for? For Inès? For the nothing she gives me, for the pain she inflicts? Fuck you, Inès. I'm going to fuck Madeleine, I am going to fuck her. As soon as I get the chance.

'Lumumba is taking money from the Soviets.'

The conversation has been rolling on. I haven't really heard any of it. I look over vaguely at the present speaker. It is Nendaka.

He says again, 'Lumumba is taking money from the Soviets. It's intolerable.'

I look at the fat bar-owner. I can't think of anything to say. I'm not interested. I'm interested only in Madeleine. I am quite drunk. To Nendaka and Houthhoofd and Stipe my lack of reaction seems to cause some consternation. They exchange glances. I'm giving the impression of a man not easily impressed.

'Is that so surprising?' I say at last.

I look across at Madeleine. Stipe starts to say something about how Lumumba has flirted with the Soviets, like he's flirted with everyone else. But taking Red gold at this point is a big statement about the direction he's taking the MNC and about his plans for the Congo post-independence.

I put my foot on the bar of Madeleine's chair. I move my leg and press against her calf. She looks suddenly up. I hold her gaze.

'We have copies of the financial records – lodgements, transfers, withdrawals,' Houthhoofd is saying.

I press. Madeleine raises her glass and takes a shallow sip. Slowly she licks her lower lip, puts the glass down, gives me a look, then turns to the others. Nendaka is announcing that he is going to lead a break-away faction of the MNC. He says he will split the party in two.

I nod my understanding, thinking of Madeleine with her palms against the wall, her swimsuit snagged around her ankles.

Houthhoofd is summing up. The MNC will soon be split. Business won't accept the party's programme. The officers of the Force Publique won't accept it. The black soldiers won't accept it. Katanga won't accept it. Patrice Lumumba, Houthhoofd concludes with satisfaction, is finished.

Over the brandies Houthhoofd stares at me, wordless and cold. I don't care. I feel like the young lion eyeing the old. Madeleine sits as far away from me as possible and fusses about her lover. Stipe tries to cover up with small talk. He's not good at it.

Houthhoofd suddenly asks if I make my living from journalism. There's a barb in his tone.

'And books,' I say.

'Books?'

'I'm finishing my fourth novel at the moment.'

He stares at me with contempt, and even I can hear how the word *novel*, spoken in his presence, sounds weak. If I'd said I liked to build model boats or collect postage stamps he would not have looked at me with any less disdain.

For the first time that night I feel disadvantaged, suddenly put down, even a little panicked, and all because of what I do.

173

Even Stipe, who loves books, thinks, at bottom, that writers are of no account. I stop fantasising about Madeleine; the semi-erection I've had since dinner shrinks away.

We set off at noon the following day, after a formal interview with Nendaka. As Auguste loads our bags into the Chevrolet, Madeleine lets drop that she will be in Leo next week.

The road back to the Kasai is a tunnel into cruelty and grief. The destruction is terrifying. Villages and hamlets are burned-out, see-through. Refugees choke the roads.

The thatched classroom has been burned to the ground. A pink piglet with a crooked hind leg snuffles about in the dirt but otherwise nothing moves. There are dark, fly-flecked stains on the ground, probably of blood. We come to a stand of acacia trees, where we find the first bodies. They hang, naked and mutilated, from the drooping branches among the abandoned weaverbirds' nests. The skin is taut and ballooned, as though pumped up with air. I walk up the desolate road with Stipe. He is carrying his gun.

'What the fuck were you thinking of last night with Madeleine?' he says. 'I thought any minute you were going to take out your thing and start waving it around.'

I do not say anything. I am embarrassed. The thought of Inès makes my heart heavy. I wish I were back in Léopoldville, I wish we were out of this awful, nameless, limose place.

Glancing about I see something lying at the edge of the track which looks repellently familiar. It is covered with a heaving mantle of buzzing flies. It is a limb, a leg, severed high up; still attached is part of the pelvic bone. A little further on is a hand, then another one. There is something lying in the grass. A length of twine. I am about to pick it up when a small cloud of flies rises up suddenly and I see it is attached to a man's genitalia. Where is the owner? What agonies did he go through?

Auguste calls to us. We walk back to the trees. He has found Cleophas. The teacher's wide, flat feet are swollen. His killers have left him his shirt and tie, but his old patched trousers are gone. And now I know who the owner is. What can we do except stare?

21

S HE HATES ME now. She loathes me. It's all right. I am proud
of what I have done and I bask in her fury. I have struck
home. At last I have hurt her.

I shout my justification, I scream it at the top of my lungs in
an ecstasy of rage. Yes, Stipe gave me the story, but every word is
true. Nendaka told me himself. The first article made the
Belgians uncomfortable, this one makes Lumumba uncomfortable. So what? That's the problem with the truth, Inès, it
falls where it will. Not that you would know anything about the
truth, how could you when all you do is churn out eulogies for
the great leader and nauseating adulation for his party and its
programme? All I was doing was reporting the facts.

Non gettare il sasso e nascondere la mano, she shouts back.
Don't throw the stone and hide your hand.

Is what you do journalism? Is it honest journalism? Not
even Grant is so obviously partisan. I hate what you do, Inès, I
hate your pointless, belched slogans. It's a degradation of
your profession. Self-interrogation is unknown to you. Where
is your independence of position? Where is your critical
distance? I should have said this a long time ago. Why I didn't
I'll never know.

And she attacks along the usual lines – that what's important is being on the side of the oppressed, of sticking with that
side even if it makes mistakes, of not being diverted, of keeping
a clear sight of what the real issues are and who the enemy is.

Grow up, Inès. Grow up and join the real world, where
things aren't always black and white. Join the world in which
irony exists, read Empson and there you will see it is possible

to believe that people are at once guilty and not guilty; you will see that principles shift and people are sceptical and weak.

Oh weak? Tell me about weak! How weak I am to deny who I am, to deny my nationality, to deny my history, my place, to deny my own name. *Seamus!* She screams at me. *Seamus!* Your name is not James. You are Seamus. Why do you talk with an English accent? Where did that come from? What are you trying to prove with that?

That none of it matters! That it's old and tribal and petty.

You're ashamed. You're ashamed when you should be proud! If you weren't ashamed it would be in your books. How can you be from Ireland and not take a side? You look, and look away.

Because it's old and tribal and petty, and because I'm a writer and I see all sides. I work in words, I am a worker in words and these words cannot be made to work for others, they are not the slaves of party or position. Maybe you look down on it, maybe you and your bitter comrades think it's precious, but the writer's words are their own justification. They have to be if they are to be true, if they are to count for something.

And you say that Dante wrote that the hottest places in hell are reserved for those who in times of great moral crisis maintain their neutrality.

Where is this great moral crisis? I see ambition, I see corruption, I see squalor, I see intrigue and vanity and self-promotion. Where is the moral crisis?

And you say, the words chilly with contempt, that there are times when it is necessary to be more than just a writer.

She's gone. She's taken her things. I don't know where she is living. It's fine. I am not sad. Actually, I feel a glorious sense of liberation. I lived in the saturation of her disdain for too, too long. I was tired of her winter words. I don't miss her. Not at all. Some days I don't even remember to think of her. She is not in the apartment, not in its fabric or walls. I cannot smell her, she has left no spoor. It's as though she's never been here.

I enjoy my routine. I no longer have to mould it around her. It is at last my own again. She was so fixed that even though she was home so little her needs always predominated. The hands of the clock turned around her coming and going. I am liberated from time. I am liberated from lying awake waiting to hear the key turn in the tumbler. I am free of all that.

I am mildly surprised that I am coping so well. De Scheut asks if I'm all right, so does Stipe. One night they take me to the Sabena Guest House and try to make me eat. I tell them truthfully that my appetite was never large and that in any case I needed to lose a little weight. I assure them that I haven't felt so well in months, years. The wine is good though. What was I thinking of, I ask rhetorically as I top up my glass. Why did I put myself through such torture? I say I am beginning to think it was no more than pride. I couldn't stand the thought of rejection, so I mounted an absurd and extravagant campaign – during which I deployed every device known to the spurned lover up to and including the tactical use of tears. Me crying! I tried everything I could think of – and more than I was proud of – to make her mine again. I believed that if I didn't win her back I would be finished. But here I am and look! – I'm obviously not finished. I have a life before me. A good life. I should have let her go when she left London and saved myself the heartache and disruption. I should have simply said, 'Go! Go, Inès. Go to the Congo and find your new heroes.' It's so clear to me now. And now she's gone and I'm fine. I'm really fine. Stipe swallows a mouthful of mussels and takes a sip of his wine. He stares at me with a funny look. De Scheut puts a hand on my arm and asks if I would like to come and stay with him and the children for a while. For a moment I am tempted – a home, a family home of which I could be part. But I'm all right. Really. I thank him for his generosity, for his concern – he's such a kind man – but no . . . no . . . I'm fine. I really am.

I work and I work. I am in a work fit. In the afternoons and evenings I talk to sources, cultivate contacts, do my interviews. I file on time. They appreciate me at the paper. They've increased my retainer. They had to. I was getting approaches. They now ask for 'think pieces' as well as straight news reports and features. Grant defers to me. In company I am the one whose eyes he searches for approval whenever he hazards a comment. I know he hates himself for his obsequiousness, but I am, for the time being, king of the correspondents' little castle, however much he resents it.

I keep the mornings for the book. It goes very well. The day Inès left I solved the problem of the novel's heartlessness. It came to me in a flash. I realized I had been trying to write something I did not believe – I realized in fact that I had been writing in an effort to please Inès (insanity – when was there ever any pleasing her?) She had been encouraging me to excavate feelings that had never been there. Phantom emotions. I had been trying to write about an anguish that had played no part in my life. My solution was the obvious one: it was to do what I do best, to revert to my usual style. I took the novel apart and put it back together, remaking it dry, mordant. I have made a virtue of its lack of feeling. The book mocks the son for thinking he can find anything in his father. There are no answers there, there never are. The book is cruel, very cruel. Sometimes it makes me laugh. I write to Alan, promising him the manuscript within a month. I start to make plans for my next book. It will be a comic novel. It will be about a serious-minded, idealistic young girl (Chinese? Russian? Czech? – possibly a junior member of a trade mission on her first foreign posting) who falls passionately for a staid, middle-aged and rather surprised man (estate agent? tax inspector?), wrongly believing him to be a fearless spy in the service of international communism. I will have fun with it, at both their expenses. At our expense.

I feel different about my writing now she's gone. I admit that my confidence was shaken. By Inès, by Houthhoofd, by Stipe – I know now Stipe has never read anything of mine, though I am sure from certain things he has said that he has had the books sent from London; I think he probably keeps meaning to get round to them. Inès saw it from the first. He was flattering me, he was doing what spies do – finding a way into someone of potential use. It hurt, I admit, because we are friends. His deception contributed to the doubts I had. I was starting to think that Inès was right, that the writer is merely an egoist who, puffed up by the respect even the mediocre published word commands and by the fact that every act and person is liable to eventual summation in print, deludes himself into thinking he is worth more than he is, so much so that he convinces himself that he is some kind of special creature, delicate and fearless at the same time, independent and yet in need of eternal protection.

But now I see my novel – whatever its merits, however it will be judged on publication – has an importance. It is the proof of what I am, of what I have title to. For the first time in a long time, and with sudden precision, I see the consequence of my profession. I understand its worth and the worth of what I do. It is undermining to be surrounded by so many people who have a role in this country and the things that are happening to it – people whose passions and interests can make the onlooker seem impotent, dilettantish. But I was allowing myself to be done down. I have my book, my words, my distance, my impartial eyes; I have the rights not just to my own story, but to theirs. The written account does endure, it outlasts all participants. Eventually it will define them. It will be the breath on which their memories live, the tongue that summons their names.

I will have the last word on Houthhoofd and his proprietorial assumptions. I will have the last word on Stipe and his intrigues. And I will have the last word on the woman I once loved. I am liberated.

Madeleine calls. Madeleine and her maw. Am I being unfair to her? My appetite, my need, is just as sharp. She's at one of Houthhoofd's houses in Leo, near the Colibri on Eugene Henry. The house is empty, she's alone. There we will consummate our hostile attraction. I shower and shave, I buy flowers and champagne. Inès had no time for the paraphernalia of seduction. I, on the other hand, have missed them.

Who am I kidding? I am in hell. I can't bear the slowing down of the day. The onset of dusk sends me into panic. In the watches of the night I go mad. I am in a maze, a confusion, I am blasted by depression. I think I hear her voice, but there is only the echo of her name on my dry lips . . . Inès, Inès, Inès . . . In the mornings I wake up and she's not there. She used to look at me with bright blue eyes and say *buon giorno*, say it sweetly, say it as though the day was bound to be good because she had found me lying beside her. I have been left with less than I had before; more had been given me, more taken away. I am the debris of what I was. I am angry and bitter. I heap recriminations on her. I was right to be suspicious when she said she was already loving me as we stood in the drizzle at the lough shore in Belfast. How could she have loved me then? She barely knew me. It was too much too fast too soon. Her love is like a struck match. It flares up suddenly and brightly and dies away in an instant. Why did I let myself be taken in? Why hadn't I treated it as just another affair? Why did I let her come close? She is incapable of sustaining any deep attachment. She spreads her feelings widely, thinly, indiscriminately, there is no possibility of real, lasting attachment. Her friends say how warm she is, but this warmth is for herself. Conscious of what they are saying, aware of her reputation, her reviews, she basks in her own glow. Is this warmth any kind of real warmth? All this giving, all this altruism and ostentatious sympathy for the downtrodden – it's about her, it's to meet her needs not others'. I always hated her holier-than-thou manner, her irrefutable justifications – how do you breathe a word of criticism against someone whose answer is that they are serving others? You end up appearing peevish and self-centred. She is one of the most selfish people I have ever met. You're selfish, Inès, that's all you are – a selfish little bitch who's convinced herself she's a saint of the cause! Why on earth did I put up with your selfishness for so long? That and the scorn with which you looked on me and everything I did.

I crumble. After pouring out my venom I crumble. I apologize to her in my head, cravenly, submissively. I beg her. I cry that I didn't mean any of it, that I'm just upset, that I'm missing her and the life we had.

Just before the elections I decide to leave the apartment. I can stand it no more. I find a house for a reasonable rent on Gombé. The night before the move I pack my last few possessions. Among them is a book, *Lettere di condannati a morte della Resistenza italiana.* It was the first present she gave me. She told me this book moved her more than any other. She said it would be good for my Italian because the language was simple. I never did more than flick through it. Now I sit down and turn the pages. I can read most of it, even without a dictionary. I come to a letter written by a partisan from Sanremo, a sixty-one-year-old tailor. It's twelve lines long. He tells his children and his mother and his sisters and brothers he has just been informed that he is to be shot. He asks his son and his daughter to be good to each other, and asks his mother to forgive him the pain he has caused her. He ends with *Baci a tutti, vi assicuro che muoio con coraggio. Baci, baci, baci.* The honesty of the feeling behind the simple words, the knowledge of the circumstances in which they were written. The man in his cell, waiting for dawn, for the step outside his door. I can't bear it. Kisses to all. Kisses, kisses, kisses. Tears stream down my face. I am crying not for him but for myself. Everything now reduces me to tears. I can't believe that I am to be deprived of her forever. It is like a death.

The following morning, waiting for de Scheut to come and help me with my things, I sit down at the little table before the window and start to write.

Oh Inès, why am I writing this when I know it's hopeless, that the one thing you'll never forgive is the thing that I have done? I lay awake all last night, alert to every sound, thinking, hoping, you might come home to me and make everything better. I did not really think that you would – I am too much of a realist – but I could not stop my body refusing to lie still, or my mind imagining you once again in my arms.

I look for you everywhere, Inès, and know I will never find you. I should never have come to this awful place. I am out of my context, and it's difficult to look well when

you have no place. Each day that went by I felt less worth-
while. There was nothing for you to see in me, no way I
could shine for you. The only friend I had you loathed.

I began to think you loathed me too. For my inability to
take a side, for my refusal to take this thing seriously. But
that's how I am, you know that – it's my work, my past,
it's who and what I am. Physically too I thought you
despised me. Hair you don't like, eyes that are always tired,
a face that is too thin and a waist that is getting fat; and
other things about myself I cannot bring myself to write
down in words. You never wanted to touch me, and I
desired you every day. I don't understand, I don't under-
stand. Is politics so important? What about love? What
about love? What about this love of ours?

Are you there, Orla? Are you reading this, my love?
Don't turn me away.

I deliver the letter by hand to the tiny office near the Marché
Indigène. Some days later when I visit the apartment to pick
up my mail I find it has been returned unopened. I knew of
course it would be. Inès is strict. She keeps her word. She told
me she would never speak to me again. She never will.

Is there something overdone about all of this? Something
inflated? Am I trying to prove to myself that I am capable of
love? Is that what all this is about?

part two

Ireland and England

THE STORMS COME after lunch. The wind gets up, the lightning cracks in brilliant, branched arcs, and day changes
in minutes to sullen false dawn. From Mont Stanley I can plot
the rain's approach some way off: it blows in from the west,
where the ocean is, a slanting grey wall, whipped over the
forests and the waterfalls, on to the city to hammer the tin
roofs and lash the tarmac of the boulevards.

After all these months I should be used to the electric
afternoons but I am mesmerized by them still. If I close my
eyes they take me to a place at the edge of memory, where I
cannot often go, where I am small and fevered and frightened. They take me to a long, white, high-ceilinged room.
The polish of the dark wooden floor gleams with the disci-
pline of a place where voices are always hushed. The wind
gusts against the glass of the great windows on which reflec-
tions dance and ghouls shiver. Further up the ward a boy is
crying in his sleep. Through the chaos of my fever I can hear
my mother's voice. The doctors and the nurses do not want
her to come to me. She is a tiny and trepid woman, she goes
in fear and trembling and dreads confrontation. But I am her
son and she will not be diverted. At the bedside she holds my
hand and keeps me safe from the long ghosts.

My father was the third and youngest son of a Derry draper,
a lay preacher and Unionist councillor in that forlorn city.
All three sons were clever but only William got as far as
Queen's, where he read English. He was an outstanding

student – brilliant, in the opinion of some of his tutors, and he had a great career in front of him. After taking his degree in Belfast, he got a job teaching at an Oxford preparatory school. By then he had converted to marry my mother.

I last saw him in London just after the war when he showed up at my digs in Islington. I had been demobbed some weeks earlier and was arranging to resume my studies. I never thought I would see him again. He found me through his mother, a kindly woman with whom I kept in touch after our family was overthrown. He looked haggard and shabby. He had aged greatly in the twelve years since I had seen him last. Gone were the dark, suave looks, gone was the confidence, the easy charm.

It was about eleven in the morning and he was not drunk. But he reeked of booze. The sour smell came off his clothes, out of his mouth, from every pore. At first I did not want to have anything to do with him, but I found it hard to turn the wreck away. Mrs Lemass made us tea and we drank it in my room with the windows open. It was late summer and warm. I could hear the traffic on Holloway Road.

He began his tales of woe. Nothing in the world had worked out for him, everything he had touched since leaving my mother had crumbled into dust. Everyone was against him and did I have a couple of pounds he could borrow? He poured whisky from a hip flask into his tea cup. I declined the offer of a nip. His Derry accent was still strong and he had the kind of Irishness that embarrasses me most – full of knowing sentimentality and exaggeration, anecdote and cunning and communication through performance. He was the kind of man for whom a well-told story, however preposterous, guaranteed escape: there was no predicament too tight, no shave too close, no allusion too uncomfortable but a story would save you. I loathed it.

The drink warmed him, made him worse. Before long his

miseries were transformed into triumphs: the fortunes he had made, the beautiful women who had loved him, the places and things he had seen. He had just been offered a job with a leading City firm at a huge salary. He wasn't going to be rushed though. He had other irons in the fire. He drank the flask dry. I managed to get him out of the room around two with a ten-shilling note and a promise that we'd meet for lunch the following week.

At the door, with Mrs Lemass doing her genuine best not to eavesdrop, there was a single moment of truthfulness. William looked at me from the bloodshot globes of his old eyes and he said suddenly, quietly, 'I've been a fool. I'm sorry.' I mumbled something about there being no need to apologize for anything. Then he gathered himself and said with a brave smile, 'Things are going to change. I'm going to change, you'll see.' He shook my hand, told me how wonderful it was to see his son, and said again, 'I am going to change.' He said it firmly, with conviction, as if saying it were enough to make it true.

When he was gone I mulled over the visit. I wasn't surprised that he hadn't asked about my mother. Even William knew guilt. But neither had he asked a single question about me; not about my academic success or about my future or my plans. Not even about my war. He was too absorbed in disguising his own failure, from me, from himself. I picked a volume of Clarendon from the shelves, opened it at random and read about the intrigues at Charles I's Oxford court.

On the day of our lunch date, as I was putting on my jacket and checking the change in my pocket for the bus fare, it suddenly struck me: what am I doing? Why should I see this man? I barely know him and I don't like the little I know; we have nothing in common, nothing to say.

I left the house but I walked past the bus stop and down as far as the Angel, where I got on to the Regent's Canal, heading east to Victoria Park. There I sat at the lock gates and watched the ducks and the barges on the water. Things were different now, I told myself, I was different. I was twenty-five years old and after nearly three years in uniform I was on the threshold of another life. My D.Phil topic had been approved: 'The political impact in England of the sixteenth-century price inflation'. I had made my first visits to the Public Record Office, I was finding my way round the Exchequer and Chancery archives, I was learning to decipher the Tudor script. Like the man who throws away his last packet of cigarettes to prove he is serious about giving up, I stood up my father to announce a final break with the pettiness and dreariness of a previous life. I would be free from Belfast. I would be free from the sadness and pain of my family.

I left Mrs Lemass's house at the end of the week, moving to new temporary digs in Clapham. I left no forwarding address and I do not know if William ever tried to find me. Somewhere in my head I can see him on the doorstep facing my old landlady, puzzled and frowning – perhaps even hurt. I can see him thanking her and apologizing for troubling her, and turning away. I do not feel guilty about this. I never saw him again.

I have seen the photographs. Nuala was a beautiful young woman. She was small and slim, with thick brown hair which she wore short in the style of the times. She was the eldest of nine children – there were two more who did not survive infancy – and she left school at twelve to work in the flax mill near Albert Street. Her own father had been born in County Antrim but had moved to Belfast in search of work; he was a quiet man who liked to play chess and smoke a pipe. Her mother died in the Fever Hospital aged forty-four, six weeks after giving birth to her last child, a club-footed boy.

At the time of her marriage to the son of the Derry draper, Nuala had dreams of finer things. The grime could not quench her youthful illusions. She had a brain, she had a mind. She managed to get out of the mill and into the telephone exchange, and from there she had eyes on a career in nursing. Her reading did not stop at the mill gates. She always had her head in a book. She loved opera. She could sing the arias from *La Bohème*. She was awed by the idea of sophistication. Little touches of those early dreamy pretensions remain today, though really she has reverted to type. A Belfast woman, born on the Falls Road. That is what she is; but it is not what, in her heady courtship, she thought she would be.

She thought William would transport her to a different world, a world she caught hints of in novels and films. This man, whom she loved with a loyalty and intensity I find impossible to comprehend, would take her into this world. There would be a fine house, there would be smart friends, clever and amusing talk, wonderful parties.

What did he get from the marriage? A beautiful wife, yes. Devotion, yes, adoration. And other things. He was a Protestant at a time when it was beginning to be fashionable in the circles to which he craved admittance to be Catholic, or better, a convert. She had simple, rock-like faith, the kind seen by some as naïve, by others as profound. To my father, faith gave his wife a captivating and unaffected loveliness, and also a kind of alluring mysticism. At Queen's he had had a special interest in the Metaphysical poets.

What else did William get? She was gay and happy, she loved to dance and she had a voice which, her sisters later said, would have taken her to the concert hall had there been money for the training. Her house was all noise and bustle. His own was silent and fearful. William's father was an angry bigot whose footfall was heavy. The councillor devoted his evenings in the Guildhall to the fight against Rome and its brainwashed slaves in the slums below the city walls. He achieved his apotheosis at Buckingham Palace years later when he received his MBE. I think of the photographs of the occasion – sent to me by his widow – and see a vain, self-loving man, elect, fanatically convinced of his own salvation. He condemned the marriage. He did not speak to William after his conversion, would not have his name spoken in the house. I have a vague memory of the visit he paid after my mother, my sister and I returned from England. We were living in her father's house at the time. The councillor, who had business in Belfast that day, was shown into the parlour. He was stiff, his gaunt cheeks were red with choler and black with beard-shadow. His sideburns were shaved to the temples. The door closed, but his rebukes were not muffled. After he had gone, leaving £5, I saw my mother weeping in a chair. Her sisters gathered round her like a screen round a patient in a hospital bed.

They joined, my mother and my father. Man and wife, Catholic and convert. They came together. But not for long. In England, William came up against his first disappointments. He was a provincial, a yokel. His colleagues laughed at his accent (which he did his best to tone down), at the Derry words he used (which he tried hard to excise), and because he was an Irishman popularity was everything. Stung, bewildered, he tried ever harder to court acceptance. He bought the drinks, settled the restaurant bill, lent little sums which with the wave of a nonchalant hand he generously cancelled when the debt fell due. He and my mother threw parties to which no one came.

He discovered that having a wife was not in itself a source of embarrassment, but this wife was. She was not brilliant and the thing that had commended her most – her simplicity – had been corrupted by consciousness of a sophistication she

192

could never attain, and which she only ever got half-right. She was bewildered by the clever epigrammatic wit and cowed by the competitive displays of learning. In the family album there is a photograph of Nuala at one of the school's social occasions. In one hand she has a cigarette in a holder, in the other a wine glass. It almost made me cry the first time I saw it, though she looks happy enough. I can see the desperation for acceptance, and the insecurity. Men have fantasies of themselves as saviours; we can't help it. Stories we hear turn into duties we imagine: a damsel in distress, a knight in armour. No matter our shortcomings in reality, we persist in seeing ourselves like this. My fantasy was to enter the photograph and snatch the cigarette-holder out of my mother's hand, then, defiantly, take her away from the people around her. And we would be heroic, because we had acted with integrity, with dignity, shunning their falseness; and we would be made more heroic because of the glares and hostility we provoked.

After that? It really is a fantasy. After that – nothing. I think that my father, when he first looked at my mother in Belfast, at the trusting and beautiful face, must have had a similar fantasy. Take her away, take her away . . . They married within six months of meeting.

But in the face of more disappointments the fantasy palled. Burdened now with a screaming, demanding child as well as a wife, William's career went badly. His confidence failed. His colleagues whispered about him, the boys complained to their parents. The second child – my sister Siobhan – was sickly; there were doctor's calls, doctor's bills.

To close on this new world he had to distance himself from the old: the old was my mother and her simple loyalties. William started an affair. He discovered he was good at it. He started another, another.

My father was not a brutal man. He was the baby of the

family, spoiled by a doting mother. In his youth he had been quiet and bookish, and on the occasions when he was confronted by violence he was shaken and appalled. He avoided service during the Great War. But to show – to his new friends? To himself? – that he had sorted out his domestic life, that it was his to order and re-order, his calculated unkindnesses turned to violence. My mother went to hospital.

For some years – I believe four – they stayed together. He was a weak rather than a bad man and there were times when guilt overwhelmed him. There were days of tenderness and love-making.

The end came on my third birthday. It is my first memory.

We lived in a small house in Banbury, but for my birthday party we were invited to the larger home of my godparents, English Catholics in Oxford. They had a lawn, long and flat with neat borders that went down to a little pond, and my father – great joy! – played with me in the garden. We played football with balloons. I was deliriously, selfishly happy. Siobhan slept in her pram under the shade of a weeping willow. The sun was out and the sky was blue. My mouth was full of giggles. My father picked me up and put me on his shoulders. He held me there in the sun and threw the balloons into the air. We ran after them and I, from my perch, tried to trap the squeaky globes in my arms. My father put me down. He took his jacket from a garden chair, hoisted it to his shoulders, put on a pair of sunglasses and smiled at me. I watched him approach the french windows, behind which I saw my mother, and behind her my godparents. My father stood this side of the window, spread his fingers against the glass, and was gone. Tears streamed down my mother's face. I can see her now in her summer dress and sandals, sobbing wretchedly. My godfather, a man for whom emotional display was never easy, put out a hand and touched her arm. His mouth worked, his lips moved in a stutter, but he couldn't find words to say.

She was from a place where there was no such thing as not knowing anyone. She could not bear the loneliness of England. I can dimly recall the night we sat in the waiting room at Liverpool docks. The boat would take us to Belfast. My legs and feet were cold. It was foggy; it is possible that sailing had been delayed for it seems to me we waited a long time. Siobhan and I sat either side of our mother in our identical fawn coats, snuggling against her, the family baggage piled before us.

At least Belfast was not lonely. She came from a cheerful family, though one well fastened by the boundaries they lived in and never sought to extend. My mother's heartbroken return was, I believe, for her brothers and sisters an object lesson in staying with what you know. She had breached some unwritten rule of her small world, had in some way got above herself, and had paid the penalty. Now she was manless, an unusual condition in that place in those days unless it came through spinsterhood or widowhood. She felt it acutely. Her confidence crashed, it never really recovered. She became terrified of saying or doing the wrong thing. She worried about conventions and appearances. 'Don't let them know you live in a corporation house,' she told Siobhan, whose school friends had invited her to a party. And she worried about money, about what would happen to us.

When I was ten or eleven there was a reconciliation. William showed up on the doorstep one day. He presented her with a bunch of lilies. My mother sent Siobhan and me out to play and by the time we came in for tea she had taken him back. It lasted almost two years. He was as hopeless as ever, and as cruel to her. After one argument he followed her into the kitchen, where Siobhan and I were trembling by the stove, and punched her in the ear. After he stormed out of the house my mother asked us to fetch a neighbour. He drove her to the hospital and my father took to making 'business'

195

trips. Sometimes he'd arrive home with flowers and presents, and he'd take my mother out to dinner. But the trips got longer and longer. One day he just never came home.

I don't think it sentimental to say he never found anyone to replace my mother. When he tracked me down to my room in Islington and launched on his tall stories I didn't challenge him. Perhaps I should have. But it is hard to strip a man naked, even the weakest, most despicable man, and parade him for all to see and mock. Everyone, I suppose, deserves some cover. So, for all its transparency, I did not challenge William's cover that day. Instead I listened to his lies.

My new post-graduate life went well, went very well. I had a circle of friends who liked my company, who were amused by me. In those days I was capable of holding the dinner table's attention with stories and mimicry. I could tell jokes against myself, I could be a clown. I didn't mind looking silly as long as I was entertaining.

I completed my thesis in four years. The *British Journal of History* and the Royal Historical Society accepted parts of it for publication. I began work on a monograph whose principal argument would be that the great political and religious upheavals of the sixteenth century owed little to ideology or doctrinal conviction and everything to the Tudor state's perpetual need for cash, a need exacerbated by the effects of the European-wide price inflation. Like all young bloods I was out to make a name for myself – I stated my case provocatively; I loftily dismissed Weber and Tawney. I had a famous and powerful enemy at Balliol whose books were littered with anachronisms about 'the rise of the bourgeoisie' and 'capitalist modes of production', and he said something about the poverty of empiricism in connection with my approach. But I had defenders as well. I took a job as a teaching assistant while looking around for a suitable full-time post.

Then one bright afternoon I left the Public Record Office with a vague sense of needing some distraction. I had been cramming in my research during the Easter vacation; the Exchequer figures were crowding me, and my head felt cluttered and stupid. I thought I might have a spring cold coming on. I wandered down Chancery Lane and up the length of Fleet Street to Ludgate, and near St Paul's I found a dusty old bookshop where, out of idle curiosity, I picked up a nineteenth-century French novel. It had been a very long time since I had read fiction. I stood on the creaking bare boards of the floor and glanced over the first couple of pages with only passing interest, thinking at the end of each paragraph to put down the book and go on to explore the history shelves. Instead I kept reading. It seemed to me that I knew the people in the story, knew them first-hand. The more I read the more I recognized their voices, the way they walked, the houses in which they lived. I knew their banality, their pretensions, their selfishness. It was almost as if the story had been set in the world of my childhood. Why had I not read this before? Why had no one told me?

I finished the book that night. I did not return to the Public Record Office for almost a week. I stayed in my room and read novels. With one eye I watched the characters rise from the page, with the other I watched my own life. It sounds solipsistic, but reading about imaginary others made me intensely curious about my real self. Before then I had sent few queries in my own direction. Once I started reading I entered a period of introspection and self-examination; fiction referred to me questions I had not even known how to formulate. It was like being forced to stand naked in front of the mirror in a harsh and unflattering light.

I did not like the reflection cast back at me. I saw vanity, arrogance, self-importance, cowardice, I saw the meanness of my own motives. I started writing, I think, because I saw in words a way to cover myself up. In fairness, I did not try to use writing as reinvention, or as an advertisement, a sign behind which I could hide and say I was better than I was. Instead I rendered everything as a kind of sly joke, including the characters in which I breathed. That way I was only one more joke among many, my failings were invisible. Long before my first efforts at fiction I had substituted James for Seamus.

At around this time I met Alan at a dinner party. He was a year younger than I and had just got his first job in publishing. He struck me at first as rather bumptious and pleased with himself; I know – he would never admit it now – he thought me prickly and awkward. I probably was. Somehow we got over our initial mutual reservations. At his invitation I sent him some things – unconnected passages, a couple of short stories, a piece of memory. He invited me to his office in William IV Street where he told me he liked them. He liked, he said, the speculation, the moral neutrality, the jumpiness. 'Keep it like that,' he advised me. 'Personal conscience is fine, it's flexible and interesting; social conscience is tedious because it's invariably rigid and predictable.' He told me of a writer whose new novel was coming up for publication. 'Boring,' he announced. 'A novel is no place to parade your political beliefs.' He reminded me that Stendhal had once said that politics in a work of art is like a pistol shot going off at a concert, and he cited Auden: 'The honest truth, gentlemen, is that, if not a poem had been written, not a picture painted, not a bar of music composed, the history of man would be materially unchanged.' The work of writers and artists who persisted in trying to prove the opposite invariably declined. Had I ever read any of Day-Lewis's *Noah and the Waters?* His worst work. Embarrassing. Alan knew, he said, of several writers of vaguely left-wing sensibilities who, when it came to their fiction, found that no matter how hard they tried they could not fly the flag for the cause. The reason was simple: politics of that sort demands conviction, fiction demands doubt.

With encouragement from Alan I completed my first novel in five months. I finished my second in just under a year – I cannot write anything like as quickly now. The advances were small, but with occasional reviews, newspaper and magazine articles, and the odd radio piece I began to make a living. I abandoned my academic career. The notes for my monograph lie in a tea chest in the cupboard where I keep my vacuum cleaner.

When I was in my early teens things were hard for us. They were hard all over town. The mills were closing, the docks and shipyards were at a standstill, and the workless – cheered on by Siobhan (she had joined, to great family scandal, a communist youth organization) – were rioting. It was after William's second and final disappearance and my mother was in a distraction over money. One Friday night she clutched us, more for her comfort than ours, as the tick man shouted through the letterbox. It was then, as we sat in the dark holding our breaths, she noticed my fever. In the panic it was briefly – and wrongly – taken for TB, and I was admitted to a ward of the Fever Hospital in which my grandmother had died. The morning after my admittance my mother, anxiously scanning the newspaper lists, saw that B19617 had been placed in Class I, among the dangerously ill. She hurried to the hospital and would not be turned away. In the mutiny of my senses I was being tormented by ghosts. They were in the windows, they were around my bed. There were devils and angels fighting over me. Outside the wind was howling. Then her voice started to come through, a scented whisper, a rustling, an echo. I could feel my hand in hers. When I opened my eyes I could not make out her features for her face was in halation and the eerie light around her was glowing, spun, white and foggy. But there was something about her presence, its intensity, its declaration that heaven and earth would be moved if that's what it came to. I understood love as a child understands it, as a thing that comes to those who are greedy for it, a thing due by right.

Some time later, during my convalescence at home, she received a letter from William. We sat together in the kitchen that night. She gazed at the fire in the stove. She was not crying, but she was away, somewhere else.

'Where have you gone?' I asked gently.

I was pretending to be more grown up than I was. She turned to me and smiled – amused, I think, and touched by my pretension – and answered that she was here, nowhere else.

I asked why she still loved him.

She took me seriously; for the first time she regarded me not as a child for whom these things are unfathomable and should remain so, but as a kind of companion, as a friend. She was quiet for some moments before she said, 'Because he's a human being and he deserves to be loved.'

Love was not joy for her, it was not happiness. That's the way I understood love. And from that day on I could not bear to be around sadness or the people and the rules which made sadness. I had to get away.

It would be an exaggeration to say that nothing grew in my heart before I met Inès. There were women, and there were good times, happy times. There was fondness and kindness. There were presents and trips and all the things that go with man and woman, including soft words and impossible, felt pledges. But the truth is it was all at a remove; I was always watching the scene, watching myself, and, terrified of sadness, of what the end of love entailed, I made sure of my impregnability by convincing myself that I took nothing too seriously, that nothing deserved to be taken seriously. If I broke a heart, what of it? It would mend, and anyway hadn't its very predictability turned disappointed love into a well-worn joke? The patterns were so pathetically familiar all you could hope for was some little variation to provide some amusement for someone, somewhere.

So I walked in and out of others' lives, always on my own terms. When things started to go wrong, when the demands and dependencies began, I had the capacity to walk away. I could sweep an angry hand over the table, clearing the mess in one go, even at the cost of breaking the good and useful along with the distracting and worthless. I left everything behind on more than one occasion, starting afresh, completely afresh, unencumbered, clean, looking for change . . .

And of course I was aware of where this was coming from. I could see the face of the man who inspired my actions. The more it went on, the greater my dislike of what I was doing; the greater my dislike of him, and me. And the harder it was to maintain the pretence that I was treating the things around me as a joke.

When Inès introduced herself at Alan's party I was at a certain point in my life. Is that why I'm making so much of the failure of our affair? 'I am going to change,' William had said, his last words to me. But there is no such thing as a change in people. We think we can change, some people try hard for change, we always hope for it. It is a kind of psychological grail. I suppose it is in our nature to feel dissatisfied with what we are and to cling to the belief, even to the day of our death, that we can in some way be better. We cannot stand the thought of remaining the same. We have to grow, we have to move forward. But we are as we are, and not even the greatest of traumas will change us.

It could never have worked with Inès. I know that now.

part three

Léopoldville, November 1960

1

The ANC colonel tells me things will be better now that Mobutu has taken control. The coup five weeks ago was a very good thing. He tells me the UN should leave the country, that the re-organized Armée National Congolais will put an end to Tshombe's secessionist revolt in Katanga and the tribal fighting in the Kasai. He tells me it would be better for everyone if Lumumba were neutralized. Neutralized? He's already under house arrest in the Primature. Exiled, the colonel says, to Egypt or Ghana, or the Soviet Union, if that's what he wants. But we both know exile is not the colonel's preferred solution. He chuckles as though at a private joke, then he drops like a stone. One second I am talking to a living person, the next I am gazing at a bloody heap on the ground. He is on his back, heedless, abandoned, puzzled, legs splayed and awkward, one arm twisted behind him, the other thrown recklessly out. There is a hole above his left eye.

There is a second burst of gunfire, a ferocious dry clacking. Only now am I aware there has been a first. I crouch, desperately searching for the source of the shooting and trying to guess the best way out of the field of fire. The ANC soldiers around me scatter for cover behind their armoured vehicles, one or two letting off wild retaliatory shots in the general direction of the embassy. But I have poor night vision and cannot make my move quickly enough. The shooting from inside the compound intensifies and I know I have lost the best moment for flight.

As the ANC men open up I throw myself to the ground and, stranded and exposed, press up against the corpse. It is my head I fear for, that and – shamefully, most unheroically – my arse, which seems preposterously vulnerable. I almost turn to check its visibility before thinking better of it. Oh, I hope I'm not shot there – the indignity. I laugh inwardly; the things that go through your mind . . . The ricochets whine on the concrete and they sparkle on the metal of the armoured personnel carriers like the splinters of gold from a welder's torch. Someone somewhere is whinnying with pain. The air is smoking, the clatter is deafening. There is a moment's let-up and I think about making a run for it. But in which direction? The shooting starts up again, even more fiercely. It's so absurd. This is not an assault on the fortified position of an opposing army. It is the Ghanaian embassy. The ambassador has been declared *persona non grata* by the new regime. Now I am lying beside a dead man in the middle of the road, sniffing his sweat and his brains and the thick black blood oozing on to the road from under the matt mash of his once handsome head.

I cannot see Stipe. He had wandered off somewhere before the embassy guards opened up. There is another prolonged burst. I screw my eyes shut. Three years in the army never brought death so near. I am conscious of my fear but I am conscious too that if I survive I will have a story to tell. A story for the paper, a good story, and a store of narrative and emotional fat for the book-writer to live off for a long time to come. The bullets strike the tarmac and concrete around me. They are getting closer. All I have to do is wait it out, wait and hope and survive. I must not panic. But what a bloody farce, what a fucking bloody farce! I draw myself to the warm corpse. Enter it, hide in it, be nowhere. The pointlessness of this! The whole thing has been a farce. Everything since independence has been a sick joke. The bullets crawl around me. I laugh out loud. I start to laugh hysterically. I laugh at the memory of all the things I have seen in this preposterous country. I laugh at the candidate we saw in the Kasai, riding into the village in his black tie and tails and white gloves and leopard skin, saturated with cruelty and power. I laugh at his election promises – Belgian money for crops, the wives of the white men, their houses, their cars. I laugh at poor Cleophas hanging prickless from the tree, at his big, splayed, dusty, gnarled, cartoon feet. There has been so much to laugh about. I'll say that for the Congo. It might be the death of me but it's been good for a laugh. King Baudouin of the Belgians – he was good for a laugh. Dressed like some Habsburg princeling on a doomed visit to a Balkan province, being driven into Léopoldville in a huge white American convertible, crowds lining the boulevard, whites cheering, the Congolese bemused. The brazen black youth who dashed to the car and snatched Baudouin's ceremonial sword. The embarrassed and outraged gendarmes who pursued him and the laughing Congolese who clapped him. Farce. Independence day was good for a laugh, with Baudouin's silly speech praising the genius and generosity of Léopold. Lumumba's vitriolic response. We are your beasts no more, the new prime minister declared. Did Inès write that line for him? It had her stamp. She was there that day in the Palais de la Nation. She ignored me, of course. How well she looked, how beautiful. She had gained a little weight, just enough to fill out her figure. Her eyes were shining. People will say this about someone's eyes, that they are shining, and they never are, but her eyes that day were more than bright. They *were* shining – light and happiness and fulfilment playing in them. Even her hair looked well, thicker, gleaming. And I knew then there had to be a man. Laugh at that. Why not? If I am to die I might as well die laughing. Why not?

The corpse moves. The thrown-out arm twitches. Once. Twice. I feel it, sense it rather than see it. Is the colonel alive? But the head wound? No one could survive a wound like that. I turn my face a fraction to see a soldier kneeling at the back of one of the APCs waving frantically to me. He shouts something, urgent and commanding, but it is not French and I can't make him out. His comrades are staring, making me frightened and paranoid, as if they know something to my disadvantage which I have not yet grasped. The soldier shouts again, but what am I supposed to do? Run for it? It's twenty yards to the APC. I'd never make it. They'd cut me down.

I stay where I am, I do not move. The soldier grimaces, giving up on me, and, turning back to the embassy, fires a random burst from his rifle. The corpse moves again and this time I realize what is happening. The colonel is taking more hits. Bullets are thudding into the dead tissue and bone. My shoe is suddenly slashed. I feel something hot, burning. Don't tell me I've been shot in the foot. Shot in the foot! How ridiculous. I mutter, not with fear or pain – there is no pain, not real pain, not yet – but with anger. My foot is burning and I am angry because this is just ridiculous. Where is Stipe? Where is he? He could get me out of here. Stipe!

Why didn't I leave when the chaos broke out? Stipe told me to go. He warned me. The day the army of Lumumba's new republic mutinied, when they poured into Léopoldville, breaking shop windows and looting stores. It was a time of unlawful and enthusiastic self-service, and of general alarm. The Belgians fled. They packed up and they fled. Tens and tens of thousands. Stipe told me it was going to get worse, but I held on. Even when the convoys of hysterical refugees streamed into Léopoldville, I held on. When the public docks were teeming with men and women beyond the reach of reason, I held on. And laughed.

The firing builds up to an ear-splitting crescendo. The burning in my foot has stopped now. Pain is setting in. If anything, the shooting is fiercer. Thousands of rounds must already have been fired. Two more ANC soldiers are down. I watch a third spin backwards. He lies in the road screaming in agony. Two of his comrades drag him by the ankles back to cover and the screaming gives way to a dreadful, pathetic whimpering.

I laughed even when I saw de Scheut and his children in the throng at the public docks. I could not believe it. De Scheut of all people. He would not look at me. A black porter came to help them on to the ferry and Julie screamed at the filthy black monkey to leave them alone. They didn't hear when I shouted my farewells. The voice in their own heads, white and implacable, speaking weird histories, lurid tales, hideous times, had them in its thrall.

But at least they survived. Maybe they did the right thing. I am not going to survive, I am not going to survive. There will be no story for me to tell. A bullet will crash into the crown of my head, a bullet will tear into my arse. I press myself into the concrete, into the corpse. How can they miss? Oh Jesus, don't let me die. I have to run. I can't stay here like a sitting duck. Run – anywhere, in any direction, it doesn't matter, just run. Get out of here.

I am about to spring to my feet when Stipe, pistol in hand, appears by the APC.

'Stay where you are, James!' he shouts. 'Stay where you are.'

As though in reply the embassy guards intensify their fire. Stipe shouts something in Lingala to the soldiers, commanding them, organizing them. I cannot bear this any more. I don't care what he says, I'm going to make a run for it. Then I hear the roar of an engine, more shouts, more clattering pangs as bullets from the embassy hit the armoured vehicle as it moves towards me.

'James!'

It is Stipe. He is standing ten feet away. He has got the

soldiers to bring the APC into the middle of the road to shield me.

'Come on!'

I leap to my feet and rush to him. We crouch and keep time with the vehicle until we have reached the safety of the buildings on the other side of the road. I collapse against a wall. Stipe looks down at me and grins.

'Jesus Christ,' I mutter. 'Jesus Christ.'

'What would you say to a drink?' he asks.

He helps me up and we leave the battle behind. We get into Stipe's car and drive to the Regina for a quiet drink. It's that simple. It's only when I am sitting on the concourse, whisky in hand, that I become aware again of the throbbing in my foot. I tell Stipe I think I've been shot. He looks down at my ruined shoe. There's a light smear of blood.

'Doesn't look so bad,' he says nonchalantly. 'Have another drink and I'll take you to a doctor.'

I feel surprisingly calm. Not even the wound alarms me. I feel pleased with myself. I have my story, I have my fat. I have the kind of authenticity which experience like this confers. I feel quite the intrepid reporter.

When Stipe returns with the whiskies I tease him. 'You must be pleased with the way things are going. Mobutu's good for the Americans.'

'Good for the Congo,' he replies with a wink.

'How much longer do you think Mobutu can keep Lumumba under house arrest?'

'Not much longer. He needs to find a permanent solution to the Lumumba problem.'

'The colonel was telling me something along the same lines before he got his head blown off,' I say. 'What would this permanent solution be?'

'Gizenga's in Stanleyville but he doesn't have Patrice's following or charisma. Without Lumumba, the revolt in

Orientale will fizzle out. But if Patrice gets to join him there it would tear the country in two. It would be full-scale civil war.'

'What would happen to Lumumba if Mobutu could get at him?'

After Lumumba was placed under house arrest, the UN put a cordon of troops around the Primature – the prime minister's residence in Gombé – very close to my own house – to protect him. Mobutu suspected that the UN might allow Lumumba to escape so he placed an ANC cordon around the UN one.

Stipe says simply, 'If Mobutu's men got through the UN cordon, I don't think we'd ever see Patrice Lumumba again. And to be frank, it would be no loss to anyone.'

Stipe has never admitted, even to me, the extent of his involvement with Mobutu's coup. But it doesn't take much imagination to work it out. On September 10th, Mobutu, the ANC chief-of-staff appointed by Lumumba himself, held a pay parade at Camp Léopold, personally handing out the soldiers' overdue wages. Lumumba's government was bankrupt – the Belgians had made sure of that – and the soldiers' indiscipline was largely due to the arrears in their pay. Where had the money to buy the army's loyalty come from? No one could say for certain, but Stipe's presence at Camp Léopold raised suspicions.

Four days later I was with Grant and Roger in the Regina when Mobutu walked in and announced that the army had taken power. Lumumba's tenure as prime minister had lasted less than three months. We dashed for the phones and telex offices. Later that night I went to look for Stipe and found him at the Zoo having dinner with his ambassador, Timberlake. They were in good and generous spirits and invited me to join them. Timberlake, whom I had not met before, struck me as a crude man, a Cold War warrior of the most extreme type. He seemed too loud to be a diplomat. Perhaps he was being open with me because he knew of my friendship with Stipe, or perhaps it was simply because he had been cheered by the events of the evening. He was openly celebrating the coup. Kasavubu had been hopeless, he said, impossible to spurt on to action. Mobutu was altogether different. He was tough, efficient, capable, dependable, honest and not anti-West, unlike – and this is how he referred to the deposed prime minister throughout our meeting – the awful Lumumbavitch. Lumumbavitch was Commie through and through. When I suggested that he was more of an pan-African nationalist than a communist, Timberlake dismissed the distinction as meaningless. Lumumbavitch, if not an actual Commie, was playing the Commie game. He had called on the Soviet Union and China to send military aid. He had accepted a flight of Ilyushin jets. He had accepted eighty Zim lorries for his troops fighting in the Kasai, he had taken the communist Gizenga into his cabinet . . .

We were joined by another American, a ruddy-faced little man with thinning fair hair and pale blue eyes to whom Timberlake referred as Dr Joe from Paris. I had not seen Dr Joe before. He did not seem to me to have much of the general practitioner or surgeon's manner. If he had ever been a doctor – which I was inclined to doubt – I imagine he was struck off early in his career for something unsavoury. When I asked how long he'd been in Leo he gave me a vague reply, and he was evasive about every other direct question I put to him, no matter how mundane. I got the impression Stipe was not pleased about my running into Dr Joe, an impression confirmed some minutes later when he made a transparent excuse to take the doctor off. In their absence Timberlake rambled on. Lumumbavitch's allies and supporters, even the lowliest clerk with Lumumbavitch sympathies, would now be rounded up and thrown in jail. Too bad Gizenga had already escaped to Stanleyville, but they would get the others: Okito, Mulele, Mpolo, Smail, and – this took me by surprise – Auguste.

I went to see Stipe the next morning to tackle him about the list of wanted Lumumbists. When talking about Okito, Mulele and the others, even when talking about Lumumba himself, Stipe's tone was neutral, but something hard and personal crept into his voice when he came to Auguste. According to Stipe, Auguste had spent a month in Czechoslovakia for cadre training and had recently risen to become chairman of the Jeunesse MNC, which he described as the terrorist wing of Lumumba's party. I was sceptical, but Stipe assured me it was all true. Then he asked a question that alarmed me.

'Have you seen Inès lately?'

'No. Not since independence day.'

'I know things between you are difficult, but if you see her, you should try to persuade her to get out as soon as she can.'

'What do you mean?' I asked.

'She should get out while she can,' he said with a shrug, and though I pressed him he would say no more on the subject.

Then, as we were parting, he told me that Auguste and Inès were lovers.

Yes, the Congo has been good for a laugh. I did not feel very much when Stipe broke the news. In fact I remember laughing in Stipe's face. Not because I didn't believe it to be true. I could see it all too clearly, in fact I had already suspected it. I knew the kind of man who excited Inès's interest. I had seen the little signs when Inès and I still lived together. But – out of deference to Inès, and partly for fear of being thought patronizing or churlish or, worse, jealous – I had never expressed my real opinion of Auguste. The truth was I had always seen him as a clown. The quoter of Erasmus, the lover of Socrates, Plato and John Stuart Mill, the member of the Association of the African Middle Classes and wearer of false spectacles and gaudy shirts. The man who was going to have a lawyer's office on Park Avenue with half a dozen pretty secretaries. How do you take a man like that seriously? How do you take a man like that as a lover? But Inès would. She would see in him other things. She would see in him suffering and struggle, heroism and resistance and self-sacrifice.

Was I jealous of this absurd man?

No.

Not remotely.

I was madly jealous – insanely, self-pityingly, violently so. The night Stipe gave me the news I went to Houthhoofd's house on Eugene Henry for one of my trysts with Madeleine. Madeleine had not fled, and she was contemptuous of those who had. She is woman of aggressive instincts and these instincts she takes with her to the bedroom. Sex with her is never gentle. There have been times when I demurred but she always egged me on. 'I want it like this,' she would say to put my mind at ease, and she would whisper, 'hurt me.' She knew me. She knew me well. She sensed the hatred massing in me that night. She did not complain. And when it was over she smiled knowingly, triumphantly, as if at last I had entered a dark place into which she had been trying to tempt me for a long time.

While she showered I lay on Houthhoofd's bed, thinking of Inès, thinking of Auguste. I knew what would happen to Auguste if Mobutu's men captured him or if Stipe found him. I had seen the results of their handiwork. During the fighting at Bakwanga, Baluba soldiers had sought revenge in the capital for the atrocities committed on their tribe by Lumumba's troops. One morning I came across a knot of people by the golf course. A Ghanaian officer with the UN forces, one of General Alexander's men, approached the small crowd. The men stood aside to reveal the body of a sleek young man lying face up on the street. I recognized the victim, had been on nodding terms with him. His name was Justin and he had been a low-level official in the MNC, an ardent supporter of the prime minister and a friend of Auguste's. Now he was dead – hacked and slashed and torn. I stopped for a closer look. The Ghanaian officer, squatting to inspect the corpse, flicked away a half-finished cigarette; it landed in the dark oil of blood by Justin's right leg. The bystanders spoke in loud voices, the officer wiped sweat from his eyes. The flies buzzed. The ash of the discarded cigarette glowed briefly in the pool of sticky crimson, then began its careless disintegration. I knew what would happen to Auguste.

I got off the bed and went into the shower. Madeleine looked at me in surprise. She glanced down at my cock and smiled. 'So soon?' she said, amused. Without another word, she slowly turned her back on me and spread her palms against the white tiles to steady herself. As I fucked her I saw Auguste's face where Justin's was. I saw him dead, mutilated, bleeding. I started to say, 'I hate you, I hate you, I hate you.' I went on and on. I was shouting at Auguste, I was shouting at Inès. Madeleine was groaning. She was bent fully over, squashed into a corner, contorted, pressed against the tiles, the water running off her back and broad, strong shoulders. There were little juddering, rippling movements in the flesh of her backside as I rammed against her. I hate you, I hate you, I hate you.

Will somebody please take me away from this? From where I am now. From what I am doing. From all this hate. From myself. Please.

'Come on,' Stipe says, finishing his drink, 'let's get you to a doctor.'

I suggest he take me to Roger's.

'Have you heard anything of Auguste?' I ask.

'He's still hiding in the city somewhere,' he replies.

'Do you think they'll find him?'

'They'll find him,' he declares flatly. 'It's only a matter of time.'

Though I make no comment on his answer, he knows it holds satisfactions for me. I am partly ashamed by my response. Partly.

2

Roger offers Stipe a drink. He downs it quickly, then says he should get back to the embassy.

'You know,' I begin sheepishly, 'I don't like melodrama any more than you, but you probably saved my life.'

He makes modest disclaimers but I can see he is pleased by my recognition of what he has done for me. He pats me on the shoulder and says he'll call tomorrow.

Roger carefully removes my broken and bloodstained shoe and cuts away the sticky sock.

'It's a graze and there's some bruising, but it's not serious. I'm afraid your shoe's a write-off, though,' he says in a voice that betrays the merest hint of disappointment; I suppose like all professionals Roger likes the occasional challenge. He points to my foot.

'You can see here the line of the bullet along the instep. I'll clean it up for you and you'll soon be right as rain.'

He gets to work and I ask how much longer he thinks he'll stay on. Though he's threatened to go many times before, Roger never seems able to bring himself to leave.

'Oh, someone has to look after things,' he says quietly. 'One never likes to speak ill of one's colleagues, but the Belgian doctors have been rather irresponsible, you know. Packed up and left like everybody else. Thought nothing of the patients. The whole health-care system's in a frightful mess.'

Roger is a kind and honourable man. Every time I see him I feel embarrassed about my dismissive appraisal when we first met in Houthhoofd's garden. And though we have become friends of a sort I regret that we will never be closer, never know each other better. We share a drink every now and then – a meal would overburden the slim frame of our connection – but even in our cups we never really talk. He is one of those reserved Englishmen whom it is easy to like and impossible to know.

'Things are turning terribly nasty,' he says, swabbing my pathetic little wound. 'The atmosphere is not good at all.'

'Lumumba made sure of that on independence day,' I say.

'I don't think it's fair to lay all the blame on Lumumba,' he says gently enough but with a conviction that surprises me for he has never given any indication of his political views; I always took him to be one of those men for whom what he did in the polling booth was as private as what he did in the bedroom, and not a proper subject for civilized conversation. What politics he had I had always assumed to be conservative; I suspect he thinks Macmillan a good egg.

'Lumumba's speech on independence day may have been a little intemperate,' he continues, 'but understandable in the circumstances. What was King Baudouin thinking of trying to tell the Congolese that Léopold had established the colony by treaties and peaceful methods! Rather a load of twaddle, frankly. Gave the natives a few bits of cloth and a crateload of gin in return for their land. The chiefs had no idea what they were agreeing to. In some cases they weren't given the chance to say no. Did anyone ever tell you what happened to the Bayeke?'

'I don't think so.'

'The chief of the Bayeke was a man called M'Siri. Terrible despot. Lived in a mud and thatch palace surrounded with skulls on sticks. The Belgians wanted a treaty because the Bayeke land had all sorts of minerals. M'Siri wouldn't give them one so they shot him on the spot. Then they asked M'Siri's eldest son if he wanted a treaty. It turned out he did, lucky for him. The treaty put practically the whole of Katanga under Léopold's rule in exchange for the son being allowed to remain chief. Is that stinging?'

'Hardly at all,' I say.

He drops the swab into a plastic bin, goes to wash his hands and prepares some lint and bandage.

'Still, I suppose the Belgians would say that the Congo was in an appalling condition when they arrived. There were cannibals, you know. Far more of them here than anywhere else in Africa. The people just didn't have enough to eat. They also had malaria, leprosy, trypanosomiasis, tropical ulcers, everything you care to mention. Frightful place, really. Slavery was the biggest problem, of course. They reckon thirty million Congolese were taken off as slaves. The Arabs were the worst. Tipu Tip – he was a friend of Stanley's. A terrible rogue. Made a fortune from slaving.'

He finishes the bandaging. It is very tight.

'How does that feel?'

'Fine.'

He goes to the sink and starts scrubbing his hands.

'The Belgians actually made Tipu Tip governor of Stanleyville and gave him a salary of $150 a month into the bargain. Didn't do their reputation a lot of good with the natives.'

He takes a white towel and rubs his hands.

'I'm not saying we haven't made our own mistakes, but I do think the British would have done it rather better,' he says, going to a cabinet by his desk. 'I'll give you some antibiotics. The wound's not serious but you have to be careful with that kind of thing in the tropics.'

'You're very kind.'

He waves me away dismissively. 'Can you put weight on your foot?'

I stand up from the chair.

'It seems okay.'

He regards me, as though hesitating to say something.

'What is it?' I ask.

'I've been asked to pass on a message to you,' he says. 'I didn't tell you straight away because I know how things are between you two.'

'Who's the message from?'

I have no need to ask. My heart is thumping.

'Inès.'

'I see.'

I have to sit down.

'She telephoned earlier. Twice, as a matter of fact. Apparently she'd been trying to get hold of you at home and you weren't in. Then she thought of me. I wrote down a telephone number. She said it's important.'

He hands me a scrap of paper and looks at me with sympathy.

'Are you all right, James? Would you care for a whisky?'

'No, thank you. May I use your phone?'

'Of course. It's in the hall.'

My hand is shaking so much I misdial twice. The phone at the other end rings only once.

'It's me,' I say.

'I need to see you.'

She sounds strange, as though having to make an effort merely to talk.

'Are you all right?'

She is not well. I can hear it in her voice.

'Yes, fine,' she says peremptorily, but unconvincingly. 'Can I come to your house?'

'Of course.'

'I'll be there in one hour.'

'Do you want me to pick you up?'

'No. It's not safe. I see you in one hour.'

I am about to tell her that I am so happy to hear her voice again, that she will never know how much I have missed her, that I love her, that I think about her all the time . . . She has put the phone down, and saved me from another humiliation. Slowly I replace the receiver. I close my eyes. I hunch my shoulders and make fists of my hands. I must be strong, I have to be strong. Perhaps they have captured Auguste. Perhaps he is dead. Perhaps she wants to come back to me. Let him be dead, please let him be dead. Come back to me, Inès, where you belong.

From behind I hear Roger ask if I would like him to run me home. I realize I have been standing alone in the hall for several minutes. I turn to him and force a wide, nonchalant smile to my face.

'Yes, that would be very kind,' I reply; and I joke lamely, 'I'm not sure how far I'd get in just the one shoe.'

'No, indeed,' Roger says, smiling back at me. 'I'll just get my keys.'

We have barely left the house when Roger asks, 'Are we being followed?'

I turn to look behind us.

'There's a black Citroen with two rather unpleasant looking gentlemen in it,' he says. 'I wonder if they might be Congolese Sûreté.'

The roads are almost empty and the Citroen's presence is conspicuous, and suspicious. But still I say I can't imagine why anyone would be following us.

'No indeed,' Roger says doubtfully. 'Probably just taking the same route.'

We get through the first roadblock without too much trouble. But at the next the soldiers are in angry mood and order us out of the car. It turns out they have heard about the shooting at the embassy and the death of the colonel, apparently a well-known and popular officer. We stand by the side of the dark, lonely road at the end of a line of frightened blacks who are waiting to be questioned by an officer with a swagger stick. The Citroen has pulled up a little way before the roadblock. Two soldiers go to investigate. Roger and I watch as the car's occupants – two black men – identify themselves.

'Why would the Sûreté be following us?' I ask Roger.

'I suppose they're suspicious of any whites these days,' he replies.

An aggressive-looking NCO approaches us.

'Better not to tell them how you got your foot,' Roger whispers. 'Just in case. You never know how they might take it.'

I make up a story to do with a falling gas cylinder. The NCO shouts at us for several minutes. He says that we are paratroopers, that we are spies. We are not Belgians, I assure him, we are not Flemish.

'*Tu miens*,' the NCO shouts into my face.

'No,' Roger replies calmly. 'We are British – British.'

The NCO jabs his rifle into Roger's chest.

'Steady on,' Roger says.

Further up, the officer pulls a man out of the line and starts screaming at him. The soldiers start to gather round, like lions round the beast they have chosen for their kill. The officer strikes the man across the face with his swagger stick. The man mumbles something. A soldier rams a rifle butt into his back and he stumbles forward only to be met by more blows. The officer kicks at his shins; another soldier gives him a savage blow to the back of the head.

'I think we should say something, don't you?' Roger whispers. 'This really isn't on.'

We both know we won't.

The beating continues. The man is on his knees. The blows rain down on him.

The NCO looks at us and grins. 'MNC,' he says, jerking his head to their victim. 'Lumumba man.' He runs a finger melodramatically across his throat. 'All Lumumba man get this.'

'We are not Lumumba men,' I insist.

'Not by any means,' Roger adds, rather shocked by the idea that anyone could mistake him for such.

The NCO asks for money, and after a little bargaining we surrender a few francs. Once he's pocketed them, he pats us on the back and chats amiably – we're the best of friends now, no hard feelings – as he escorts us to the car. Lumumba man are all going to die, he tells us cheerfully. The communists will be killed. Then the Congo will be free. We drive off and leave the Lumumba man on his back surrounded by the officer and the soldiers, weakly, vainly, trying to fend off their attack.

Roger drops me at the gate of my house and asks if I can manage. I assure him I'm fine. He reminds me about the antibiotics and tells me to pop in to see him tomorrow to have the bandage changed. I thank him for the lift and he pulls away.

As I go inside I check the street. There is no sign now of the Citroen. Either Roger and I were jumping to conclusions or the Sûreté men got bored and called it a night.

3

S HE HAS COME back to me. It is after midnight by the time she arrives; she is very late. I open the gate in the garden wall and she is there, small and trembling. She falls into my arms and I don't care that it's the malaria. I am made strong again, though I would prefer her need to be of another order. I put an arm around her and help her to the house, drinking in every moment of our physical contact. She has not washed her hair. It has the smells of the things I imagine and fear belong to a new and different life: rain and earth and wood smoke and palm oil and spices. They are ordinary but seem somehow alien to me, so far from what I am and how I live and the way the things around me are. She has been defying the fever but is now at the end of her resistance. Her voice is small and far away. She tells me she had trouble getting through the road-blocks and this is the worst possible time for her to be sick. Things are about to happen. She has a part to play and she is afraid she will not be able to play it, and now I must help her.

'Let's get you inside,' I say.

'Please,' she pleads, 'I know this will be hard for you, but you must help.'

The lover who leaves patronizes the lover left, retains enforceable claims, the most significant and hurtful of them sexual. Inès knows that all she has to do is ask. What can I refuse her? How? I tell her I will help and I sweep her up and take her inside, to my bedroom.

Her stomach is boiling, her eyes are yellow-clouded and her

224

blood dreams. Since the delirium took hold, her words have been without destination or purpose, but once, in the early hours, she cried out for her father, and I was there: a father to her now, watcher, nurse – a kind of lover once more. I do not know what she saw or heard when I whispered her name. '*Mi fanno male le ossa*,' she told her dead father. 'Yes,' I responded, 'yes, I know, darling.' Perhaps it was the sound of a language she had not expected to hear, but her gaze sharpened momentarily and she regarded me for an limpid instant with the frank and abstracted curiosity of a child. 'I am sore in my bones,' she said in English. It was a small moment of lucidity. It seemed as though she were looking inside her head for a memory, a connection – a reference with which to reconcile where she was now with what she was and what she knew and who she was with. The effort exhausted her and her eyes closed. I kissed her brow, the way a father might, and stroked her damp hair while under the sheet my hand found her breast. She made a little noise, I think of gratification, before she was borne away again to the furnaces where she is – for a time at least – lost to her causes and found to me.

Auguste waits for her. There is a plan, she said. Two nights from now an Egyptian plane will land at Njili; Nasser is a friend of the Congo. Lumumba will escape from the Prima-ture, and he and the wanted MNC people still in Leo will make their way to the airport and be taken to Stanleyville where Mobutu's writ does not run and Gizenga is still in control. Auguste will go with them, but now he needs help. He is hiding with Smail's friend, Harry, the Indian diamond smuggler, but Stipe and Mobutu's men are looking for him everywhere and the net is closing. I must go to Auguste and tell him that Smail has been arrested. The prisoner will be tortured and when he talks the soldiers will go to Harry's shack. Auguste must be moved to a safe place until the plane arrives. To my house.

'This house isn't safe either,' I told her. 'They know about me and you, and they know about you and Auguste. They will make the connections, Inès, they will guess.'

'They will not suspect you,' she insisted. 'You are known as the friend of Stipe and Stipe is the friend of Mobutu. Bring Auguste here. They will never think to look for him here. Keep him just one night, then take him in your car, they will not stop you. Only as far as the airport, only as far as Njili. It was my role, I was going to hide him, but now I cannot, and Auguste is waiting for me and I cannot help him.'

I countered. I told her about the roadblock and the Citroen.

The fever was taking her, inch by inch, surrounding her, consuming her. She found it harder to concentrate, harder to be rational. Please help Auguste was all she could say.

With sudden desperation I said, 'Inès, things are out of control now, there's nothing you can do here. They've won. Mobutu and the Americans have won. Come back with me to London. Leave this place. We'll build a life together again. It'll be a happy life, a good one. Please come back with me.'

She gave my hand a little squeeze and said in a whisper, 'They want to kill Auguste because he believes in the freedom of his country. Stipe wants to kill him because he does not accept to be the puppet of the Americans. I cannot leave.'

What were my wishes when compared with hers but selfish and petty? I spoke of happiness and of building a life; she spoke of struggle and of saving someone from death. As always there is a higher justification for what she wants. Perhaps I should have conceded the virtue of her reprimand. But I didn't. Instead I felt angry with her for getting involved in the unnecessary melodrama of all this. Let these people get on with their bloody feuds. Both sides are as bad as each other. What's it got to do with us?

'Are you going to Stanleyville as well?' I asked with bitter petulance.

'I don't know,' she struggled to say. 'I don't know what to do. I'm so tired.'

'Why are you trusting me with this?' I spat the question at her. 'How can you trust me after all you've accused me of?'

She said softly, almost inaudibly, 'Because you are a good man.'

'If I'm so good come back with me.'

I felt a delicate finger move lightly in the palm of my hand. Her yellow eyes flickered. She was sinking in the bed, going down with fever's fires raging around her. I could hardly hear when she said, 'I trust you because I am still loving you.' Then she slipped away into malaria's moiling confusions.

At five it is barely light and the bats are returning to roost. I hear them scratching the wooden planks of the ceiling above us. The river drones and gushes. In the garden the first of the birds hazard their calls. I lower myself to her, forehead to forehead. Where do you go in your scalding dreams, Inès? Do you come to me, to where I wait for you? I say her name over and over so she will know where to find me, but other voices, hot, demented, compete with mine, dousing my pleas and promises. I force the chloroquine into her mouth and go to the kitchen, limping slightly on my throbbing foot.

I take my coffee out to the white-walled garden at the back of the house where I sit at the table between the mango tree and a giant white flame of the forest. I can smell the faint morning perfume of the frangipani, and the hibiscus and bougainvillaea are in bloom. The house is large and win- ningly ramshackle, with a covered patio and spacious rooms with high ceilings. I have never known such luxury. For a moment I see myself with Inès in a place like this, happy and contented, secure and comfortable. Then I laugh to myself. How she would hate it. *Secure and comfortable* – she never wanted that. But maybe some other kind of life together is possible. I tell myself it's not such a hopeless dream. Only a few hours ago I was sure we would never speak again. Now she tells me she is loving me still. Now she lies in my bed. She came to me, after all. Of all the people she must know in Léopoldville she chose me to help her. The more I think about it, the more I see the way her mind is working: she wants out of what she has got into. She wants to come back to me. It's the only explanation. I could snatch her up now, drive to the airport, get her on a plane and we could be in London tomorrow.

And then my sense of realism returns. There is nothing in this for me. She doesn't want me, only what I can do for her cause, and for her lover. Resentment seeps into me. I sip the coffee. It has gone cold. I will not snatch her up and take her away. Instead I will go to Auguste, to where he hides. He will be suspicious. I will be the last person he expects to see, the lover of his lover, the friend of his former friend, the man who now wants him dead. But he is desperate and I am all there is. I will tell him that Inès has asked me to do this, that she trusts me. But I worry that I don't trust myself. What will I say, what will I do when I find him? Will I look at his mouth and see the marks of her kisses? Will I look in his eyes and see what he has seen as Inès waited for him in their bed? What things did he do to her? And she to him? I hear the catch in her voice, the way she sounds when she comes. I hear it so clearly, so vividly. I turn suddenly because I hear them together behind me. I knock the table. The coffee spills in the saucer. There's nothing of course, only my bitter, inward imagination. I do not trust myself. Not at all.

I look around at my garden and my house as though for the last time. I watch a line of ants file through the coarse grass to and from their nest in the soft black sandy soil. The bulbuls are squabbling in the trees and singing their pleasant, piping song. I know that soon I will give up these peaceful surroundings and all my unmerited comforts. This thing has run its course, the interlude is over. My novel is finished, the manuscript is with Alan in London. I shall hear from him any day now. Regardless of his verdict it will be time to return to my real life. I shall leave Léopoldville and the Congo. I shall say goodbye to Stipe and to Roger and to Madeleine. Helping Auguste will be my last act here. There is no life to be had with Inès. I can delude myself no longer. It is time to go.

Charles, the houseboy, opens the gate and wheels his bicycle into the drive. He hails me solemnly with his habitual *nókó*, which I have long since given up trying to discourage. Who was I kidding anyway? I am his *nókó* and Charles is comfortable with boundaries that are known. So am I.

'*Káwa, nókó?*'

'Yes, more coffee, please, Charles,' I reply.

He claims to speak almost no French. I have been forced to improve my Lingala.

He props his bicycle against the wall and goes inside. Ten minutes later he reappears with a tray. His hair is steel grey and receding. His face is unlined, his arms rangy and thick-veined. I once asked him his age but he treated the query as too personal even to acknowledge. He is a private and unsmiling man who has a habit of not hearing my questions, or not understanding them. I think he may be illiterate. The notes I leave for him go disregarded. He could be sixty, he could be forty. He never looks me in the eye and I never escape the feeling he doesn't like me.

'I have to go out today,' I explain as he sets the tray down for me. 'I don't know what time I'll be back. Late, I expect. There is a friend of mine staying here. She's not well.'

'*Maláli?*'

'Malaria. I am going to arrange for the English doctor to come and see her, but I would like you to stay with her until I return. Will you do that?'

'*Íyo, nókó.*'

By the time I have finished my fresh coffee I decide the hour is reasonable enough to phone Roger. He says he will come over before midday.

'Roger,' I say hesitantly, 'if you should be talking to Stipe, I wonder if you wouldn't mind keeping this to yourself.'

There is a pause at the other end of the line. I hate putting him in this position. A decent man like Roger doesn't deserve to be caught up in the troubles of others.

'I rarely see Stipe,' he says at last.

I finish dressing. I sit on the bed and look at Inès. The fever will break soon. She will wake, weak and wracked. Roger will take care of her.

Charles goes to open the gates. I look over the grass and ask him to cut it before the rain comes this afternoon. He nods automatically; his expression is blank, as always, his eyes turned away. I hesitate before getting into the car. I have never talked about the political situation with Charles and I have no idea where his sympathies lie. He is Bakongo and probably a supporter of Kasavubu. The former president has been in exile since Mobutu's coup, but relations between the two men are said to be good and there are rumours that Kasavubu will be returning soon to join Mobutu's regime. Would Charles know who Inès is? Would he know she is a confidante of Lumumba's? If he is a supporter of Kasavubu is it safe to leave him with her?

'Did you hear about the shooting at the Ghanaian embassy last night?' I ask, thinking to draw him out. 'Mobutu wanted the ambassador out of the country because he was a friend of Lumumba's.'

Charles shakes his head. '*Tĕ, nókó.*'

He hasn't, so he claims. This is unlikely. Word would have spread all over the city by now.

'Yes,' I continue, 'the Ghanaian guards killed an ANC colonel.'

He affects no interest whatsoever.

'Perhaps things will be more settled now that Mobutu's in charge,' I say in a final gambit.

'*Mbele.*'

Yes, perhaps. I give up. He will not say anything on this.

'My friend is too ill to see anyone,' I say. 'Don't let anybody into the house apart from the English doctor. I'll be home as soon as I can.'

'*Íyo, patron.*'

I search his face for hints of secret calculations, for the possibility of betrayal. Am I doing the right thing? The sky is low and whitish-grey. The sun will not appear today and there will be a thunderstorm later. I get into my car, a Mercedes no less. I picked it up at the public docks the night de Scheut and his children fled. A hysterical engineer who had driven five hundred miles from Coquilhatville, stopping only for fuel, arrived with his wife and four daughters, sleepless and hungry and in a state of high distraction, expecting at any moment to be set upon and torn limb from limb. The engineer, wild-eyed and trembling, insisted on selling me his car after discovering there was no room on the ferry. I did not want his car and even if I had sold everything I owned in the Congo I had nothing like what it was worth. The man pleaded. He had left everything behind, he needed all the money he could lay his hands on. He needed it at once. Bemused porters looked on. One of the market women offered a basketful of *capitaines* and catfish. The engineer cursed her and she went away chortling. He would accept whatever I could give him on the spot, for the last thing he wanted was for these black bastards and rapists to have his precious Mercedes. Roger and I emptied our pockets and came up with 3,200 francs.

I start the engine and drive out to the street. There is no sign of the Citroen, no sign of anyone taking an undue interest in me or my comings and goings. I wave at Charles as I go. As usual he pretends not to see me. It's easier that way, I suppose. It saves embarrassment for both of us.

I drive past the Primature. Both sets of troops have settled into the rhythm of their standoff. They look forward to another boring day. How will Lumumba escape? Are his supporters planning an assault? They might take on the ANC soldiers, but would they fire on the UN troops? I think of the fiasco at the embassy, of the dead colonel and the whimpering of the wounded soldier. Is there to be more blood? A little further on I pass a small throng of people gathered at the roadside. They are inspecting a new corpse. What am I getting in to?

4

THE VILLAGERS ARE about to scatter when I pull up in the car, but Auguste, after a momentary look of alarm, gives me a terse nod of acknowledgement and they gradually settle down again. I stand at the edge of the clearing while he resumes his talk. Squatting outside one of the mud huts, he speaks in Lingala, without eye contact with his listeners. His speech is unemphatic and punctuated by long silences during which people look vaguely at the ground or the sky or the trees. Occasionally he takes a spoonful of rice and beans from a tin plate at his feet. He chews the food with great deliberation and follows each mouthful with a sip from a Coca-Cola bottle. Whatever I have come to say he seems in no hurry to hear it, though he must know my presence here portends something out of the ordinary. There is never any urgency in the tropics. I know that now. *Du calme, du calme.* Always. There is resignation and withdrawal. There is watchfulness. Sometimes there is a kind of faintly optimistic indolence. There is never exigency, never emergency. Even when lives are at stake. A black hen with a single yellow chick in tow pecks at the earth around my car. The day is hot and humid and brooding; we will soon be in Léopoldville's worst season.

A listless hour passes before Auguste gets slowly to his feet and comes over to me, and for the first time there is no smile, no craven, clownish grin. His gaze is level and self-assured. I have never seen him like this. Even his clothes are sober now. He wears a simple white shirt with short sleeves and an open collar. It hangs loose outside dark grey slacks. The jewellery is gone.

'It is good to see you again, James,' he says in English. 'Are you well?'

The voice, like the gaze, is confident. The people, gathering at his back, murmur among themselves and gaze at me without expression.

I tell him I am well enough, and I tell him that Inès is at my house, ill with malaria. I tell him why I am here. He nods slowly, taking in my news. There is no indication of panic or fear, nor is there any sign of discomfort at being face to face with the man whose lover he has taken. I look him over. He's about the same height as me, perhaps an inch shorter, but he's younger and leaner; there is not an ounce of spare flesh. His back is straight and his shoulders strong. He is muscle and bone, the perfect mesomorph. His skin is perfect too. I look for flaws to make me feel better, and can fine none: he is, I see for the first time, a beautiful young man. How shabby I feel. How jaded and bitter. I take a deep breath. I must do what I am here to do. I tell him that Inès is afraid Smail will be tortured and will give away his hiding place. I tell him he can stay in my house until the Egyptian plane arrives.

Auguste looks into my eyes. Is he asking himself if he can trust me? He waits a long time before saying anything; then, simply, 'I will get our things.'

Our things.

Watched by the silent villagers, we walk together to the car and drive the rest of the way along the dirt road. I see Harry tending a little garden of beans to one side of the shack. He looks over at us as we pull up, mutters something to Auguste, ignores me, and goes back to his labours. I climb the steps to the crude verandah – constructed, it seems, from broken-up wooden pallets of the kind that litter the docks and warehouses in Leo – and enter the diamond smuggler's stuffy, grubby two-roomed hut.

A narrow iron cot dominates the bedroom at the back

and I realize that Inès has been living here with Auguste. This is the bed they have shared. Her things – *their* things – are scattered about. Her suitcase, her typewriter, some old clothes, a few books and pamphlets. I look over the titles – *The Origin of the Family, Private Property and the State; Anti-Dühring; The Part Played by Labour in the Transition from Ape to Man:* Engels was always a great favourite, more readable than Marx, she used to say. There is an edition of Gramsci's prison letters and, on a rough box by the side of the bed, a history of the Communist Party of Italy under fascism. Auguste puts the suitcase on the bed and starts to gather up their possessions. He lifts from a chair a dress of heavy silk, dusty pink – Inès's favourite, the one she kept for the few occasions when she had to look smart. I almost shout get your hands off that. I bought her that. Me! You know nothing of it, you have no right to touch it . . . but he doesn't hear the thunder I want to strike him down with, doesn't see the fury in my eyes. He lays the dress on the bed, slowly, carefully, lovingly, and smoothes it with his gentle, fine hands. Black on pink. He seems lost in a memory, recalling her and the feel of her through the material. I can't bear that he has the right to touch it – and so casually, as though they had been together always, as though I were the stranger. I have to turn away. I remember the day I bought the dress. I remember it very well. I had been up to see Alan in Highgate and was on my way home when I passed a second-hand shop in Camden. There in the window was the tailor's dummy on which the dress was draped. I am not good at buying clothes – I have no eye for it – but I knew at once it was for her. I bought it and took it home. She gabbled away as she put it on. She said she could never get away with a dress like this, but she was terribly excited. And when she stood in front of the mirror and saw the colour, the fit and the cut – saw that everything was perfect – she became suddenly quiet, and I did too. Something changed in the room and made everything there was between us yet more intimate, more intense. When she turned to me there were tears in her eyes. 'It's a dress, just a dress,' I said as she hugged me. She sobbed against my chest and I forced out some weak laughter and made poor jokes. But the truth is my own eyes were moist. A dress, a simple dress. It had made her so happy. Why hadn't I bought her a hundred? A thousand? What does Auguste know of this? Nothing. I look again at the bed. What things did he do here to Inès? How well did he do them?

'Are you all right, James?'

I hardly hear him.

'James?'

He is looking at me but he doesn't see. I fight down the urge to tell him he can go to hell, that he can escape without my help. To cover my emotions I pick up the history of the Communist Party of Italy from the makeshift bedside table and go to where it is bookmarked. The paper is cheap and thin and spotted with brown. It smells musty, faintly like geraniums. She has underlined a passage. I was always horrified by her habit of scribbling on the pages of what she was reading, but she insisted books were not ornaments and that broken spines, torn dust jackets and annotations were proof the author's work had been appreciated. I read the lines she has singled out for attention. It is a quotation from someone called Eugenio Curiel, a party member: '*The major effect of fascism in Italy is infinite scepticism, which kills all possible faith in any ideal, which derides the sacrifice of the individual for the sake of the welfare of the community. This is, at bottom, the most conspicuous conquest made by fascism and will remain its bitterest legacy.*' Inès's bed-time reading.

'I suppose we should take these,' I say, indicating the books.

'Yes,' he says, 'Inès will want them when we get to Stanleyville.'

'Is she definitely going to Stanleyville?' I ask with studied casualness as I gather the books and pamphlets together.

She had told me she didn't know if she would go. Was that just a ploy to get me to help her? Or do I know something Auguste doesn't?

'Yes. Inès will come to Stanleyville. It will be safer there.'

'Will it?' I ask harshly. 'I mean, I know it will be safe for you, but is it going to be safe for Inès?'

'I did not say it would be safe, James,' he replies calmly, 'only that it would be safer than here. In Stanleyville Patrice will reorganize the movement to fight back against Mobutu and the military dictatorship.'

'I asked if it would be safe for Inès,' I shout at him. 'I don't care about anything else.' I gather up a handful of Inès's clothes and throw them angrily into the suitcase. 'I don't care about Patrice or Mobutu or any of them, and frankly I don't care about you. This whole thing is a mess and it will be a mess whichever incompetent, vicious lot of you takes power.'

I drop the books on top of the clothes in the case. Auguste, standing still on the other side of the bed, regards me quietly. His affected calmness enrages me still more.

'Who do you think you're kidding, Auguste? You're no revolutionary. Six months ago you were proud to be a member of the Association of the African Middle Classes. Remember? Remember you were going to be a lawyer on Park Avenue? Remember you were going to have an office full of pretty secretaries? You can try your man-of-the-people act on with simple villagers, Auguste, but, please, not with me.'

He looks at me without responding.

I gather up the rest of Inès's things. I am cursing her inside my head. What right had she to ask me to help the man who has replaced me? Auguste is now in mortal danger but that has nothing to do with me. It is her responsibility. She put him in this position. She is the one who convinced him that the world was a place where anything was possible if you ignored the rules they made for you, if you were brave enough to disregard the boundaries. But boundaries exist, Inès, boundaries exist. Lines on maps, lines between peoples, between individuals and men and women, between colour and class and profession and belief. They are there, even in the skies. You can negotiate them, one by one, you may cross them on occasion, but you cannot behave as if they don't exist. It is your fault that Auguste is in danger. You convinced him that there were no boundaries except those the Belgians had placed in his imagination. And because of your fault all my faults are exposed. All my pettinesses and jealousies. This isn't fair, Inès.

I grab the typewriter, leaving him to bring the suitcase in which their clothes are mingled.

'Let's go,' I say, 'before the soldiers get here.'

I walk out to the rickety verandah. There, before the house, the entire village seems to have congregated. Harry works his little garden as though nothing out of the ordinary were happening. He keeps his head down, ignoring the crowd, ignoring me. What an infinite capacity people have for overlooking what they do not want to be part of, even when it is going on outside their own house. Auguste appears behind me and a murmur goes up from the villagers. A woman in an electric-blue *pagne* with a design of golden telephones holds up a baby as though for Auguste's blessing. As we descend the villagers throng round us, reaching out to touch Auguste's face, his hair, his back. He puts down the case and they take hold of his hands. He stands among them like a prophet among the faithful, his eyes calm and vatic and kind. A girl with short hair and a necklace of small blue and white stones stands before him and smiles bashfully.

'Maybe she can be one of the secretaries in your Park Avenue office.'

He gives me a brief glance. There is an infuriating forgiveness in his gaze.

'Come on,' I say, bored with this, and irritated. 'Tell the true believers your girlfriend's waiting.'

Still he makes no move to hurry. What has he said, what has he done that these people should treat him this way? What has prompted this devotion? It is a long and slow leave-taking. The villagers press close as he gets into the car beside me. Hands come in the window for a last touch of their seer. I start the engine.

'What did you tell them?' I ask maliciously as we pull away, 'that their dead relatives would rise from the grave when Lumumba was back in power? That they'd find Belgian money growing in their fields?'

He gazes back at the villagers. They are waving farewell.

'The people thought you were *mundele ya mwinda*,' he says when we have left the shack and the village behind.

'What's that?'

'It's what the old people used to call the Belgians. The white man with a light.'

'Why did they call them that?'

'When the Belgians came to the villages, the men would hide in the forests. So the Belgians would round up the women and children as hostages and rape the girls and threaten to kill them all unless the men returned. When the men came back the Belgians took them away to work on the rubber plantations and the railways. They worked with steel rings around their necks with chains linking one to another. They were whipped and beaten. They had their hands cut off as punishments for not producing enough rubber or ivory. So the next time the Belgians came to the villages, all the people – whole clans and tribes – would flee into the forest to escape

239

the mutilations and rapes. Then the Belgians sent the police into the forests at night with powerful torches and so the people called them *mundele ya mwinda*. White man with a light. Many people thought the whites were demons with magic lanterns.'

The rain has started. It beats down on the windscreen and drums on the roof.

Auguste continues, 'I was telling the people that the whites are not our enemies.'

'Do you really believe that?' I ask.

'There are many who are,' he replies, 'but you are not one of them.'

'I'm neither a friend nor an enemy,' I say.

'If you are not a friend of the people, why are you helping?'

'It has nothing to do with sympathy for you or Lumumba or the MNC,' I reply bitterly.

'Inès says you are not really so detached.'

'That just proves you can live with someone for years and never really know them.'

'Perhaps you cannot see what your real motives are.'

'Oh, I've always had a good view of my motives, Auguste. But I think perhaps you're in the dark about your own.'

'You think it is wrong to want justice and equality?'

'Those aren't motives – just words, and rather over-used ones at that.'

'I disagree.'

'They're not words that motivate me – or anyone else I know.'

'They motivate the people I know.'

'Obviously we move in different circles.'

We drive on towards town through the torrential rain.

'There's a roadblock about a kilometre from here,' I say to Auguste. 'It would be best if you hide in the back.'

As he climbs into the boot and waits for me to close it we realize we are thinking the same thing.

'Have you any idea how I feel about you?' I say.

He flickers.

'Have you thought even for one second what seeing you does to me?'

He hasn't. It never occurred to him to spare a thought for me. One of love's privileges is to excuse the lover from the normal, everyday duties and responses. We allow the newly in love certain dispensations. We condone, at least for a time, their self-centredness. But that doesn't make this thoughtlessness any easier to bear. I look down at him. We both know he is entirely in my power. I could deliver him to the soldiers at the roadblock. Or to Stipe. I could make up a story for Inès. I could be rid of my rival for ever. I slam the boot shut. We both know I could do this. We both know I won't. I know my motives better than he. They drive me in one direction. He is safer with me than he can imagine.

5

Passing the Regina it occurs to me to make a precautionary telephone call. I park the car on Avenue Moulaert and shout back to Auguste, still hiding in the boot, that I will be five minutes. The storm has passed and the rain has eased a little, but it's still heavy. I leave the car and make a dash for the hotel. Inside I see Grant talking to George, the UN Secretary General's press officer. They shout their hellos and ask if I will join them for a drink. I make my excuses and go straight to the public telephones. I dial my own number. There is no sense in being amateurish about this, there is too much at stake. The phone rings twice.

'Hello?'

It is Roger.

'It's me. Is everything all right?'

'Ah, James. I'm glad you've called. I'm afraid there's been a little activity. You've had some callers.'

My heart thumps in my chest.

'Yes?'

'Military.'

'I see,' I say, my voice uncertain. 'Is everything all right?'

'I think so.'

'Did they say what they wanted?'

'Not in so many words, but they were rather keen to come in.'

'Is Inès all right?'

'Oh, yes,' he says brightly. 'Don't worry. I sent them packing. Told them not to come back unless it was with a warrant.'

I laugh with relief. I can imagine the scene: Roger facing down an armed body of ANC soldiers with nothing more than the unshakeable conviction of the English middle classes that officialdom must always act legally and correctly. It wouldn't have surprised me to hear he had cited Magna Carta in support of his refusal to allow the soldiers entry.

'However,' he continues, 'I think it's probably not a good idea for Inès to stay here much longer. I have the feeling they may be back.'

'Is she fit to travel?'

'A short distance only. She's a little better, but still quite weak.'

I fall silent, trying to work out a solution to this latest complication. I am not sure how much I can ask of Roger.

Before I can say anything he speaks again, 'I can take her to my house, if you'd like. The coast seems clear now.'

Relief and gratitude flood into my voice as I thank him. But then I think of the possibility that they might raid Roger's house now they've seen him at mine. Nor do I feel comfortable about asking him to shelter Auguste as well. I am sweating heavily in spite of the hotel's air-conditioning. I glance around, trying to marshal my thoughts. Grant and George are having their drink at a white table near the swimming pool. I feel terribly tired and sticky. My feet are hot and swollen. I wish I could take off my shoes and all my clothes and dive into the pool. I wish I could float face-up with my eyes closed and my ears below the surface. I wish I could lie down. I think of Madeleine. It was here, by the poolside, she flirted with me, and I with her.

'James? Are you there?'

Madeleine. The solution comes to me.

'Yes – yes, I'm still here. I've thought of something.'

I give him the address of Houthhoofd's house on Eugene Henry.

'And Roger,' I add, 'it's probably a good idea not to let anyone see that you have a passenger.'

He says he understands. He will put Inès in the back seat and cover her with a blanket.

On my way out I run into Stipe talking to two UN officials on the concourse. He seems different, cooler towards me, as though he knows something. I tell myself I'm being ridiculous, that of course he doesn't know, that he's often like this when he's 'working', that it's only my nervous imagination. But even when he asks about my foot there is a hardness in his tone. Just a scratch, I say, smiling too much. Nothing to worry about. As the officials move off I spot someone coming towards us.

'Isn't that Dr Joe from Paris?' I say, eager for an opportunity to divert him.

Stipe's face darkens and he signals to Dr Joe to wait a moment. The bizarre little man stops and tries to look inconspicuous.

'One of your shadier friends,' I say lightly.

'Just someone who's here to do a job,' he says.

'What job would that be?'

Stipe looks at me with small, hard eyes.

'You wouldn't be trying to fuck me, James, would you?'

'What?' I say, shocked by the question and the tone.

He stares at me.

'It's just that there are rumours,' he continues.

'What rumours?'

'Certain MNC sympathizers and people who have been under surveillance have dropped out of sight. They've left their houses, their jobs. Other people have been overheard on the phones taking care what they say, obviously talking in code. Something's going on.'

'You'll tip me off, won't you, whatever it is?' I josh matily. 'You know I don't like to miss out on stories. It makes the paper think I'm not doing my job.'

He looks at me like a parent who suspects his child of lying, but – short of a full confession – cannot prove it. I know all I have to do is keep my mouth shut, but part of me is desperate to confess.

'I know as a matter of principle you don't like to get involved,' he says. 'This isn't the time to change the habit of a lifetime.'

'You've lost me, I'm afraid.'

'Have I?'

'Very much,' I say, struggling to maintain my act.

His mouth tightens. 'I hope so,' he says. 'I really do. I won't bullshit you. Inès is in a lot of trouble.'

I don't have to act. I can feel the blood drain from my face. I am like a drunk fighting to keep upright, concentrating on keeping the contents of my stomach where they are.

'If she comes to you—'

'I'd be the last person she'd come to,' I put in quickly.

Perhaps too quickly. He stares at me bleakly.

'If she comes to you,' he repeats slowly, 'you can do her a big favour.'

'What would that be?' I ask.

'You can tell me where she is.'

'Why would that be doing her a favour?'

'Because I'd try to keep her alive.'

I let out a nervous little laugh.

'This is all suddenly terribly melodramatic,' I say as lightly as I can.

He glares at me.

'You find the idea of Inès ending up in a torture cell in the Central Prison amusing?'

'Would they do that to a foreign journalist? Would they torture a white woman?'

Stipe snorts, amazed by my naïveté. He looks me up and down.

'You really don't know where Inès is? You're telling me the truth?'

'I'm telling you the truth.'

'Call me if she tries to get in touch. I can help her. I can help you too, because if she drags you into this you're going to need help.'

He nods to Dr Joe who scuttles over. The little man's chin is coarse with blond-brown stubble. There is an odour about him like bad eggs. He avoids looking me in the eye.

'Let's have a drink soon,' Stipe says.

He and Dr Joe leave together. I follow after them. The rain has stopped. I watch as they walk past my Mercedes to their own car.

I am trembling as I get in behind the wheel. I do not immediately start the engine. I sit and think about Stipe's offer of help. Was he being truthful with me? Would he help Inès? And if he did, what would be the price? The total price? Surrendering Auguste might be a down payment only. He might want more from Inès and she would give nothing. I see Stipe's Chevrolet make a right turn, heading down to Boulevard Albert I. I think about driving after him, stopping him and confessing everything. I watch as the car stops at the bottom of the street, indicates left, waits for a space, pulls out and disappears.

'Are you okay?' I ask Auguste.

There is an answering murmur from the boot. I turn on the engine and put the car in gear.

I close the gates behind us and – leaving Auguste locked in the boot, which gives me a malicious little thrill – walk to the back of the house where the windows of the washroom are not shuttered. I lift a stone from the garden, check to make sure I am unobserved, then break the glass.

I am coming out the front door when I hear a car pull up in the street. I hurry to re-open the gates and let Roger through. Together we help Inès into the house. The fever has broken but she is exhausted. We take her to the main bedroom and set her in a chair while I prepare the bed in which Madeleine and I have spent many afternoons and nights.

'Auguste?' Inès says in a whisper.

'Don't worry,' I tell her, 'Auguste's safe. Everything's going to be all right.'

I ask Roger if he thinks they were followed.

'Not as far as I could tell,' he says, looking around the room. 'Rather nice place.'

'It belongs to Bernard Houthhoofd,' I say.

Roger raises an eyebrow.

'Don't worry. They'll never think to come here. Houthhoofd's in Katanga and there's only one other person who uses the house.'

'What if he shows up?'

'She won't. I'll make certain of it.'

I leave Roger to tend to Inès and go to the Mercedes. Auguste stretches and rubs his shoulder when I let him out of the boot. I give him the suitcase and I take the typewriter. As we enter the house he asks about Inès.

'She's in there,' I say sourly as Roger comes out of the bedroom.

Auguste goes to her.

Roger, a little embarrassed in a situation the like of which I feel certain he has never encountered before, says matter-of-factly, 'By the way, I hope you don't mind, but I let the houseboy go for the day. He kept on about having to cut the grass, but I wasn't sure it was a good idea to have him around, what with the military and so forth.'

'No, indeed.'

'Well, I think I should be on my way,' he says, glancing at his watch. 'I'm playing tennis with one of the UN chaps. American. Terribly decent fellow. Might have dinner at the Zoo if we can get in.'

'I don't know how to thank you,' I say.

'Think nothing of it,' he says quickly, as though to stave off an embarrassing display on my part.

He checks his bag and pats his pockets for his keys.

'I didn't have a vote, of course,' he says on his way out, 'but if I had, I would never have voted for Lumumba. Not likely. Rather too headstrong for my tastes. But the point is he won the election and I know we're all supposed to be grateful to this Mobutu chap for restoring order, but there is actually a principle here.'

'Yes, indeed,' I say, though I am not too clear about what principle Roger has in mind.

'Dictators always arrive with excuses,' he continues. 'Mussolini had his and so did Hitler and so did Franco. But the fact is one shouldn't have any truck with them. It's quite wrong.'

'Yes,' I say.

I find myself absurdly moved by Roger's simple precepts, particularly because there are risks he does not seem aware of. I give him a brief version of what Stipe told me in the Regina. He is blasé.

'Don't worry about me,' he says. 'I'm a personal friend of the ambassador. If they try any monkey business with me they'll soon find out who they're dealing with. Same goes for you. You're a British citizen.'

His insouciance is infectious. I feel suddenly as though a great weight has been lifted. Confidence sweeps over me. I can see Stipe's threats in perspective. We will come through this. I extend my hand and when he puts his in mine I squeeze it with emotion, grateful not just for his practical help but for the lift he has given my spirits. None of this seems to register with him. He appears utterly oblivious both of the gratitude and the feeling behind my gesture. He says only that he has left some more chloroquine for Inès on the bedside table. I go out to open the gate for him. He gives me a polite little nod as he drives off for his tennis game and his apéritif and his dinner. When he is gone I feel as though I have lost a trusted friend.

I walk to the bedroom door. Inside I see Auguste on his knees by the side of the bed. He holds Inès's hand in his and whispers to her. She makes little sounds in response. He strokes her brow and I can stand it no more.

I go to the kitchen and fix myself a gin. It is only just after three, but I suddenly feel exhausted. I remember that I did not go to bed last night. I have not eaten all day. I will go home. I will have a shower, then call Madeleine. I will suggest she come to my house instead of meeting here as we usually do. She will agree to that. I have never allowed her into my house before. She will be curious; perhaps she will think the invitation presages some new development in our relationship. In any case she will come.

I hear a noise behind me. It is Auguste.

'You'll have to be as quiet as possible here,' I say. 'There are a few tins of stuff in the cupboards and there are beers in the fridge. I wouldn't turn on the lights. It might attract unwelcome attention. Better just to get an early night. I'll be back tomorrow evening to pick you up. What time should I get here?'

'Before eight,' he says. 'The plane will be at the airport at nine.'

I down the last of the drink.

'I ran into Stipe at the Regina,' I say.

Auguste's face betrays no reaction.

'He seems to have lost his sense of humour,' I continue. 'He was very serious.'

'Stipe was always very serious.'

'I used to find him more ironic.'

'I think you may have misread him, James. When things were going his way Stipe could afford to pretend he didn't take anything too seriously. But the moment things went against him and his interests, the real man showed himself. Don't feel bad that you misunderstood this. So did I.'

I rinse the glass and leave it on the draining board.

'He has been plotting to assassinate Patrice,' Auguste says.

I laugh. 'I think that's going a little too far – even for the new Stipe.'

'No distance is too far for the Americans in this. They have brought a scientist to Léopoldville. He is a poisoner.'

I laugh again. This is sounding like an overblown Jacobean revenge tragedy.

'They call him Dr Joe,' Auguste continues, 'but his name is Gottlieb. His mission is to kill Patrice with a special poison.'

At the mention of Dr Joe I straighten up.

'How do you know this?' I ask.

'The Americans are not the only spies in Léopoldville.'

It's too absurd. But I don't laugh. I think of the ridiculous looking little man scuttling about with Stipe. I know Stipe wants Lumumba off the scene for good. But would he go that far? A shiver runs down my spine. The sense of well-being brought on by Roger's words drains away. Stipe's threats ring in my ears and again I find myself thinking about going to him.

I take a last look at Inès. She rests more easily now. She gives me a wan smile when I sit on the bed.

'The plane tomorrow night is the last chance to get out of here,' she says in a small voice.

'I know,' I say.

'We're depending on you. If you don't come to pick us up, we have no chance.'

'Does that mean you're definitely going to Stanleyville as well?'

She does not say anything.

'I'll come,' I say when I know what the answer is. 'You can depend on me.'

There is so much more to say, and nothing to say at all.

Pulling up at my house, I beep on the horn before remembering Roger has sent Charles home. As I get out of the car to open the gates, two ANC jeeps come roaring up the road. I stop to watch them pass. But they don't pass. Instead they screech to a halt and a squad of soldiers, led by a captain, jump out and surround me. The captain is a stocky man with wide-spaced eyes and a flat face. His teeth are individual, discoloured stumps. They have been filed and filled with gold. He asks if I am James Gillespie. I say, rather haughtily, as though it's none of their business, that I am. He says that I am to come with them to the Central Prison for questioning. Thinking of Roger's example, I demand to see his warrant. The captain's reaction is immediate but at the same time unhurried, almost languid. He simply turns to the soldier next to him, takes his rifle and casually smashes the butt into the side of my head. What I feel first is not pain, but nausea, an overwhelming desire to vomit. It's a new experience for me – nausea not from the stomach but from the head. As I retch, I try to bend forward but the world is no longer ordered the way I know it to be. Sky and earth are moving, they are intent on changing places. The horizon jumps up to my face, then careers away again. My legs are giving way, I am sliding down. Blinking, I took up at the massed brains of the grey-white clouds above. They swirl around and I am sick again. I splutter and choke as the vomit settles back in my throat. It is not easy to breathe. The captain stoops over me. My eyes are not working as they should. He is in vision for a second, sways away, comes back into view. My head spins.

'Where is Auguste Kilundu?' he demands.

I hear him clearly. My ears are working at least.

'Where is Kilundu?'

I try to speak, but nothing comes. I am not sure what I want to say. To tell him I don't know where Auguste is or that I do. I concentrate on getting some words out. The effort causes a wave of nausea to rise. I shut my eyes. The next thing I feel is a blow to my stomach and suddenly my lungs are airless. I let out a groan and gasp to breathe. I feel a sharp pain in my temple. Someone may have kicked me in the head, but I cannot be sure. Panic grips me. I am thinking about brain damage and ruptured internal organs. I am worried they will go too far, that they will kill me before I get to the Central Prison. I want to shout out that I will tell them everything.

I feel myself being dragged to my feet. I think I may have pissed myself. The captain is laughing through his filed, peg teeth.

6

I LIE CURLED up, the side of my face pressed against the oily, ribbed metal of the jeep's floor. The captain, sitting with his feet at the small of my back, bellows and screams and every now and then he jabs a rifle butt into my side or kicks at me. The kicks are not hard. His boots are restricted by lack of space. I keep my eyes shut and pretend not to hear or feel. All I want is blackness. I want to embrace numbness, to fold into nothing. I want to trust in others. The ambassador. My editor. Alan. Stipe. Grant. George the UN press officer. Roger. Anyone. They will do things. I cannot do anything. I do not want to do anything. I just want to lie here wrapped in the cocoon of my pain. I do not want anything to change. If they change they will get worse. Better not to think. I do not even want to try to get my fear under control. The effort is too much. Easier just to give way, to let things take their course, to be led – even if it's to the torture chamber. To think is only to create in the present the terror of what is to come.

The captain leans forward and puts his mouth to my ear. He screams so loudly I cannot hear the words. He straightens up again, muttering something to his men in a tone of disgust, and – almost as an afterthought – slaps my ear with his open hand. He pulls up my left hand and yanks the watch from my wrist. Someone else is going through my pockets. The captain spits at me and I feel the tickle of his phlegm sliding down my neck. He kicks my arse. The blow causes my legs an involuntary jerk, and I feel the wetness. I *have* pissed myself.

The embarrassment of this. I don't want to be here, I don't want this to be happening. Let me go, please, it's nothing to do with me. If you call Stipe he will explain everything. He will tell you that I'm not a Lumumbist. I'm not on their side, I'm not on anyone's side. I see all sides. My craft demands it. I am against things, yes, I admit that. The things of intolerance and illiberalism. I am against dogma and certainty and ideology and all the things that close our options. I am against. I am not *for*. I am *for* nothing. I can't be. *Je suis un homme-plume.* I live for words, my life is in words. You must understand. Only words, and words cannot be for because they have already described everything. They know too much, they know where everything leads. They undercut, they expose, they stand apart, they refuse to be drawn in. They are not involved and I am not involved. Not in anything. *Je suis un homme-plume.*

The captain kicks me in the head.

It's useless. I know it. My justifications will not work. I must think. If I am to survive I must force myself to think.

The jeep jolts sharply. My head bangs on the metal. At least the nausea is subsiding. My senses are making an unsteady return. I run my swollen tongue over my teeth. I think they are all there. But there is blood, thick and salty and sweet tasting. I find the source, a gash on my lower lip and I suck at the blood. I suck hard because the hot liquid is me; I am taking myself in, I am reassuring myself, loving myself, reminding myself of me. I am real. My blood makes me real and worth preserving. I must think. I must work out a version of events to give them. The journey to the Central Prison will take fifteen to twenty minutes. Once I am in the interrogation cell there will be no time to concoct a story. I must come up with one now. Something plausible. I must use these precious, shuddering minutes.

What do they know? Start there. What do they know? Think. Think. Think. The black Citroen. The car that seemed to be following us last night when Roger gave me a lift home. Was that the Sûreté? Were they following us, keeping us under surveillance? If they were they may already know everything. They would know that Inès came to me after Roger dropped me off, that I drove to Harry's shack the next morning – this morning; ages have passed. They would know that I went to Houthhoofd's house, that Roger joined me there later with Inès. They would know that Auguste was there as well.

But they don't know. A triumph! Yes! They don't know where Auguste is. So they weren't following me, at least not all the time. Then why have they arrested me? Think. Think.

They're going on a hunch. It has to be that. They know about me and Inès and they know about Inès and Auguste. They are doing what investigators anywhere would do. They are bringing in a known associate of a wanted man for questioning. They have nothing specific against me.

Confidence starts a slow infiltration into my head. Perhaps this situation is not as impossible as it seems. I can deny everything, including the most compromising fact of all, the thing that started this: I can deny that Inès was ever in my house. There is a blow to my knee. They are all kicking at me now, front and back, and they are spitting. There are gobs in my eyes and nose and chin and hair. It's all right. It doesn't matter. I can handle this. I'm in the clear. I can deny everything.

I can deny everything.

Yes.

Absolutely everything . . .

Charles.

Oh no. Please no.

Charles.

Think.

The houseboy will tell them everything. Why would he not? He has no loyalty to me. I inherited him. He came with the house. Part of the goods and chattels. I kept him on. I tried at least to be a reasonable employer, paying slightly over the going rate, being flexible about his hours, but he rebuffed all my attempts to get any closer. He doesn't like me. Why would he not tell them about Inès? He is Bakongo, and they are no lovers of Lumumba. He has probably already told them. There was a white woman in the *nókó's* bed when I arrived for work this morning. A small white woman who was sick. The *nókó* told me not to let anyone in to see her except the English doctor.

They will guess the woman's identity immediately.

What does this mean for me?

Nothing good, nothing good.

It's hopeless, it's useless, hopeless.

The English doctor.

It's getting worse. They will go to Roger. Why did I involve him? Accomplices always betray. How long will Roger's high principles hold out? Not long. Roger is a law-abiding man, and these people will soon convince him that they are now the law. He may make a protest, he may deliver an indignant lecture, but the protest will be small, the lecture brief, they will be for form's sake. Then he will tell them.

I can still deny it.

Why not?

His word against mine.

What if they search the house and find something of hers? Is there anything of hers to find? A piece of clothing perhaps. All right, so there's a piece of woman's clothing, but that doesn't mean it belongs to Inès. Or that she left it there last night. They won't believe me.

We must be near the prison now. A minute or two away.

They won't believe me. I was wrong to start thinking. Why didn't I stay in my womb of pain and bruises?

Time is running out. I have to get my story straight.

I make my decision. I shall deny Inès was ever in the house. I will say I haven't seen her since – when was the last time? Independence day. I saw her in the Palais de la Nation on independence day. June 30th. On the press benches. Almost five months ago.

And Auguste?

I have not seen Auguste either, not for many months. I certainly would not help him, in any way. I can use his theft of Inès from me to give this statement extra weight – I will keep this in reserve. A trump card; I will not play it too soon. As men they will understand. Why would I help the man who cuckolded me?

What else? I must work through the corollaries of my denials.

I saw Roger last night but only because I picked up a slight wound in the shooting outside the Ghanaian ambassador's residence. I have not talked to him since. Whatever he says. Keep it simple.

My movements this morning?

Where can I say I have been? I cannot risk giving them the name of a third party. The lie would be too easily exposed.

I went for a drive.

I went for a drive to look for 'colour' for an article. I am a journalist. Yes, a drive around Leo. An observer. A watcher. Collecting details for an article. No. This sounds too much like spying. And if you are a spy you are a Belgian and if you are a Belgian you are a para. Colour for a novel. *Je suis un homme-plume*. Nothing more, nothing more.

The jeep judders as though passing over a ramp. We are arrived. I cannot stop myself from trembling. We come to a halt. I hear the sound of a heavy gate closing behind us. The soldiers' boots hit the concrete. At least I have got my story straight. It has the advantage of being a simple series of denials; it has the disadvantage of being untrue.

The soldiers grab me and haul me out of the jeep.

We are in some kind of courtyard. To one side is the perimeter wall and main gate, to the other a low grey concrete block. Three men in shabby uniforms lounge by the block's entrance, a rust-coloured steel door. They regard me with little more than mild interest, though they cannot have seen many white men in here. I may even be the first. Then I remember that Smail has been arrested. He may still be here.

The captain shoves me from behind and the soldiers frog-march me towards the block. One of the shabby guards unlocks the steel door. He shares a joke with his friends as I pass inside.

I have the impression the captain may be insane. In the dark tunnels below the prison he screams and laughs hysterically. I do not think he is putting on an act. The two soldiers who have continued with us are quiet now and I notice they avoid his eyes. He jabbers sometimes, as though to himself, rapid, disconnected speech.

At the end of a long, gloomy passage, we come to a barred gate beside which a man in drab and dirty civilian clothes sits at a desk. Before him is a large book, like a hotel register. The captain pushes me forward and I flop against the gate. The two soldiers pull me roughly up and push me back against the wall. The captain commands the man in civilian clothes to open up. There is an exchange in Lingala. I understand enough to know that the civilian is asking for the prisoner's details – name, age, nationality, suspected offence. The captain shouts angrily. The civilian insists. He also seems to want the captain's signature. This the captain refuses to give and he starts to rant. The civilian, in a reasonable tone, tries to interrupt, but nothing can stop the captain. He goes on and on.

I use the distraction to review my story. Deny everything. Inès did not come to the house. I have not seen Auguste. I don't know where he is hiding.

There is a flaw. There is a terrible flaw in my calculations.

Auguste and Inès are at Houthhoofd's house. What if Madeleine should go there tonight? What if she brings another lover to the bed in which Inès and Auguste now lie? My plan had been to divert her, but now I cannot. She will want to go to the house. She will call me and when she can't get me she will call another. She will open the door and realize immediately something is wrong. Her senses are sharp. She knows smells. She will smell another presence, she will smell a woman, she will smell the malaria. She will sniff out the *macaque*. She might confront them. She may even be armed. Madeleine often carries a gun. She knows how to use it.

Everything is lost. I was right. This is hopeless. I should never have brought Auguste to Houthhoofd's house. What was I thinking of? I thought I was being clever but I've led myself into a trap.

The captain continues his rant. The civilian remains impassive and unimpressed.

I drop my head. I bend over and put my hands on my knees to rest. I feel depression and despair close on me. My legs are weak. My head is dizzy. And then – with the sudden blinding clarity of religious revelation – I understand that I am protected. They can do nothing to me. I feel the despair lift in an instant. I have more protection than any ambassador, any editor, friend or politician, can provide. My knowledge is my protection. I don't have to undergo torture, I don't have to die. I don't even have to be here. I can tell them what I know. Why should I help Auguste? I hate him. There are times when I could have killed him myself. I ask myself could I live with the knowledge that I had betrayed Auguste? I picture myself in London, in my flat, ten years from now, twenty. Would I sleep at night? Would I be tormented by feelings of guilt? Would I look inside myself and see only blackness and weakness and selfishness and hate? And I know the answer. Inwardly I'm already apologizing to Inès. It's not difficult. I have let so many people down over the years that I carry my apologies with me always. Still, part of me means it this time. I am sorry, Inès, for all that I've done, for all that I am about to do.

The captain, still by the desk with the civilian, looks over at me and shouts something, a command, a threat. The soldiers haul me up and shove me back against the wall. I must stand, not slouch, the captain commands. I ignore him. I am not afraid. I must talk to Stipe. Telling the captain will guarantee me nothing. I shout out that I want to talk to Mark Stipe at the American embassy. I shout out two telephone numbers and repeat the name – Mark Stipe, Mark Stipe.

The captain screams at me to be quiet.

I take a breath and go on. I want to talk to Mark Stipe at the American embassy. He is a friend of Mobutu. He is a friend of mine. He will want to know I am here and he will want to talk to me. I have important information for Mark Stipe. Only for Mark Stipe.

The captain strides over to me. He slaps me hard across the mouth, grabs my hair and bangs my head against the wall. With his other hand he pins me by the throat and screams into my face. I am fascinated by his teeth. I understand nothing of what he is saying.

He turns quickly and marches back to the desk. The civilian says something, the captain sweeps the register from the desk to the floor and glares at him. The civilian slowly pulls open a drawer and removes a bunch of keys. He pushes back his chair – careful to show he is in no great hurry – and gets up to open the gate. The captain says something sarcastic, then beckons his soldiers.

We pass into a corridor with solid cell doors on either side. Is Smail here? The place smells faecal. There are stains on the concrete walls. At the far end, on the left-hand side, is an open door. They push me forward. I have never in my life been locked up. I do not want to go inside.

'I want to speak to Mark Stipe,' I say quickly, doing my best to keep my voice intact. 'Together we can help you. We can help you find Auguste.'

All this succeeds in doing is to provoke more screams from the captain, and his screams set off someone else's. The whole place erupts. The mad howling from the cells sends shivers down my spine.

I must not admit that I know where Auguste is for then the captain would decide to beat it out of me. I must tantalize him. I must make him understand that he will only get what he wants in the presence of Stipe.

'Look,' I say as we near the open cell, 'I know you want to find Auguste and I want to help you, but I have to talk to Stipe.'

For the first time the captain does not respond with screams and threats. We are at the cell's threshold. I glance inside. I must at all costs prevent the door from closing behind me.

'Look,' I say reasonably, sensing headway, 'there's been a bit of a misunderstanding, but if you bring Stipe here I'm sure we can clear it up in no time and then we can all go home.'

Still no screaming. Even the howling from the cells has subsided. There is complete silence. The captain looks at me

261

with his wide-spaced eyes. His mouth hangs open slightly, like a punch-drunk boxer. Then he starts to chuckle. It is not a pleasant sound.

He says in French, 'You lied to the American. Stipe is not your friend any more.'

'You're wrong. Stipe is my friend, my very good friend. He will want to know that I am here. He will want to come to see me.'

The captain's chuckle lengthens into a weird, thin laugh. The two soldiers glance at each other. They want to be out of here.

The captain says, 'Stipe already knows you are here, and he doesn't want to see you.'

He puts a hand square on my chest and shoves me inside. The door bangs shut and I am alone in the pitch black.

I put out my hands. I bump into a wall. I turn, put my palms and back flat against the concrete and slide to rest on my hunkers. There is the smell of urine. I can see nothing. I might easily be sitting in a puddle of piss. I put a hand down. The floor seems dry. The smell is revolting. Then I realize I am the source. I pinch the inside of my trouser leg and tug away the material. The skin feels prickly and irritated. I need to see. Perhaps there is a light. Gingerly I get up – pain is taking hold everywhere, in my legs, my sides, my chest, my stomach, my head – and like a blind man I run my hands over the four walls. There is no switch I can find. I slide to the floor again.

Stipe. Was the captain lying? Surely he was. I think of all the times Stipe and I spent together. We shared so much. From the very start he showed the solid marks of friendship. We talked about books and writers and irony and women. He told me about Rita, his college sweetheart. He told me about Rita, the wife who no longer loves him. I told him about Inès and her childlessness. We shared meals and drinks. We went places together. He gave me material and I wrote articles. Last night he saved my life. We were friends. We are friends.

I understand. It's the same as it was with Auguste. Stipe is a generous friend. He is in his own way a needy man. He is strong, he is powerful, he knows what he wants, but he needs to be liked. He gives – perhaps with a little ostentation, but generously – and he asks nothing in return except the loyalty due to a good friend. First Auguste betrayed him. Then me. Of course he is bitter, of course he is angry. Only a few hours ago in the Regina he told me he could help me if I told him first. I did not tell him. I fucked him. Now he is fucking me.

I stretch out on the floor. I don't care what I am lying on. I don't know what might crawl over me. I don't care about anything.

7

I MUST HAVE fallen asleep. I don't know how. The floor is hard and every part of my body aches and my mind has never known such confusion and fear. Still I slept. I do not know for how long. I have no idea of the time. When they arrested me it was not yet four. Half an hour, three-quarters at most to get to the cell. I may only have been asleep for minutes. It might not yet be even five o'clock. Roger might still be playing tennis with the UN man. Madeleine might be in her bath, preparing for an evening with a lover. I laugh at the thought of her finding a *macaque* in the bed she uses. She will not like that at all.

Inès. Oh Inès, how did it get to this? I veer between love and hate for you. I wish I could be free of you. But no one has ever provoked in me what you have provoked. You discovered me, and then you didn't want me any more. This happens. It's nothing unusual. It's everyday stuff. I think I could have coped if only you'd dealt with it better. If you'd said to me one morning, tenderly, as though it mattered to you that you were going to hurt me, if you'd put out your hand and touched my face and said to me that things had changed, that your feelings had changed, that you were sorry . . . But there was none of that. There was no kindness, there was no consideration. Just impatience, and coldness and disregard. And I know I made it harder for you by demanding reassurances. But I think I deserved better. Not because I was good or blameless or . . . I cannot think of what else I can say I was or wasn't. I can only say I deserved better for the simple reason that I loved you and was bewildered and sad. Love has responsibilities. The last of these – the most arduous perhaps – applies to the end of love, when the spurned love has a right to demand help, and this responsibility you ignored. You went off for your higher things without regard for me.

I can't help myself now. I have to tell them what I know. It's not revenge. At least I don't think so. It might have been earlier, when I thought Stipe would come here, but not now. Now it's a question of survival. And I'm sorry. I really am. I can hear the howling again. Oh Inès. Come to me, hold me.

The door swings open. I think I must have been sleeping again but I cannot be sure. I cannot remember closing my eyes, or opening them. I remember no dreams.

The light from the corridor is not strong, but still I blink. I put my hand in a peak over my eyes. I hear a voice. It is not the captain's. It is quieter, more educated, but it is still peremptory.

'Get up.'

I do as I am told.

'Where is Auguste Kilundu?'

'I have no idea,' I reply at once.

I don't know why I say this. Perhaps simply because I've been saying it since they came to arrest me and it's embedded in my head, or because I've made a swift calculation about the likely benefits to me of telling them at this point.

'Come.'

Movement is not easy. During the night – if it was the night – my body has tightened. At each step part of me rebels.

'Come,' the voice snaps. 'Get a move on.'

'I need water,' I say.

My visitor says nothing.

Keeping my eyes down, I limp into the corridor. Once there, someone grabs me by the arm and marches me down to the barred gate. I wince with the pain and stiffness. It means nothing to my escort of course. I chance a look. There are three of them, all in civilian dress. They have the look of policemen, bored and well-watered and fed. As we emerge from the cells area one of them goes to the desk. The same man is still on duty. He doesn't bother to look at me. The policeman signs in the register, turns and signals to his two companions and we move on. We turn right into another passage. We come to a staircase. We go up. We go through a door into a short passage. We go through another door. We come out into the blinding daylight. I shade my eyes with my free hand. They half-lead me, half-drag me across the court-yard towards another building, another door. The light sears. It goes into the back of my brain and burns. I blink, I screw up my eyes. I see the silhouettes of what I think are armed guards standing before the new door. As we approach I begin to make out small details, a little relief, some colour. One of the policemen opens the door. I am pushed forward. I glimpse the guards as we pass. One of them seems to be white. I pass within a few inches of him. He is definitely white.

'Mark?' I whisper hoarsely.

Stipe – if it is Stipe – does not respond.

'Mark? Is that you? Help me, Mark.'

There is nothing from the white man. Before I can say anything more the policemen have pushed me through and closed the door behind us.

They pull me down another corridor. At the end an open door leads into a bedroom. Bedroom? There is a man lying on a bed, sound asleep. My eyes are adjusting to the light. The man in the bed comes into focus. Except it's not a bed. It's an office table. They push me into the room so violently I have to put a hand out to stop myself from falling over. I touch the sleeping man. He is cold and clammy and soft. I snatch my hand away. The man is not sleeping. I look around the room. In one corner, grinning to himself, is the captain.

I look again at the body. The head is hideously swollen. The bruising is so severe and so widespread that at first it's not easy to see that the body is white. It is Smail. His testicles are the size of cricket balls. There is blood at the tip of his stubby penis.

'Where is Auguste Kilundu?'

The voice comes from behind. The question registers but in my shock I do not understand that it requires an answer. One of the policemen spins me round.

'Where is Auguste Kilundu?'

I have no voice.

'We will leave you here with your old friend and the captain,' the policeman says, 'unless you tell us now where Auguste is hiding.'

'I'm very thirsty,' I say. 'I'd like some water. I also want to see the British ambassador.'

The policeman swings a fist into the side of my face. The blow is hard, though not enough to fell me. I go down anyway to avoid more punches. All three kick at me. The captain gets up to join them. He is carrying a heavy stick. I put up my hands to protect my head. He lashes me across the neck and shoulders. The room is small and they are in each other's way. I find some protection under Smail's table. One of them takes hold of my ankle and starts to pull me out from under the table. I grab the legs. The blows come down on the exposed part of my legs and lower torso. Someone is stamping on me. I hold on to the table and try to pull myself under. It moves. They continue to pull. The table moves, it slides on the floor, it topples over. Smail is lying on top of me. Suddenly the beating stops. One of the policemen says something. A few moments later the door closes and there is total silence. They have left me alone.

I lie still. I lie under Smail's body, my face pressed into the cold death-sweat on his chest. Then, as if only understanding at that moment the horror of my situation, I panic and flail about to struggle out from under him. I kick my legs free and when I am free I gaze in revulsion at the corpse. I crawl to the furthest corner. I wipe my face and bare arms, any exposed skin, to be cleansed of the touch and smell of him. The air is putrid. I take deep breaths. I concentrate, count, breathe. Calm. Calm, be calm . . . I have another story. A fantastic story, better than the killing of the ANC colonel. Zoubir Smail, Lebanese-born diamond merchant, Communist Party member, close associate of deposed prime minister Patrice Lumumba, widely rumoured to have organized and facilitated secret Soviet funding of the MNC, murdered by Mobutu's secret police. Eyewitness account of tortured body in Léopoldville's Central Prison. I can use all of this – along with my own arrest and beating – for novels, stories, plays. It can be the dramatic set-piece around which my work will turn. I will be able to make something of this. Yes. As long as I can make the deal with Stipe. I gaze at Smail. *Does a man die at your feet, your business is not to help him, but to note the colour of his lips.* I must gather my wits. I must note the colour of his lips.

Listen to me.

There is a dead man – not a friend, but a man I once knew – lying in a pathetic heap not ten feet from where I am and I am thinking about my own advantage. I feel suddenly repelled – utterly disgusted – by my own callousness. Is this all I have ever been? A selfish, egotistical watcher? I let out a groan. I bury my face in my hands and start to sob, from fear, from despair, from loathing of myself. I never said I was brave or idealistic, but I kept my weakness from myself. I always managed to do that.

This is me talking now. No tricks, no artifice, no writer's advertisements. No false self-accusation that will make me look well. There is nothing hidden or complicated or deep or doubting. I am banal and self-serving. This is the truth. I have disguised myself with words. Fiction words. Lie words. Others – not all, but many – are taken in, but I am no longer taken in by myself. Fiction words once made me feel well, but no more. They serve the liar who arranges them, the solipsist who designs their effect, the egoist who veils their sly, unpleasant insinuations and passes off brass as gold. Other people? Other lives? Where do others come into this? What room is there in this, in what I do, for others? My every waking thought turns on myself. I am at the forefront of my own imagination. Others – insofar as they exist at all – move around my sun. They live in my light and my darkness. At my whim. I have never had a single genuine concern – real, heartfelt – for another human being. I have never been honest. I have never once given up anything for another person. This is not exaggeration. I am not making myself look bad to make myself look good. I have got away with it until now because like the clever criminal I leave no fingerprints at the scenes of my crimes and I am always careful to go masked. Poor Smail. How small he looks in death, how reduced. I will lay him out. I will get him back on the table. I crawl back to him. Where the skin is not bruised it seems blue. It's the blue of blood in the veins of very old people, the men and the women with pale, papery skin who wait for death in rooms which smell of fish paste and moth balls. I will get him on his table. He's heavy and I am not strong. I take him, hands under his arms, and strain against the weight. His bloody swollen head lolls forward. I strain, pull, hoist. It's no good. I try again but I can't get his upper body on to the table. I let him down gently. I roll him on to his front, crushing his big bruised balls under him. I say out loud, sorry. Sorry. I stand over him. The ends of his fingers are black, as though frost-bitten. I lean down and take him by the waist. I heave with all my strength. He's doubled over, bent in the middle, head on the floor, knees and feet on the floor. Sweating with the effort I swing him round to the table. He's slipping from my fingers. I let out a groan as I make a final effort to lift him another few inches to get a part of him, any part, on the table. I can't do it. I don't want to drop him, but he's slipping from me. He crumples to my feet.

The door opens. It's Stipe. He barely glances at Smail.

Staring at me, he says, 'I've seen you looking better.'

'Look at what they did to Smail. Look at what they've done.'

He looks at the body for a second. His face registers nothing. Boredom perhaps. I know his work now. I hate him.

'Let's concentrate on you for now.'

'No, let's concentrate on you!' I shout at him. 'Let's concentrate on what you're doing here . . .'

'You asked to see me.'

'. . . Here in this country.'

He shrugs. He says, 'I'm trying to make this country a safe place.'

'Safe for who?'

'People like you.'

'Leave me out of it.'

'You always want to be left out of things, Gillespie,' he says scornfully, 'but you're involved in this. I don't mean just because you have connections with the people we're looking for. You're involved the same way we're all involved. People like you don't like the dirty games people like me play, but you benefit every time we play and win. You won't admit it, you'd probably deny it even to yourself, but you want me to win, because if I lose, then so do you. You lose everything. All your privileges. Writing, publishing, journalism – to mention only the things of particular interest to you – they're only possible in a certain context, and my job is to make sure that context continues to exist. Sometimes that means doing unpleasant things, sometimes it means associating with unpleasant people.'

'Like Dr Joe from Paris? Or Dr Gottlieb, as I believe he's called.'

Stipe flickers. For once I have surprised him.

'A poisoner?' I say, pressing forward while he is momentarily off-balance. 'That's more than just unpleasant, Mark.'

'There are a lot worse than Dr Joe. They're not the kind of people you feel comfortable inviting to your house for dinner. But you do. You have to. They come and sit at your table and it can be real hard to swallow your food in their company, but you make the effort. You eat the dinner, you drink the wine because you know if you don't, our context – our precious context – disintegrates.'

He pauses. He glances at the floor, at Smail.

Keeping his gaze on the corpse he continues, 'What am I doing here in this country? I am making sure that the biggest and richest country in central Africa – one with huge strategic importance – doesn't fall into the hands of the people who want to destroy our context.'

'Keep it up, Mark. You'll soon be telling me it's better to be dead than Red.'

'No,' he says casually. 'It's more of a Hobbesian thing with me. Better led than dead. I've always been a believer in strong leadership. I've always believed in doing what is necessary. It's the one thing I have in common with Inès, I suppose. How is Inès?'

The mention of her name jolts me back to the reality of my predicament.

'I don't know.'

Stipe nods slowly. 'You haven't seen her?'

'No,' I reply quickly and unequivocally. 'I told you I

271

haven't seen her since independence day.'

'Not even around town? Not even at press conferences?'

'We move in different circles, and you know Inès: she thinks press conferences exist so journalists won't get the story.'

There is a thin crack of a smile from Stipe. It is followed by a long silence.

'Just so there's no misunderstanding,' he says evenly, 'if you don't tell me where Auguste is, by nightfall you're going to look exactly like Smail there and there's nothing I can do about it.'

'That's a lie, Mark,' I reply fiercely, unintimidated by his threat. 'There's everything you can do about it. You can go to your ambassador and your ambassador could tell Mobutu to order my release and I would be out of here in twenty minutes.'

'Okay,' he says with a small smile, acknowledging my point, 'let's say there's nothing I would feel inclined to do about it.'

'I can't tell you where Auguste is.'

'Think about this, Gillespie.'

'I can't tell you because I don't know.'

He looks at me and I hold his gaze. I haven't convinced him, but I may have created the beginnings of a doubt.

'What did you do after I left you at Roger's?' he asks.

'Roger cleaned up my foot and drove me home. I had a drink and went to bed.'

'Did you see Roger yesterday?'

I stick to my story. 'No.'

'Talk to him?'

'No.'

He pauses before continuing, weighing my answers. They have been straight, unambiguous, confident. Am I creating doubts in him?

'Ask Roger if you don't believe me,' I say defiantly. It's all I can say. It's the logical challenge of the innocent man. A meaningless one, of course, because he will already have made plans to talk to Roger. What will Roger say? I can't think of that. I have to hope. And there is reason to hope, I realize. It's day. A night has passed. That means Madeleine has not discovered Auguste's hiding place. Perhaps she didn't go there after all. Perhaps there is no other lover. Perhaps I am the only one. I feel a strange surge of tenderness towards her.

'What did you do yesterday?' Stipe asks.

'Yesterday? I didn't have much on.'

'What exactly did you do?'

'Got up, did the usual things. Coffee in the garden. I didn't have anything to file, I've finished the novel, so I went for a drive, just to look round.'

'Where did you go?'

'The docks, along the boulevard, nowhere special. I called in at the Regina for a drink. I bumped into you there. You and Dr Joe the poisoner, if you remember.'

'Where's your houseboy?'

'Charles? I don't know. Isn't he at the house?'

'He didn't turn up this morning. Do you know where he lives?'

'In the cité somewhere. I don't know the address.'

He studies me closely. I have answered his questions without hesitation, almost believing my own lies. But I am a fraction of an inch from collapse. I have to concentrate to keep from trembling. If he presses I will go down. To divert him I take the initiative.

'What makes you think I would know where Auguste is?'

'He's been in hiding since the coup. Then, about a week ago, Inès dropped out of sight. She stopped going to her office at the Marché and moved out of the place she was staying in Rue de la Tshuapa. Disappeared. My guess is that she joined Auguste and I have good reason to believe she has been trying to organise an escape route for him. It's logical she would have approached you.'

'It's not logical at all. Not after what happened between the two of us.'

He turns away and puts a hand to his mouth. He tugs at his lower lip like a professor lost in thought.

'I've been meaning to ask you, Gillespie, what goes through your head when you think of Inès and Auguste together. I mean, you must think about it – right?'

'I try not to,' I say.

I know where this is going . . .

'That's wise, very wise,' he says with unpleasant smoothness. 'No sense in torturing yourself with comparisons. I mean, they're not exactly flattering.'

. . . but I cannot stop myself. I can see before my eyes . . .

'You're a middle-aged man who's spent most of his life behind a desk of one kind or another. You're soft. There's an overhang at your belt, your bulges are in all the wrong places.'

. . . the things he is taunting me with . . .

'You're a long way past your prime and Auguste – well, that boy's in the middle of his. And what a prime we're talking about. I've seen the man, you know, the full man, if you understand me, and . . .' – he chuckles to himself – 'it's impressive. Very impressive. You look at it and you think Jesus, that's just not fair. You understand what I'm saying? I mean it is huge.' He laughs. 'What do you think Inès thinks when she looks at it? I bet it makes her a very happy girl.'

It's pathetic that something so crude can do this to me, but the collapse is coming. Inside, things are giving way. I shut my eyes but I can't shut out his words.

He continues, 'You know, Auguste was always pretty open with me when it came to women. We had long talks. These guys, you know, they fuck all night. I mean all night. You can just hear Inès, can't you? Squealing.'

I should be able to ignore this, to dismiss it for what it is. There are hot tears on my cheeks.

'I love that sound, don't you? That sound a woman makes when she's being pleasured. I was in a hotel room in Managua one time. The walls were very thin. I heard this couple making out every night. The woman – oh, I can't tell you the noise she made, the little groans, the cries. Drove me crazy. Just think. Someone somewhere in this city is listening to Inès right now. Can you hear her, Gillespie? Can you hear her now? Listen. That's her, she's on her way, she's starting to come.'

I can hear her. Stipe steps up to me.

'You know what Auguste told me? What he likes best?'

He puts his mouth to my ear. His breath smells of toast, of biscuits.

'In the ass. Think of that, Gillespie. Old Auguste turning Inès over, spitting on his fingers, moistening her up, popping a finger inside and she's waiting for it. She knows what's coming. He's got his thing in his hand, it's ready. He pushes it against her ass. Think of that. Think of the noise she's making now. Can you imagine if there were pictures of that?'

I can see her.

'What do you think her face looks like when he's doing that to her? What does she say when she comes, Gillespie? What does she say?'

She says *amore mio. Amore mio.* They're my words, they're words for me, not for Auguste, not for anyone else, for me, me. Me. Her words. My words.

'What does she say? Because she's saying it now. Can you hear her? I can. So can Auguste. Auguste can hear her very well.'

I am lost in my tears.

'Leave me alone!' I scream.

'How do you feel about Auguste?'

I loathe him.

'Gillespie? How do you feel about the man who took your woman?'

I despise him, I hate him . . .

'Tell me where Auguste is.'

. . . if I had a knife I would stab him in the heart.

'Tell me. Everything will be okay. We can work it so that Inès will never know it was you. We can even arrange it so you end up looking like a hero, and you know how much she goes for heroes. The two of you belong together. You know that. You can be together. You can go back to London or Rome or Bologna or Ireland. You can start a family. I know she can't have kids, but you can get married and adopt. And if you have any problems with that, I can help you there as well. Trust me. Trust me, James. I can get Inès back for you. You believe me, don't you?'

I nod. Like a child before its parent.

'And you want that, don't you? More than anything else in the world.'

I nod again.

'So, where's Auguste?'

I snivel. I wipe the last of the tears from my eyes.

'Where's Auguste?'

'I don't know.'

He slaps me across the face with the back of his hand.

'You're lying to me! You're fucking with me!'

I let out a long sigh.

'Mark,' I say with the calm that comes from total defeat, 'I'd give him to you. Believe me. If I knew where he was I'd take you by the hand and if you gave me a gun – I don't know, I might even shoot him myself. But I don't know where he is and nothing you or any of those other people can do to me can make me tell you what I don't know.'

He stares at me with contempt in his eyes. His face is red and the thick branched vein pulses in his forehead.

'You've been very stupid and you're going to be very sorry,' he shouts.

He walks out, slamming the door behind him.

I look down at Smail, at all his wounds. I did not know him well. Hardly at all. He was a friend of Inès's, a member of the Party. I doubt, had I got to know him better, whether we would have established any kind of friendship. He was a believer, like Inès, and with only one exception I have never got on with believers. But no one deserves to die like that. What could his last hours have been like? His last minutes? Perhaps soon I'll know. We will be united in that at least. I kneel down beside him. I roll him on to his side. I pull up one arm. I work my other hand under his knees. I pause to get my breath, to gather my strength. I hoist the body over my shoulder in a fireman's lift and rise, staggering under the weight, to my feet. My heart pounds in my chest and I think I will faint. I step up to the table and I lay him down as gently as I can. And then everything drains away from me. I don't fall. I sink down and close my eyes.

The door opens. Two of the policemen enter. Come, they say. There is nothing else for it. I follow them without complaint. We retrace our route back to the cell. They lock me inside. In the dark I am not afraid. I don't care if Stipe questions Roger and finds out that I'm lying. I don't care if Charles turns up and tells them about Inès. I don't care what happens to me. I feel at peace, ready for anything.

There is no interrogation. At five minutes to five they release me. I know the time because the civilian at the desk notes it in his register. A single policeman escorts me through the tunnels and out to the main courtyard. A guard opens the gate and I step through. No one says anything. No one gives me any reason for my release. Outside there are thirty or forty women and children. Some are standing, most are sitting on what look like makeshift beds on the pavements. They regard me blankly. They are the wives and mothers and sisters and children of the men inside. The gate closes behind. I look up and down the street, trying to get my bearings and thinking about where I might find a taxi.

Before I can make a move I hear a gentle voice call my name. It is Stipe.

'Come on, James,' he says, 'I'll give you a ride.'

'I'd rather get a taxi.'

'Look at yourself. What taxi driver's going to pick you up? Come on.'

He leads me to his car, opens the passenger door and helps me inside. I wonder about my ribs. With every breath I feel a stabbing pain in my side.

Driving to Gombé, Stipe says, 'You really don't know where Auguste is?'

'I really don't.'

'Roger's in Brazzaville. It seems he has a patient over there who got sick yesterday. Interrupted a game at the tennis club to go over to see him. Did you know he had a patient in Brazzaville?'

'I don't know very much at all about Roger's practice.'

'They were talking about you, apparently, at the tennis club. It's a small town, Leo – you can't keep anything quiet for long. His tennis partner works out of the UN press office. It seems he'd heard rumours about your arrest. He mentioned it to Roger because he knew Roger and you were friends.'

I say nothing. I suspect, as Stipe may, that Roger, hearing of my arrest, decided to take the ferry across the river and await developments in safety.

'Did you get me out?'

'Yes,' he says.

'Thanks.'

'I hope when I eventually get to talk to Roger,' Stipe continues, 'that what he tells me squares with what you told me.'

'If you're going to threaten me, Mark. I'd rather walk the rest of the way.'

'I'm not threatening you.'

'I told you – I don't know where Auguste is.'

Stipe looks straight ahead. I am certain I have convinced him.

As we near the house, he says, 'I'm sorry about what I said – about Auguste and Inès, I mean. I had to try. You understand that, don't you?'

'I understand.'

'I hated having to do it, James. It made me feel sick inside. I'm sorry.'

'I could tell your heart wasn't in it,' I say.

He puts a hand on my arm and pats me affectionately.

He pulls up outside my house.

'I have some news you probably don't want to hear,' he says. 'First thing tomorrow morning you're going to receive official notification that your presence in the Congo is no longer welcome. They'll give you three days to wind up your affairs. It's for the best, James, believe me.'

'You don't have to convince me. I was going to leave anyway.'

'We should get you a doctor.'

'Yes. Get Dr Joe. I'd love to have a talk with him.'

I give him a hard stare.

'Remember what I said about preserving the context,' he says.

'How can I forget?'

'Let's have a drink at the Regina before you go. It'll be on me.'

'That would be nice.'

'Call me.'

He beeps the horn and gives me a friendly wave as he drives off. It's as though he were doing no more than giving me a lift home from work. Why not? For him it has been a normal day, I suppose.

The house has been searched. My clothes and papers and books have been thrown about, ripped, torn, broken. It's not important. There was nothing of any value here. I won't need three days. What affairs have I to wind up?

I go to the bathroom and look in the mirror. I snort with amusement at my hideous reflection. It's authentic at least, the result of genuine experience. One day I will draw on these cuts and bruises and the terror and pain they caused. I run a bath and soak in it for an hour or so. If anything, the pain seems worse when I get out. I drop the towel and stand naked in front of the mirror. I pinch the spare flesh at my belly and sides. What Stipe said about me is true. I am old and shabby.

I should know better, but I am only half done. I pat myself dry taking care to avoid the more tender areas around my ribs. I put ointment on the cuts and swallow four painkillers. My lower lip is torn and badly swollen. It will need attention.

Driving into town, I wince with each gear change, each turn of the wheel. I keep a close watch on the rear view mirror. I make a U-turn on the boulevard and drive back almost as far as the turning for Avenue de la Gombé. I pull over, pretend to look for something in the dash, and glance around as I start off again. There is no one behind me. I should know better but I head toward the house on Eugene Henry anyway.

I cannot decide whether I have been heroic or silly. I can be stubborn and resentful and sometimes buoyant, hard to wear down. But that's not why I did not tell them what they

wanted to know in the Central Prison. I did not betray
Auguste because if I had I would have lost her. And because I
kept silent I will lose her forever. I should know better. This is
the stuff of farce, not tragedy. I can see myself on the stage,
and I am laughing.

8

L UMUMBA STANDS AT the front of the *barque*, his glasses glinting
in the last of the sun. Behind him, the old boatman works
the craft across the river. The clumps of water-hyacinth drift
past, the spotter plane circles above. Little Roland is bleeding
and crying. His mother is in a distraction. Inès and the others
of our convoy who have not already crossed the Sankuru walk
to the jetty in their own trance. They cannot believe he is
re-crossing the river. Nor can the soldiers. He had slipped away
from them yet again. Now he is coming back, of his own
accord. We watch in stupefied silence, as at the inexplicable
workings of some strange natural phenomenon. We all know
what this means and are at a loss to understand. Why would a
fugitive come back to face his own death? As the *barque* nears
us, Inès cries out, 'No! Patrice, no!' He makes no sign that he
has heard her. His long, thin form is still, his face sculpted and
disheartened. Only when the wood of raft and jetty meet and
the Baluba soldiers rush forward to take him does he tremble. I
see fear penetrate him then, a prevision. At Mangai this morning he told his followers he would be betrayed and tortured
and killed. The soldiers jabber with excitement as they bundle
him towards their lorry. As we – his companions on this
reckless, planless flight – gather round, the soldiers push at us,
angrily, violently. They haul Lumumba up to the first of the
lorries. An NCO tries to tie his hands behind his back, but the
soldiers are already beating him. They are beating him like a
dog, settling scores for the massacres in the Kasai. The NCO
struggles determinedly but the whirl of limbs and fists defeats
him. Exasperated, he complains to his comrades. Around me,

people turn away, unable to watch. I look. Of course I look. It is in the nature of my profession. It is in the nature of me. The soldiers leave off their beating to allow the NCO to fulfil his orders and secure the prisoner. Once his hands are tied they start again, as though the referee had blown a whistle. The lorry jolts forward. We stand in its diesel-drenched wake and watch until it disappears from view. The remaining soldiers hustle and harass us, demanding to see our papers, checking identities. I turn to look for Inès. She is by the sky-blue Peugeot with Pauline and Roland. She gazes across the river. Somewhere on the other side Auguste is hurrying through the bush. She hopes he will find safety. She hopes they will be united again. She did get to kiss him goodbye. The spotter plane is gone. One of the women sitting by the baskets of boiled eggs and *pilipili* and the mounds of little silver fish folds some sweaty banknotes and pushes them between her breasts. She has made a sale. There is always time for spectators to eat.

This didn't have to happen. The whole episode has been shambolic, ludicrous, unnecessary. In three days we covered only four hundred miles. Poor going. The roads are not so bad, the rain has for the most part held off. We should have been within striking distance of Stanleyville by now. Our failure . . . I keep inadvertently slipping and saying *our, we.* It comes from nothing more than the fact that I am here in this place with these people; the meaning beneath my presence is clear to everyone. I am still not part of this. I am here through accident, default, chance, caprice, stupidity, bad judgement . . . Our failure is not surprising. What I have seen since we left the capital has been time-wasting, disorganization and incompetence. I have seen confusion and blundering, lack of direction and leadership. Sometimes panic. We have been constantly at the mercy of rumour. I did not see a plan. I did not see anyone who could think fast on his feet, who could come up with viable and realistic alternatives once things began to go wrong, and they went wrong right from the start, when the convoy approached the airport only to be told there was no Egyptian plane. They held one of their interminable meetings, even though Lumumba's escape might be discovered at any minute (*escape* is hardly the right word here, it is to imply drama and daring when in fact all he did was crouch on the floor of the car that left the Primature and drove unchallenged through the UN and ANC cordons). Some argued that they should wait, that Nasser would not let them down, that the plane would come, others that they should try to get to Brazzaville. In the end they decided to make for Stanleyville, where Gizenga has organized an army to fight against Mobutu and his new ally Kasavubu. They would need cars for the long journey. Good cars. There were so many people. They needed my car. I could easily have handed over the keys. I was going to abandon it in any case within three days. Instead I went along with them. I went for the exactly same reasons that I said nothing in the Central Prison. I went along, a bit player in the farce of his flight. It was an uncomfortable, exhausting journey for my aching body and I found it difficult to eat because of my gashed lip. But there was compensation – the compensation I had been relying on. For almost the whole three days Inès was beside me. We were not alone. In the back there were never fewer than three of her comrades. Not Auguste though. Once we got underway he transferred to Patrice's car. The leaders had to confer. I think Inès may have been a little disappointed that she was not invited to partake in their decisions. She was quiet at the beginning. Then she became more talkative, at first with her comrades, then with me. When we stopped at Bulungu they held an impromptu rally. We were wasting time, but there was no persuading him. She came to me then and looked at my wounds. She is a good and loving carer. The smallest sign of illness in me always brought out her nursing instinct. She kissed me and hugged me, a friend, a sister. She asked questions. I did not tell her much. I did not tell her about the captain or Stipe, but I did say that I had seen Smail's body. Her eyes filled with tears, but she set her jaw and fought them back. 'I have made a rule,' she said, 'no more tears.' She put her little hand in mine and I closed my fingers around it. The sounds of Lumumba's speech and the murmuring crowd came to us softly on the wind. I was reminded of a balmy day when I was a boy at school and the masters decided to take the whole school to a field on the mountain. We sat in the sun, an easy breeze riffling the pages of our books, the hum of our teachers and the other classes a low buzz in the air around us. It was special, different, there was a kind of magic about it. It was the sort of day which made a child think that life had other, hidden possibilities, that it was not all on the surface. I felt like that with Inès. I felt dreamy and warm, and when she spoke of her hopes and plans I held down my usual irritation and listened, happy just to hear that voice again, to let myself be lulled by her song, to be convinced – if only for a moment – that there are other ways of seeing things, that it's not all on the surface.

There is another way to describe what happened at the Sankuru River. Another way to tell the story of Lumumba's escape from house arrest, the race to the airport, the disappointment there, and the long journey which ended at the crossing near Port Francqui. My way, Inès would say, is inadequate. Were she to hear it, she would claim not to recognize the events it purports to describe. Hers is the other way.

They see him as a fugitive, even those closest to him like Auguste and Mulele and Kemishanga, but that is not how he sees himself. He is the elected prime minister, the leader of the independent Congo, head of state, and he carries himself as such. And soon everyone sees that this is what he is. They see the dignity of his bearing. He is a man who is always in motion, who is always going here and there, who is never still. His movements are graceful, never hurried or jerky. He puts people at their ease at once, for though he is the prime minister and all the world knows his name he has not forgotten what it is to be of the people. At Bulungu, our first stop after a night of driving, he goes to buy provisions in a little store. The people recognize him at once, for his face is striking and handsome. Word spreads and by the time he is ready to leave the villagers have gathered. Stay and talk to us, Patrice, they say. Explain what is happening. Tell us why the Belgians sent their paratroopers to kill and burn. Tell us why they sent arms to Tshombe in Katanga. Tell us why the UN have come and why they refuse to go. Tell us why the Americans have helped Mobutu and Kasavubu. And he talks, explaining everything. They bring us food to eat and beer to drink. They do not want him to leave, they want their prime minister to stay with them. He promises he will never desert them, that he will be back, that the cause he and so many others have served will triumph. He tells them that they have the right, which no one can take away, to an honourable life, to unstained dignity, to independence without restrictions. He tells them that the Belgians and their allies have corrupted some of their compatriots and bribed others, that they have distorted the truth and brought independence into dishonour. He tells them that his own actions have been criticized, that some said he spoke too rashly in the Palais de la Nation and that he has spoken too directly many times since. But how could he speak otherwise? Dead or alive, free or in prison, it is not he who counts. It is the Congo, it is the poor people for whom independence has been transformed into a cage. He tells them he knows in his heart that sooner or later the people will rid themselves of all their enemies, that they will rise as one to say No! to the degradation and shame of colonialism, that they will regain their dignity in the clear light of the sun. And he tells them they are not alone. In Africa and Asia, the free liberated people will always be found on the side of the millions of Congolese who will not abandon the struggle until the day when there are no longer any colonialists or mercenaries in their country. Mulele and Mungul and Auguste and Pauline all urge him to be on his way, that the soldiers cannot be far behind. He says that neither brutality nor cruelty nor torture will ever bring him to abandon the cause to which he has dedicated his life. If they capture him, he will never beg for their mercy. He would prefer to die with his head unbowed, his faith unshakeable, and with profound trust in the destiny of the Congo rather than live under subjection and without principles. History, he tells them, one day will have its say, but it will not be the history that is taught in Brussels, Paris, Washington or the United Nations, but the history that a free Africa, north and south of the Sahara, will write. A glorious and dignified history. At last they get him into the car. But it is the same again at Pukulu, and the same again at Mangai. He tells the people that their independence has to be defended, that he will defend it, even with his life. Pauline tugs at him, pleading with him to come away. Some say there is a spotter plane in the air, that the soldiers are on their heels. He speaks gently to his wife and caresses her, he lifts up his infant son and kisses him. He is the husband you know would always be kind, the father who would be loving and just. Pauline pleads with him and he would do anything for her. We run into a checkpoint on the other side of Mangai. The soldiers surround him and start to beat him but he talks to them and he explains the truth of what is happening to the Congo. And instead of beating him, they take his hands and hold them. And they cheer him on his way when he leaves them. Some of the soldiers are crying. They shout, Long Live the Congo! *Depanda! Depanda!* See what this man is. See how loved he is. And at the Sankuru River, when he could have made his escape, he gives up his life because he will not leave his wife and child behind. Even though Pauline shakes her head and silently begs him to save himself. He steps on to the *barque* and commands the old boatman to deliver him to his enemies. How can you say this is a farce? Which of us would have made such a gesture? He gave up his life because he believed in something.

This is how Inès sees it, because she sees dreams.

In Léopoldville, two days later, Grant tells us that he saw Lumumba and the soldiers arrive. It was a carnival, he says, a sick and vicious carnival. Mobutu stood with folded arms and watched the soldiers slap and abuse their prisoner. They pulled his hair and threw away his glasses. One of the NCOs sarcastically read out Lumumba's declaration in which he had affirmed that Mobutu's coup was illegal and that he was still head of state. When the NCO had finished, he rolled the paper into a ball and rammed it down Lumumba's throat. Lumumba did not flinch. He stood his ground, bearing the indignities and the pain. He was taken away. Grant and the journalists were not able to see what happened next, but they heard the screams.

Inès and I go to Gombé, to my house. She waits while I pack. I am done in less than an hour. Then we drive to the public docks and take the ferry to Brazzaville.

9

WE ARE BOTH waiting. She for word from Auguste, I for . . . what? For the end, for the very last moment of our story. She still calls it that. Our story, our affair. I have not corrected her. I never will. Our affair is over, but our story will continue a little longer, until the day there arrives a letter or messenger. Then it will be time for her to go, and time for me to accept what she has told me.

Brazzaville is not so bad. The shabby, chaotic streets teem with noise and life and incident. On crossing the river we found a cheap hotel and spent the first week in a double room that overlooked the market. We slept in twin beds, but she was not distant from me. She took me to see a doctor, who strapped up my ribs and stitched the gash in my lower lip. We found a house to rent on the riverfront. It has a garden, nothing like as big as the one I had in Gombé, but it is walled and secluded and tranquil. I love to watch the birds in the morning. The bulbuls bicker in the branches and beautiful blue and brown and lilac rollers come to perch on the telegraph wires.

Inès and I talk a great deal. We talk about the Congo, about independence and the way the Belgians emptied the treasury, bankrupted the country and did everything they could to sabotage Patrice's plans. We talk about de Scheut and the colonists who fled. We talk about Mobutu and Kasavubu and the UN and Tshombe and Katanga. We talk about Stipe and Houthhoofd and the articles I wrote. We even talk about Madeleine and Auguste. There is no acrimony, no blame. It is a review of a shared past, a recension, sympathetic and sad, by two people who were apart but who are, in some uncertain, uneven way, discovering again what they have in common.

One day we talk about us, about what went wrong. She hugs me and tells me that she knows she was hard but this was because she had to defend herself from herself, from the subversion of her own emotions, her own weaknesses. I clasp her to me and I can't help myself. I say for the last time don't turn me away. I bury my face in her hair. She puts a hand to the back of my neck and waits tenderly, patiently, and I think sorrowfully, until I get myself back under control, which I do. I never really thought she would change her mind, but her manner now – so loving, so kind – makes me feel a little better about things, and about myself.

I have given up writing for the *Observer*. I see now that everything I did for the paper was tainted by Stipe. My stories were true, they were accurate. But, as Inès would say, truth and accuracy are not always the point. They can be made to serve particular interests just as lies can. She spends most of her time at her desk writing articles about Lumumba's escape and recapture. She writes with passion, anger, indignation. She protests at his detention with Okito and Mpolo at Camp Hardy. She urges the UN to intervene and save the prisoners; she believes Patrice's life hangs by a thread. She writes a furious denunciation of Mobutu when he orders Lumumba and the two others to be sent to Élisabethville and there placed in Tshombe's 'care and protection'. When nothing is heard of the trio after a week in Katanga, Inès writes a piece in which she says the deposed prime minister and his companions are almost certainly already dead. She quotes from Lumumba's last letter to Pauline. *I am writing these words not knowing whether they will reach you, when they will reach you, and whether I shall still be alive when you read them. Do not weep for me, dear wife. I know that my country, which is suffering so much, will know how to defend its independence and its liberty. Long live the Congo! Long live Africa – Patrice.* We do not know for sure if Lumumba is dead, but I say that Pauline might have wanted his last words to her to have been more personal. Inès shakes her head slowly. No, she says, Pauline knows how much he loved her, that when he crossed the Sankuru it was for her. She would always know that and no words he could write could say as much to her now as his action then. Better to use the few words he was permitted to assure her that his life had not been in vain, that the thing he believed in and sacrificed himself for will one day come to pass.

She finds the silence from Auguste hard to bear. She doesn't know if he made it to Stanleyville, if he's dead or alive. Sometimes I see her at her desk, gazing into space, sad, lost. *Persa.* She tries to conceal these moments of distraction. She knows what they do to me.

We tend to keep to ourselves in these sequestered days. Others hold little interest for us, and, though we talk, much of our time is touched with silence. We go to walk in the market in the evening when it's cooler and not so crowded and the last of the vendors offer their wares at bargain prices. I love the fruit here. I buy bananas and mangoes and oranges, pineapples and berries. Inès chooses the vegetables and sometimes a chicken or some fish. It's harder to find good wine so we buy beer from a young girl who has a little bench at the beginning of the meat market. She overcharges us, but Inès has taken a shine to her and cheerfully pays what is demanded.

Occasionally Inès will slip her hand into mine. I don't look at her when she does this. I just give her hand a light squeeze and we walk home together like that.

After dinner we sit on the patio overlooking the garden

and I read to her. She has always liked my voice, though in truth it tends to monotone and because my breathing is untrained I stutter and get into trouble over the phrasing. Sometimes I will look up and see that her thoughts are away somewhere else, with someone else. But after a moment or so she will ask why I have stopped and I smile and start again. We sleep in separate bedrooms.

One morning a letter arrives.

> *Dear James,*
>
> *Please forgive my tardiness in writing to you. The delay was due to the usual things – too much going on in the office, a mountain of correspondence to get through, not to mention a neurotic and demanding young author to nurse-maid through his second novel – he seems to think I exist solely to pander to his needs.*
>
> *Your book is wonderful – funny, though it shouldn't be, and enigmatic. Both Peter and Rosamond have read it now and are of the same view. (Part of the reason I held off writing to you was because I was waiting for their reactions.) Rosamond hasn't stopped talking about it. She thinks it far and away your best work to date. So do I. True, it's disturbing and hardly optimistic, but in its cold, terrifying way it's utterly compelling, and the irony is patrician – I mean that as a compliment, as you know.*
>
> *I've just come out of a meeting with the marketing and publicity people and the plan is to publish in May. Everyone is terribly excited. You will be back by then, won't you? Your presence will be enormously helpful.*
>
> *I don't know what to say to you about Inès, except that I'm sorry. Are you over it yet? I do hope so. Are you writing anything at the moment? Think about a swift follow-up,*

won't you? It would be nice to get a little impetus going.
Very best wishes and I look forward to seeing you soon.
Alan

I take the letter to show Inès. She is in the middle of an article demanding that Tshombe provide proof that Patrice is still alive. She puts aside her work and reads while I stand by the desk. She shows no reaction at first. Then she nods slowly and looks up from her chair. She smiles and gets up and hugs me. *Bravo,* she says, *complimenti.* She always took pleasure from whatever success came my way. Nothing that has happened between us has changed that.

Later, after our visit to the market, we walk along the riverfront. The fishermen are coming in and the women and the children are bathing. The sun is low and the river golden. She asks me quietly what I will do now. I say I suppose I will go back to London soon, that there will be the proofs and the cover to look at and various meetings to attend, and a lunch or two, knowing Alan. We walk on, sometimes brushing against each other, sometimes pausing to look across to Léopoldville. The sun slides down. In its last moments the descent is very sudden. We stand together in silence. I am aware only of her breath, her presence. Our thoughts are scattered, there's no chasing them, no catching them. The night bears them away. Eventually I say it's dark now, we should go home. She doesn't move and I ask if she's all right. She nods and we start back for the house.

On the patio I seem to lose my voice when I am reading to her.

'Go on,' she says softly, 'don't stop now.'

'No,' I say. 'I don't find this book particularly interesting. I think I'll get an early night.'

I leave her and go inside. I feel empty. Alan's letter said

all I wanted to hear, but it has brought me no joy. How different it would have been had we still been together.

I am awake when she comes to me.

'Is everything all right?' I ask, anxious and confused.

She sits on the bed. I can't look her in the face. It's too upsetting. She runs her hand through my hair and closes her fingers around it and gently tugs at it, as though to pull me out of my silence.

'Do you really want to go to Stanleyville?' I ask. 'Who knows how long Gizenga can hold out against Mobutu? The whole thing could collapse any day.'

'I know,' she says, 'but I have to go.'

'Why do you have to go?'

She closes her eyes. She says, 'The world divides in two and sometimes I wish I could be in your world, James, where you don't care about politics, where you can see all points of view.'

'What's so wrong with that?'

'There's nothing wrong with it. But few people have this privilege. When you are on history's losing side, when you are poor and cursed to eat bread, to accept your enemy's point of view is to accept starvation and slavery.'

I make a sound of exasperation. This kind of vocabulary is too hysterical for me. I take her hand and put it to my lips and I ask if there is anything I can say or do that will make her change her mind. She tells me that she still loves me. For a moment my hopes rise. And then there are those awful words. She says she will love me forever. Ah, that kind of love.

And yet that night there is love. She does not move to go to her room. She sits at the end of my bed and we talk. As the night wears on she pulls the sheet around her bare legs and shifts closer to me. She leans her head against my chest and I touch her ear and throat and neck. She puts her hand on my arm and brings up her face. We kiss. I lower myself and she climbs on top of me. I pull the dress over her head. I lick her little breasts and push my hands down the back of her knickers. She straightens her legs to let me get them off. I say to myself that I will not allow this to stop. I will stay inside her all night, I will never let her get away.

I think I have been asleep, I don't think for long. Some seconds. I hope seconds, only seconds – I cannot bear the waste of slept time. The sound of her breathing fills the room. I know her when she's like this, on her side, curled, her back to me, sleepy and vague and satisfied and wet and in my arms. I know I can please her more and I don't have to wake her. Rub her gently from behind and whisper things to her, not in a way that will wake her. I don't want her dreams disturbed. I want her protected and safe and mine, always. I bring my hand up to the nape of her neck. I can smell her on my fingers.

In the morning she is gone. I leap out of bed and run to her room. She's not there. She's not at her desk and she's not in the garden. I throw on my clothes and, my mind in turmoil, rush out to look for her.

I find her hurrying through the market on the way back to the house. She has been at the AP office. She holds up a sheet of paper. There has been an announcement about Patrice. She is going to Léopoldville now.

'You can't go,' I say. 'It's not safe.'

She will not hear of my objections.

'I go.'

I will not be parted from her, not now. We will risk it together.

On the ferry she shows me the AP report of a statement released in Élisabethville by Tshombe and the Katangan minister of the interior, Godefroid Munongo. In their version, Lumumba, Okito and Mpolo escaped from captivity

295

soon after their arrival in Katanga. They had abandoned the stolen car in which they were travelling after it had run out of petrol. The Katangan government had offered a reward for their recapture, but before the forces of law and order caught up with them all three men were massacred by the inhabitants of a small village in revenge for the atrocities committed by Lumumba's troops on the Baluba people. The villagers may have acted somewhat precipitously, the statement went on, but their actions were excusable and they would collect the reward. Neither the village nor the gravesite would be identified for fear of reprisals by Lumumbists. When one reporter asked the minister of the interior if he and Tshombe had had anything to do with the deaths, Munongo responded, 'I will speak freely. If people accuse us of killing Lumumba, I will reply, "Prove it." '

Today of all days. Couldn't this news have waited another twenty-four hours? At times like this Inès is never mine.

'There's something else,' she says.

My heart narrows.

'Auguste?' I ask.

She nods. I look out over the river, at the boats and the sandbanks.

'A messenger from the party came to the house this morning when you were asleep. He's in Stanleyville.'

'I'm glad he made it,' I say. 'Does he want you to join him?'

'Yes.'

'Will you go?'

She does not say anything. There is still hope.

Our entry into the Congo without the proper papers is facilitated by payment of a small consideration to the two senior policemen on duty at the public docks. We hurry up to the Regina, intending to talk to George, the UN press officer, or, failing that, to Grant or one of the other correspondents. My heart is not in it, but now is not the time to press Inès.

As we reach the hotel we see a small black woman come out. She wears a dark blue *pagne* but is naked from the waist up, her hair is shorn and her eyes are downcast. A small crowd of people follow her out of the hotel and stare after her.

'It's Pauline,' I say.

We stop and watch as she makes her way down to the boulevard. Word is spreading. The curious are coming down from the cité.

'What's going on?' I ask George.

'She came to ask if the UN would help to get her husband's body returned,' George replies. 'The trouble is, I'm not sure there is a body.'

Grant, standing among a small group of reporters and photographers, comes up to us.

'My God. I didn't expect to see you two here again.'

He seems genuinely pleased to see both of us. We shake hands and he asks if we've heard the news.

'The story about the villagers is a transparent lie,' he says, 'and Tshombe and Munongo couldn't care less that no one believes them. I've been piecing together what happened when they sent Lumumba to Élisabethville. Apparently on the plane, Lumumba, Okito and Mpolo were roped together. The soldiers beat them so sadistically that the Belgian Captain had to send the co-pilot back to tell them to pack it in, they were actually endangering the craft. By the time they got to Élisabethville airport – so the Swedish UN soldiers there say – Lumumba and the other two could barely stagger off the plane. Then they were forced to run a gauntlet of Tshombe's soldiers. It seems that night they were taken to a farmhouse owned by a Belgian. I'm pretty sure they were done in then and there, though after God knows what kind of treatment. I'm pretty sure too that Tshombe and Munongo were there to watch it. Munongo may even have given Lumumba the *coup de grâce* himself – a bayonet in the chest is what people are saying.'

Inès says she wants to go after Pauline.

A photographer with a London accent asks Grant, 'What's with the black bird having her tits out?'

'It's the traditional way women mourn here,' Grant replies icily.

He suggests we take his car and catch up with Pauline on the boulevard. Inès and I get in the back, one of the other reporters gets in the passenger seat beside Grant.

'Have you seen Stipe?' Grant asks as we set off.

'No,' I say.

'I'd stay out of his way, if I were you. He wasn't too happy when he realized you'd pulled a fast one on him.'

He takes General Tombeur de Tabora, one of the smaller avenues that runs parallel to the boulevard.

'By the way,' he says, turning to look back at me, 'I heard about what happened at the Central Prison.'

The other journalist, who as far as I know I have never seen before, likewise turns round.

'Yes,' he says, admiration in his voice. 'That took some guts.'

I feel Inès glance at me.

'I don't know why I did it,' I say vaguely.

Inès puts her hand on top of mine.

'*Tu lo sai,*' she says.

Inès may think she knows, but she doesn't. She thinks my motives honourable, possibly even heroic. They weren't.

At Avenue du Marché Grant turns right. He finds a place to park and we walk down to Albert I. There is the most incredible sight. The traffic in both directions has come to a halt as Pauline walks forlornly down the boulevard. People are pouring from the side streets. Young and old, men and women and children. Hundreds of people, thousands of people. They fall in behind her and around her, a great, silent throng. We start down to meet them. I work my way to be next to Inès. I can hold off no longer.

'Do you know what you're going to do?' I ask her.

She stops and looks at me. Grant and his companion walk on.

'Yes,' she replies, and because she says the word sadly I know what her decision is.

'I'm being selfish, I know,' I say. 'I'm thinking only of myself. I know there are important things, that there's no comparison between what I want and what you want, but what can I do with this love I have for you? Please don't go.'

She is crying. I look away. I look at the trees and houses and the cars. I concentrate on those things. I take her hand in mine.

'Don't go.'

I feel someone brush against me, then someone else. The vanguard of the march. People surge past. A river, an unstoppable black river.

I look at Inès. She gives me a small smile.

'Is this it?' I say.

'Yes, *amore mio.*'

We are knocked and buffeted. I hold on, I try to hold on, but her hand is jolted from mine.

'Inès!' I cry. 'Inès!'

She moves on with the crashing current, carried away by it.

'Inès!'

I scramble after her but it's impossible. I see her look back briefly and try to raise her hand in farewell. Then I cannot see her any more. I dive into the crowd. I struggle and fight my way through. But I cannot find her. I stare blankly into the crowd for a long time. She is gone.

A white man is elbowing his way through the crowd. He is coming towards me. Stipe. He stands before me glaring angrily. He looks me up and down. I am vile, I am a figure beneath contempt. He has no words for one such as I. The crowd surges past, knocking us, shoving its way through us, around us.

'You lying fuck,' he says. 'After all I did for you.'

'You didn't do anything for me, Mark. You got me to do things for you and the pathetic thing is I didn't see that until it was too late.'

'Jesus, what did Inès do? She must have fucked you last night. You sound just like her.'

His ability to put his finger right on a thing has not deserted him.

'No,' I say, 'I'll never be like her. I just don't see the things she sees and I never will. But I see what you've been doing, Mark. Inès was right about that all along and I hope she and Auguste succeed in whatever it is they're trying to do. I hope that what they want happens. I hope they kick you and Houthhoofd and Dr Joe and all you people out of this country forever.'

The crowd streams past the two white men glaring angrily and insignificantly at each other.

'That's not going to happen,' Stipe says. 'Auguste picked the wrong side. When he's caught and they put him up against the wall maybe he'll realize then he should have listened to me. Maybe then he'll know I was a better friend to him than Inès could ever be.'

'That's always been your way, Mark,' I say. 'As long as the other person takes your advice there's no problem. The minute he thinks for himself he's dead.'

His face is red, the pulse in his forehead throbs. He can contain himself no more.

'It's always good advice. He should have listened,' he says. 'And so should you.'

He slams his fist into my face. Such is Stipe's strength that even though he had little room to swing, the blow knocks me down. He stares coldly at me on the ground, then turns and fights his way through the crowd, muttering at people, commanding and cursing them. I try to get to my feet but the marchers trample over me, staggering, losing their balance. A nervous murmur goes up from the crowd. I try again to get up but am knocked down once more. A woman falls on top of me, her legs caught up in a tangle with mine. She starts to panic and fights me like an enemy in order to be free. Someone else falls. Another. Another. People are screaming now and flailing madly. The crush is terrifying.

Then, from nowhere, I feel powerful, unwavering arms take hold of mine, an unshakeable grip, and I am lifted, pulled clear by an irresistible strength. '*Malámu, nókó?*'

I look into the houseboy's smoky eyes and for the first time he holds my gaze.

'Are you all right, Mr James?' Charles asks in French.

'Yes, Charles. Thank you. I am better now.'

The fallen marchers are being helped back on their feet, the panic is over. Charles smiles and guides me by the arm. I find his step and walk on beside him. The crowd lets a sudden deafening roar.

Depanda!

And for a moment – a split second only as the sound breaks over me – I think I glimpse the dreams Inès can see.

part four

Bardonecchia, August 1969

1

I HAVE FRIENDS in Rome. Some people are very kind. They ask why I come here to the cold north, but the isolation suits my purpose and in any case by mid-June the weather has usually picked up. I have been spending the summer here for three years. I arrive in May when the last of the snow has gone from the streets, and the ski-runs are clear and the only tourists are weekend visitors from Turin and Milan or day-trippers from France. I usually stay until the end of August. There are few distractions. I can get on with my work. I write for three or four hours in the morning, have a light lunch, then walk up into the mountains. There are a number of routes I take, but my favourite leads west from town on Via Modane. Keeping the cold, slate river to my right, I climb up past the ruin of the old tower. I cut across the snaking road which runs to the French border until I reach the hedge-lined path. It will take me to the derelict stone farmhouse. Beyond the farmhouse are the steeply sloping woods where the deer and foxes are, and beyond the woods is the mountain with its scree and rocks and dirty white blankets of left-over snow.

In the evenings I dine at the Gaucho, the restaurant near the top of Via Medail. The atmosphere is relaxed and friendly, the food excellent. One of the waiters there, Angel, a beautiful and sad-faced Argentine, will, during his less busy moments, come to my table and ask politely if he can sit for a while. He likes to talk to me about South America and Italy and things of the heart. He used to own the restaurant, but something he does not talk about went wrong and he sold it to Gaspare, the blue-eyed Sicilian who came to the mountains eight years ago. Sometimes, if I arrive late, I will eat with Gaspare and Tommi, the other waiter, and Massimo, the pizza cook. Occasionally we are joined by Maurizio and Mattia from the little stationer's and bookshop on the other side of the railway line, whom I got to know during my first stay when they fixed my typewriter. They are all amused by how much I drink, though I do not think my consumption excessive by any means. I finish the evening with a cold *limoncello* or a grappa, sometimes two. Their talk is always lively. It's an easy fellowship and makes the loneliness – self-inflicted – easier to bear. They still ask, after three years, what I am doing here. 'Why Bardonecchia,' they say, 'the lost place?' To write, I tell them, in peace and quiet, though of course there is far more to it than that.

This year Alan has come out to join me for a week. His reputation as a publisher has grown in tandem with mine as a writer. It is a moot point who has done more for whom. We do not explore this. We accept that our lives and careers are bound together, and we know instinctively that the best way to avoid a falling-out which would damage us both is not to go into the detail or history of our connection. Like many middle-aged, professional, urban men we have developed a keen amateur interest in the natural world, an attempt at an antidote, I suppose, to our paper lives. And so, kitted out with our boots and field glasses and pocket guides, we spend the afternoons sharing our finds: the snow finches and stone-chats, the ringlets and skippers, the scarce coppers and silver-washed fratillaries.

On our last day together, as we are coming down from the mountain, he asks about my next book.

'I thought I might try something historical.'

'Really?' he says, surprised. 'That would be something new for you.'

'I was having a clear-out of the flat,' I say, 'and I came across the notes for my D.Phil. There was a very interesting infanticide case. Well documented, too, for the times. I thought I could make use of the material.'

'Sounds very interesting,' he says.

I can hear the disappointment in his voice.

'You don't approve?'

'I'm sure it will be a marvellous book.'

'Is there something else you think I should be writing about?'

'No, no,' he says. 'Not at all. The last thing I'd do would be to try to tell you what you should be writing, James.'

'You're protesting rather too much, Alan.'

He points to a little treeless tussock away to our left. A rodent scurries to its bolt hole. 'Is that a marmot?'

'Yes.'

'I've never seen one before.'

'They're quite common here,' I say.

Back at the apartment we take our cold beers to the little balcony and sit in the last of the sunlight.

'Do you want to use the shower first?' Alan asks.

I tell him to go ahead. I help myself to another beer.

Why Bardonecchia? For six years I resisted coming to Italy at all. I trained myself to avoid anything that would remind me of her. We had parted well, at least as well as one can in these affairs; we had made up some lost ground and there was that last sweet night with her. But none of that stopped resent-ment and acrimony visiting me later. I admit I was for a long time – for too long a time – desperate and unhappy. I lost myself in the murk of my work. I wrote that novel, the one for which the idea came when Inès first left, the one about the idealistic young girl and the lecherous middle-aged man and the confusion of their motives and identities. Bitter, splenetic, comic, and much-read. It was a great success.

I eventually wrote Inès out of my system and I wrote myself out of my gloom. I was after a time able to get on with my life. I had affairs; some were quite important to me. During a motoring holiday in France one year I ended up in Modane. The woman I was with suggested a day's excursion on the Italian side of the Alps. Of course, why not? I had put her out of my mind, I had my own life, my work, a lover – she figured no more. Italy was safe. It held no memories, evoked nothing from the past.

We crossed the border and came to Bardonecchia. The moment I heard the language, saw the gestures, tasted the sweet strong coffee I began to tremble. I made some excuse and we cut short the outing and returned to France. On the way back to England all I could think about was her.

I was not honest with myself about coming here. I said it was to escape the interruptions of London, to write in peace and quiet. But it didn't need to be Italy. I could have gone anywhere. The truth is I came for her, again.

I have not seen her since the crowd swept her away from me on the Boulevard Albert I. I have not spoken or communicated with her in any way for almost nine years. In the Gaucho one night – it was during my second summer – I heard her name spoken by a young man at another table. A wave of jealousy crashed over me. I looked at the speaker – young, good-looking, beautifully groomed – and for a mad moment I imagined he was her lover. Angel, who was sitting with me, asked if I was all right. I got him to translate what the young man was saying to his friends – my grasp of Italian remains as poor as ever. Angel listened and told me the talk was about Vietnam, something to do with an article in the paper that morning by Inès Sabiani. Inès Sabiani, I said vaguely and disingenuously, I know that name. Yes, Angel replied, she's one of Italy's best-known journalists. She's been doing a series of special reports from Vietnam and the young people are all talking about them. Angel asked me about Ireland, what I thought of what was going on there. Stupidity, I say. Why can't Ireland just grow up? He asks me to explain what it's all about. Bigotry, hooliganism, intransigence, a refusal to look the modern world in the face. The madness seems general and bound to get worse. It has infected my sister. And my mother, who should know better. They are enthusiastic marchers in the cause of civil rights. My mother even walked some of the way with a band of students called People's Democracy who were marching from Belfast to Derry to highlight some injustice or other. Siobhan wrote and told me the students clapped the old woman when she left them at Glengormley. When I talk to my family, which is not often, I avoid this subject.

Inès has been in Ireland again. I can read enough Italian to see that she has not changed. Her articles in *L'Unità* are as passionate and denunciatory as ever. I have asked my friends in Rome about her. They know friends of her friends. I have found out that she and Auguste are no longer together, but I haven't been able to discover why she returned from Stanleyville, or even exactly when. There are different accounts. In one she and Auguste left the Congo after the Simba rising was put down and spent a short time together in Gabon before parting for some unspecified reason. In another, she left while Auguste stayed behind to take part in another luckless campaign against Mobutu. In London I ran into Grant outside Hatchards. He was an old Africa hand by then, well regarded as a journalist, and he had just published a book of his own. I bought a copy and he signed it for me and we went for a drink in Piccadilly and talked about old times. He told me that the last positive sighting of Auguste was shortly before an ambush in the

Kasai, when the small mixed force of Congolese and Cubans of which he was part was surprised by South African mercenaries. But only a few weeks later another correspondent told me Auguste was living comfortably in Senegal, that he had a job at the university and was married to the sister of a government minister. The same journalist also told me that Stipe had resigned from government service and returned to the Congo to become a manager and kind of general trouble-shooter for Bernard Houthhoofd and his business interests there.

Alan comes out of the shower. I finish my beer and go into the bedroom.

Inès never contacted me. I'm sure she must know that I asked about her. Even after nine years, when I'm in London, I haven't lost the habit of arranging as far as possible my morning around the increasingly unpredictable delivery of the post. For the first year I was certain a letter would come. I always thought that at some lonely point, at some moment unfilled by danger or excitement or others, she would think of me and want to get in touch. She never did.

At the Gaucho Gaspare, Maurizio and Mattia hail us excitedly. Have we been watching the television? The pictures from Derry and Belfast are incredible. Amazing things are happening. War has broken out. Alan is more interested than I. He hurries me when I'm eating, refuses dessert and coffee. He wants to go back to see the news.

We settle in our chairs in front of the television. Brick-strewn streets, burned-out cars, gutted buildings, milk bottles filled with petrol, youths with scarves around the nose and mouth, rioters, refugees, police, soldiers. He is transfixed.

'My God,' he exclaims. 'Had you any idea this was coming?'

I say that I had not, and I say that I think I'll have an early night.

In the morning I walk Alan to the station. He tells me he has had a wonderful time.

'I don't suppose you'd want to write something about what's happening in Ireland?' he says as his trains pulls in. 'You could set a novel there. Terribly interesting background, don't you think?'

I think of the television pictures. The place holds no interest for me.

'No,' I reply. 'No, I don't think so. It's not for me.'

'No,' he says after a while, 'I suppose you're right.'

I help him aboard with his luggage and we shake hands. Alan has his ambitions, he can sometimes be pompous, but he is a good man. I am sad now that he is going.

I do not feel like working when I go back to the apartment. Instead I walk up Via Medail, over the bridge and along Via Modane, following my favourite route. I pass the ruined tower and the old stone farmstead with its garden of nettles and its caved-in roof and mossy grey timbers. I walk through the woods and up the rocky slopes where the scree underfoot has the tinkle of broken glass.

I sit on a boulder overlooking the valley. Inès told me once in a letter – I still have it – that she wanted me to know where to find her, and how. It's taken me a long time to understand what she meant. I had to look in a place where sceptics like Stipe and doubters like me, like Grant, like Roger, like most of us, do not believe anyone really wishes to be – anyone sane, adult, mature, reasonable. It's a place we laugh at, we scorn, and we sometimes say does not exist at all. But I caught sight of it at the Sankuru when Patrice stepped on to the *barque* to recross the river, and again on my last day in Léopoldville when the silent crowds followed Pauline down the boulevard and Charles picked me up from the road. I

311

glimpsed it when I was with Inès. She encouraged me, beckoned me forward. She promised that was where I'd find her. But I could never join her there. I was always too much a watcher, too much *l'homme-plume*, I was divided, unbelieving. My preference is the writer's preference, for the margins, for the avoidance of agglomerations and ranks. I failed to find her and I know this failure will mark the rest of my life.

There is no one on the mountain. I am here, safe in my anomie. There is only the screech of the kites, the barking deer and the quiet work of the melt-water. I think I must leave this place and not come back.

AUTHOR'S NOTE

THIS IS A work of fiction. Those with expert knowledge of the Belgian Congo will see that certain episodes have been bent to the demands of the novel's narrative. That said, the general outline of events and much of the detail is true. The literature on the Congo's independence is too large to catalogue here, but I would like to acknowledge the debt I owe it. I have taken Stipe's definition of neoteny from Wiliam Jordan's *Divorce Among the Gulls.*

I would like to thank the Society of Authors for financial assistance in helping me undertake a research trip to Zaire in 1995.

A version of Part Two appeared in the *London Review of Books* in 1992.